Air Warfare, 1917

A "LINE" OF BRITISH FIGHTING SCOUTS

Air Warfare, 1917

The Aviation War as it was being Fought
from the Allied Perspective

ILLUSTRATED

Airfare of Today and of the Future
Edgar C. Middleton

Events in the Air
E. W. Walters

LEONAUR

Air Warfare, 1917
The Aviation War as it was being Fought from the Allied Perspective
Airfare of Today and of the Future
by Edgar C. Middleton
Events in the Air
by E. W. Walters

ILLUSTRATED

FIRST EDITION IN THIS FORM

First published under the titles
Airfare of Today and of the Future
and
Heroic Airmen and Their Exploits (Extract)

Leonaur is an imprint of Oakpast Ltd
Copyright in this form © 2023 Oakpast Ltd

ISBN: 978-1-916535-40-4 (hardcover)
ISBN: 978-1-916535-41-1 (softcover)

http://www.leonaur.com

Publisher's Notes

Contents

To Mother
A Humble Appreciation

Author's Note

With Aviation we may say that we have reached the fifth step in the cycle of world progression. The exploration and the mastery of the seas opened up a hitherto unknown world to the peoples of the Middle Ages. Later the development of the steam engine pushed on civilization and commerce apace. After came the steamer upon the seas. Electricity gave the world a new and far-reaching motive power, and almost entirely replaced manual labour. But the advent of Aviation changed for all time the conditions of the world. As a factor of war, it revolutionised every military principle and theory. As vessels of commerce, aircraft will have reduced time to a minimum, and rendered distance almost oblivious; bringing every far corner of the earth within easy reach of the more populous centres. So much has already been accomplished in ten years, that one dare hardly predict what the future holds in store.

I would like to take this opportunity of thanking the Editors of the *Daily Mail, Daily Express, Evening Standard* and *Flying* for their courtesy in permitting me to use, in a few instances, material embodied in articles appearing in their journals; also, the courteous privileges extended to me by J. A. Whitehead, Esq., of the Whitehead Aircraft Co., Ltd., Richmond, in gathering necessary material.

Edgar C. Middleton

Aerial Dictionary

(Slang And Technology)

Angle of Incidence (The). The angle a wing makes with the direction of motion relative to the air.

Ballonet (A). An air-bag within the gas-container of a balloon or an airship. Its function is to control the pressure of the gas.

Bank a Machine (To). To lower the inner wing, to counteract the centrifugal force of the machine.

Body or Fuselage (The). The main portion of the craft, which contains the engine, pilot and observer's seats, and the fuel tanks.

Bump (A). A point where two currents of air conflict.

Bus (A). Pilot's slang for an aeroplane.

Chassis. The undercarriage.

Control Lever (The). The lever that manoeuvres both ailerons, wings, and elevators.

Drift (The). Of an aircraft is the distance by which the craft is carried out of its course (drifted) by an air-current.

Elevator (The). Is used for steering and balancing in the up and down directions.

Gadget (A). Popular aeronautical term for varied appliances, great and small.

Gasbag (A). Every aeroplane pilot refers contemptuously to airships as gasbags.

Glide (To). Is to descend with the engine cut off.

Gun-bus (A). A fighting aeroplane.

Head-resistance (The). The total resistance in the line of motion.

Hun (A). The Royal Flying Corps term for a beginner.

11

Joy-ride (A). A trip up aloft is invariably referred to as a joy-ride.

Joy-stick (The). The air-pilot's slang for the control lever. Lift. A matter of varying pressures on given surfaces. Nose-dive (To). When the craft is descending in a vertical direction to the earth.

Pancake (To). Is for the craft to fall flat to the ground. Prop (The). Abbreviation for propeller. Pusher Aeroplane (A). With the engine and propeller at the rear.

Pylon-Pilot (A). A gentleman who is biased in the matter of preferring a large and admiring audience to fly over.

Quirk (A). R.N.A.S. term for a beginner.

Sausage (The). Slang for a kite balloon.

Screw (The). Of a seaplane is the slang for propeller.

Side-Slip (A). Meaning obvious slipping inward of the craft.

Skidding. Slipping outward of the craft.

Spin (A). The most unpleasant sensation possible in mid-air. It usually occurs after over-banking, with the result that the aeroplane spins round like a top, and finally, nose-diving, crashes to earth.

Streamline. A certain definite shape on the plan of which all aeroplanes are constructed. This plan allows the lines of the craft to follow the direction of the currents of air caused by the head-resistance.

Stunt (A). Any trick in the air.

Tractor Aeroplane (A). With the engine and propeller to the fore.

Undercarriage. The framework beneath the body of the craft. It serves both the purposes of landing and of absorbing the shock thus caused.

Volplane. To glide.

CHAPTER 1

The Navigation of the Air

THE SURFACE OF THE EARTH

A map of the surface of the earth is to many people hardly more distinguishable than a Chinese love-letter or the American Morse Code. The markings are crudely unmistakable; but a maze of colours and angles and shapes. Yet this same evil contraption, given the geographical position of the North, and a distinguishable point on the surface of the earth, is simple to read as an open book. With the airman, however, the angle of perspective is different and certainly more bewildering. He has no single point but the entire earth at his feet, stretching away to the oblivion of the sky-line in the direction of every point of the compass. The general position is harder to grasp, and map making and reading form no small part in the curriculum of his education. While navigation is as important to him as it is to the sailor.

There is much in common between sea and air. The elements are similar. The traditions and precedents of the older Service will, in time, apply equally to either.

With regard to navigation and pilotage the main differences are: whereas the view of the sea navigator is on the level, that of his brother of the air lies always below and covers an extremely wide area.

What does the surface of the earth look like viewed from above? The first view over the side is both curious and bewildering. It is a Lilliputian world, over which swarm numerous ant-like figures. It is pleasing to the eye; a regular, unorthodox riot of colours. The colour scheme strikes one more than any other element. The grouping of towns and cities, villages and hamlets is peculiar. The roads and railways in the more populous districts intermingle in puzzling fashion. Naturally the sharpest division is that between land and sea. The blue of the one borders the grey of the other, with a thin dividing line of yellow sand of the foreshore. This yellow on the sea fringe is conspicuous: and from a certain altitude over the sea the bed is thrown up in bold relief.

These details are all supplied in the contour maps. But the map to the airman is more than a voiceless jumble of shapes and colours. It bespeaks a glorious panorama of brown-smudged altitudes, blue-lined rivers, green-tinted plains, grey-blotted towns and villages, straight, black-lined railways, that are criss-crossed into squares to be criss-crossed again, and given ugly appellations as Ac 31, Df 22, maps that are to be read only by compass and by scale.

Piecing together the intermediate colours in the grey background of the land, we have, most conspicuous, the blue of the rivers and lakes. As landmarks they are the most easily distinguishable, excepting in wet weather, when they overflow their banks and change materially the appearance of the country for miles around. Next in order of importance are railway-tracks, distinguishable by reason of their regularity and directness; they connect up the principal centres of population like network. Tunnels are at times apt to be disconcerting. The track will disappear from view for half a mile or so. But here again reference to the map soon enables the pilot to pick up the broken thread.

Large towns and populous districts are unmistakable. The key to their identity is the plan of the diverging lines of roads, rivers and railways.

Passing to the open country, woods are conspicuous, but above an altitude of 2,500 they present the surface of a level meadowland. Fields of crops differ in shade with the varying seasons of the year. Wheat in summer presents a golden-yellow appearance; in autumn, brown; in spring, green. Stubble fields are lightish brown in appearance, and dark green fields are usually found to be roots.

Roads follow almost exactly the system of railways. First-class or main roads are easily distinguishable from their width, the blue steelish appearance of their surface, and the lines of telegraph and telephone wires along either side. The old Roman roads in England are most easily distinguishable by reason of their directness. Among other conspicuous objects are golf-links; the greens and the yellow sand-bunkers stand out prominently, and glass-houses that glitter dazzlingly in the sun.

Above an altitude of two thousand five hundred and three thousand feet the entire surface of the earth, hill and valley, wood and field, appear to be at the same level. Landmarks are most difficult to distinguish when flying either at an extremely low or extremely high altitude. The time on sunny, cloudless days passes with great rapidity; in dull, cloudy weather it drags, until the seconds seem minutes, and the minutes hours. The natural course of the machine is never a direct one. It is apt, first, to veer to the left, then to return to the direct course, and then branch off again to the right.

Factory chimneys and railway locomotives are useful to the air pilot. Their smoke indicates the direction of the prevailing wind, so necessary in the matter of landing the aeroplane, which must be performed head against the wind, as also getting off from the ground.

The difficulty of aerial navigation may be gauged from the fact that a pilot recently lost his way when flying between Hendon and Chingford. Another affair of the same kind was the cause of numerous questions in the House of Commons, and concerned an aeroplane of the latest type that had been flown across Channel to the firing-line, and landed in the enemy's country on its first trip. A German pilot, in similar fashion, flew down the Belgian coast, and landed at Calais in mistake for Ostend, there to be promptly made a prisoner. And yet another instance is on record of an R.F.C. pilot who, setting out one fine morning from somewhere in Kent, ran into a dense bank of fog, and eventually landed in Norfolk. Unaccustomed to the broad dialect of the natives, he imagined for the moment that he had found his way across Channel and landed in the German lines, and was about to set fire to his machine when he discovered his happy mistake.

The majority of these errors can be avoided by reference to the map and the use of the altimeter, another name for which is the statoscope. This instrument is contained in a large metal case and registers the altitude in hundreds of feet. Beneath the face is an opening, into which is fitted a taut rubber membrane, with a small rubber tube leading to the outer air. By pinching the latter between the fingers, the outer air is excluded from the membrane. When the craft ascends, the air in the statoscope will expand, when it descends it will contract. Contraction or expansion both react on the rubber membrane, which will be sucked inward in descending, and when ascending be blown outwards. By means of delicate internal machinery these movements are conveyed to the indicator hand on the disc. But the altimeter only registers height above sea-level.

Thus, an airman setting off from an aerodrome that lies some 2,000 feet above the level of the sea, would fly on with the altimeter registering, let us say, four thousand feet; yet in reality he would only be two thousand above the level of the land, and in constant danger of collision with altitudes on the surface of over two thousand feet.

The matter of altitude varies considerably with the nature of the flying. For war work, usually well over 8,000; for commercial purposes, anything from between 2,000 to 6,000 feet. The greater the altitude the safer is the flying. The engine of a machine failing at a height of 8,000 leaves the pilot a radius of, roughly, ten square miles in which to choose a landing-place; at 9,000, twelve square miles; and at 10,000 ten, and so forth.

A comparison between the altitudes of the highest mountain peaks of the world and flying offers matter for interesting thought. We discover that the war altitude of flying ranges from the height of the Catskill Mountains to the peak of Teneriffe, and that the crest of Mount Everest is double the height of the present-day flying altitude. We have no great mountains in this country, but the hills tower sufficiently to form a continual danger to passing aircraft. No doubt in time to come such danger spots will be topped by aerial lighthouses and beacons.

Contour, from the airman's point of view, is the important characteristic of the map.

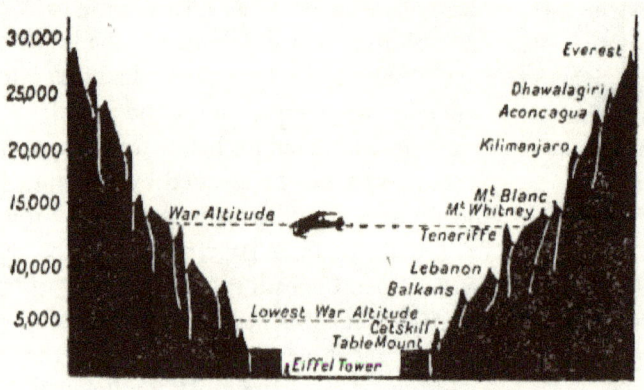

FIG. 1.   A COMPARISON OF FLYING HEIGHTS

A map after the style of the Mercator's Chart would be an ideal map for the air. It would be constructed on the following principle. The Rhumb lines on the earth's surface would be represented by straight lines on the chart. And angles on the earth's surface would be equal to the corresponding angles on the chart. The only markings would be contour, roads, railways, rivers, and towns.

A map of London on this principle would appear after the fashion of Fig. 2.

16

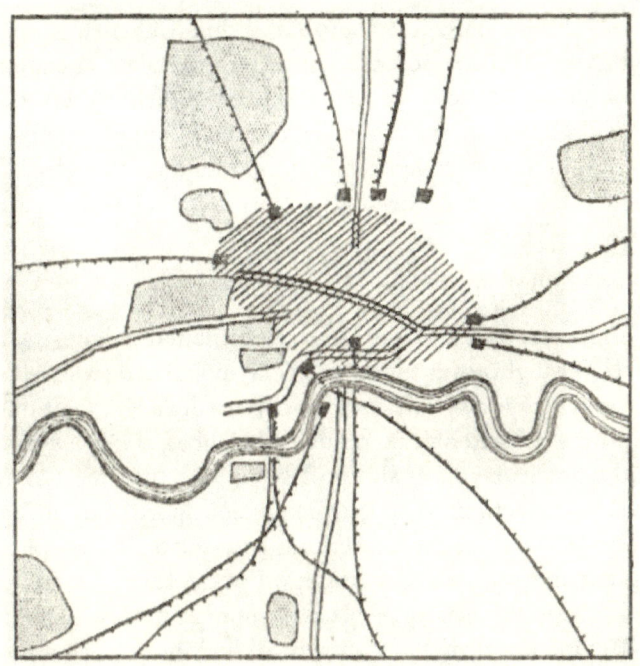

FIG. 2. HOW LONDON APPEARS FROM ABOVE

LAWS OF THE AIR

Naturally so vast an area as the air calls for special regulations and laws. And as long since as 1902 a conference of balloonists met at Brussels. The meeting devoted the better part of the time to discussing the differences between military and civilian types of craft, the use of a distinguishing flag for each craft, and the organisation of the lately formed Fédération Aéronautique Internationale, a body that now governs aeronautical matters of almost every nation of the world, and to which is affiliated our Royal Aero Club.

The latter institution has been instrumental in drawing up various rules and regulations regarding flying in Great Britain, the majority of them as a safeguard to the aviator himself. For instance, to avoid collision in mid-air:—

Two aircraft meeting each other, end on, and thereby running the risk of a collision, must always steer to the right. They must, in addition to this, pass at a distance of at least 100 metres, taken between their nearest adjacent points.

Any aircraft overtaking another aircraft is responsible for keeping clear, and must not approach within 100 metres on the right, or 300 metres on the left of the overtaken aircraft; and must not pass directly underneath, or over, such overtaken aircraft. The distance shall be taken between the nearest adjacent points of the respective aircraft. In no case must the overtaking aircraft turn in across the bows of the other aircraft after passing it so as to foul it in any way."

Again, the R.A.C. issued the following notice: —

Flying to the danger of the public is prohibited, particularly unnecessary flights over towns or thickly populated areas, or over places where crowds are temporarily assembled, or over public enclosures, or aerodromes at such a height as to involve danger to the public. Flying is also prohibited over river regattas, race meetings, meetings for public games and sports, except flights specifically arranged for in writing with the promoters of such regattas, meetings, etc. Any disregard of the above prohibitions will render the aviator liable to censure, fine not exceeding £20, suspension of the competitor's certificate, and removal from the competitors' register.

In 1913 the government passed the Aerial Navigation Act, that dealt with the specified areas over which the navigation of "every class and description of aircraft" was prohibited. These areas comprised dockyards, fortresses, arsenals, harbours and barracks.

No aircraft from abroad is allowed to make a landing in this country, except in special areas. The person in charge of such aircraft must be in possession of a clearance of a British consular officer from the country in which the voyage was commenced. No person in any aircraft entering the United Kingdom shall carry or allow to be carried in the aircraft (a) Any goods, the importation of which is prohibited by the law relating to customs, (b) Any goods chargeable upon importation into the United Kingdom with any duty of Customs, except such small quantities as have been placed on board at the place of departure as being necessary for the use during the voyage of the persons conveyed therein. (c) Any photographic apparatus, carrier or homing pigeons, explosives or fire-arms; and (d) Any mails.

The person in charge of the aircraft shall not continue his voyage until he has obtained a permit from the authorised officer, for which a fee of £3 will be payable in the case of an airship and £1 in case of an aeroplane.

Foreign naval or military aircraft shall not pass over or land within any part of the United Kingdom or the territorial waters thereof except on the express invitation, or with the express permission, previously obtained, of His Majesty's Government. Such aircraft shall enjoy such exemptions from the foregoing Orders and be subject to such special conditions as may be specified in the invitation or permission.

Nothing in the foregoing Orders shall be construed as conferring on a person navigating an aircraft any right to land in any place as against the wishes of the owner of the land or other persons interested therein, or as affecting the rights or remedies of any person in respect of any injury to persons or property caused by any aircraft.

"Any person navigating an aircraft in contravention of the foregoing Orders is liable on conviction to imprisonment for six months or to a fine of £200, or to both imprisonment and fine.

NAVIGATION AND PILOTAGE

Of the various zones, tropical and subtropical lend themselves more easily to aviation. The explanation is that the weather there is more reliable. The various seasons are more sharply defined. There is no unpleasant intermingling of calm and stormy weather. To a degree one may be certain twenty-four hours previous what the weather conditions promise to be. And the tepid air is favourable to aviation, never the warmest of professions.

Per contra the difficulties encountered in a temperate zone, as the one within which this country lies, are enormous. Rain, sun, snow, fog, all are possible within the incredibly short space of twenty-four hours. For days on end flying will be impossible, and the pilot thus kept idle and useless.

Closely akin to this matter of weather is the contrast between night and day flying. It is common knowledge that flying is mostly confined to daylight. The darkness holds many different dangers and terrors. First, the surface of the earth is lost to view. This intensifies the dangers of landing, always a hazardous enterprise. To some extent this difficulty is overcome by the use of landing flares, which in a darkened country stand out with prominence. The most favourable of these night-lighting schemes is that recently adopted by the enemy.

A large white light is placed in the centre of the landing-ground, sunk into a trench in the ground and covered with thick glass to withstand the weight of an aeroplane. At a distance of about 250 feet from this light, and also sunk into the ground, are four red lights corresponding to the cardinal points of the compass. Each of the red lights is connected by subterranean cables to a windvane, mounted on a mast or tower at some convenient point.

At night the central light glows constantly, while the red light in the direction of the wind indicates to the pilot the wind conditions where the landing is to be made. It is understood that a system of altering the lights has been devised, so that an aviator must understand the code in order to know his whereabouts. Thus, enemy airmen are prevented from using the lights as guides.

Another method is to extinguish the lights immediately the pilot has left the ground and wait for his return signal before relighting them. This signalling is performed by firing a bullet of a certain colour from a Very's pistol at a low altitude.

However, night flying is an art in itself, and is only permitted to experienced pilots; the principal reason being, as previously mentioned, that darkness obliterates all landmarks, which brings us to the matter of pilotage and navigation.

The former is accomplished by the aid of landmarks and the map; a compass is unnecessary. On the other hand, navigation is steering a course out of sight of landmarks by compass. And though the compass is said to be the best friend of the sailor, yet more so is it of the airman.

It is a similar instrument to that employed on a ship. The variation—that changes slightly every year—is similar; also, the deviation this latter being a matter to do with the metal in the framework and the engine of the machine, which is in manner similar to the natural magnetism in the earth that causes the variation of the compass needle from true to the magnetic north. Deviation again varies the compass further from the true north, and is compensated for by the arrangement of certain magnets that draw the needle back to the correct position.

Later we learn, *vide* the *Scientific American*, of the invention of an airman's compass which is visible at night by its own light. With this compass:—

A knowledge of navigation is not essential for laying a course. The first step is to set the instrument upon the chart at the spot indicating the user's location. The zero mounting of the outer ring, in line with the arrow point on the glass crystal, should point toward the north or top of the map. Any course desired (or the direction to be travelled in going from one location to another) may be found by elevating, to an angle of 45 degrees, the arm of metal attached to the outer ring and then sighting over its top and the niche in the magnifying glass bezel ring to a pin stuck in the chart at the point of destination. Such a process illustrates one important advantage of this compass over similar instruments, namely, that parallel rules for sighting are unnecessary and may be dispensed with.

In order to travel from any location to a particular destination it is essential to apply the magnetic variation. With other compasses it is necessary to add or subtract this magnetic difference, depending upon whether the variation is westerly or easterly. Doing so gives the magnetic head to be travelled, read on the centre dial in the bowl. In using this compass, however, both adding and subtracting are done away with. It is merely necessary to move the lubber's line, indicated by a white line and arrow painted on the crystal, to the point of destination. This line becomes the lubber's line to be followed in actual travel.

The present compass, measuring an inch and a quarter thick and two and three-quarter inches in diameter, contains no steel except that in the magnet, so the needle cannot become deranged by being attracted to another part of the compass. The bowl is made of bronze and painted, while the fittings are of brass. A magnifying glass, mounted in the bezel ring and fitted over the dial, enlarges the figures on the latter so that they may be read more easily. A nickel ring attached to the outside of the bowl is for convenience in carrying the instrument with a strap, if desired.

To increase the accuracy of this compass, the card is mounted in a mixture of alcohol and distilled water, thus rendering the magnetic float more buoyant and sensitive. The markings on this compass are readable at night in the light from the radium dial, which is graduated every 5 degrees and numbered every 20 degrees. The last zero is omitted in all numbers to avoid crowding.

Another deterrent to flying an accurate course are cross-currents of air. To avoid this difficulty, it is usual for the pilot to plot out a true course by mathematics preparatory to leaving the ground, making due allowance for the cross-currents and the mileage. Inappropriate word! Despite the fact that aerial is so remarkably similar to sea navigation, the R.F.C. still persist in talking of flying at so many miles an hour. How much better it would sound than saying: an aeroplane was making fifty miles an hour, to say, it was making forty-five knots—never knots an hour. A knot is equivalent, roughly, to 6,080 feet or 2,026 yards.

So much for today. In the future, within the space of a very few years we will find beaten tracks in the air as today they lie across the great oceans. There will be special trade routes and commercial tracks. But they will, without exception, all lie eastward of the United Kingdom.

CHAPTER 2

Climatic and Geographical Conditions

Aviation develops more and more day by day. To the uninitiated such development is regarded with interest, but not appreciation. This by reason of the strenuous times in which we live, and the necessary military secrecy which prohibits public discussion concerning the development of the various craft. To the man in the street aviation provides a pleasing interlude to the grim chorus of war. It is spectacular, thrilling, heroic! Beyond that it is not realised that the aeroplane and airship are no longer units but decisive factors in battle.

Yet the air is common to all. To every Power that has the necessary craft it provides a free highway, for good or evil. And what is common to all cannot be held by all. One alone can control. In time past it was the sea that was the common element. From the time of the Roman Empire the dominating Powers of the world have held the sea before conquering the land, and, incidentally, been possessed of ample seaboards. Spain is witness to the latter fact, as also France, and later our own Empire. We mastered the sea: we mastered the world! Now the air, by reason of its accessibility, has superseded the sea. In the future, the mastery of the air must mean the dominion of the world.

But before further discussion it will be well to consider the types of craft. They are three in number: aeroplane, seaplane, and airship. The former operates entirely over land; the seaplane, as its name would imply, over the sea; and the latter, over both land and sea. Which of the three offer greater possibilities in the future? For the nonce we will adopt the aeroplane, by reason of its already extensive field of operations.

Studying the map of the world, from the point of view of the air, what do we discover? Not five continents and five oceans, but one great tract of land that stretches from Hammerfest in the north to Capetown in the south, westward to Lisbon, eastward to Vladivostock, comprising three entire continents. For the rest the main group is surrounded by the great oceans, in which lie the distant continents of Australasia and America.

How does this redistribution affect Great Britain? Our islands will lie on the extreme western edge of civilization. No longer will the activities of the world turn on a hub so distant from the centre. No longer will this country be an island. For many years to come the uncertain climatic conditions of the Atlantic Ocean will protect our western shores. But to the east we shall be at the mercy of the world. In the future our lines of communication, our lines of supply, will all lie eastward.

Today the radius of aircraft is roughly 150 miles, with airships 300. Already many of our cities, manufacturing centres, and positions of military importance lie within easy reach of Amsterdam, Paris, and Brussels. When that aeroplane radius extends to three, and the Zeppelin to 600, it will include Metz, Cologne, Bremen, Milan, Berne, Innsbruck, Vienna, Berlin, Hamburg, Copenhagen, Saragossa (Spain), Christiania, and Bergen (Norway).

World supremacy for us then will be mastery of the air. Such mastery can only be achieved with an unceasing, unlimited supply of money and craft. And the future of aircraft lies in the hands of the constructors. Insufficient encouragement will entail the loss of valuable ideas and future prestige. With regard to the actual flying, aircraft are affected by climatic conditions even more than sea vessels. The latter have land-sheltered harbours to anchor from the gale. For the airman is no refuge. Inclement weather renders flying impossible.

Of all these elements, wind affects flying most. It is a matter to do with the speed of the craft over the surface of the earth. The speedometer of an aeroplane may register 80 m.p.h., but is influenced solely by the power of the engine. In reality the speed of that machine might be ten miles over the ground, that is to say it might be flying ten miles in a backward direction. The wind against which it is flying is one of ninety miles, or ten more per hour than its maximum speed.

Fog is a most dangerous condition to the airman. Once in a fog he loses all sense of direction and proportion. Earth and sky, and all landmarks are alike obliterated. Rain is blinding to the eyes, and affects the lift of the machine. And snow covers the surface of the earth with a treacherous regularity, rendering the landing of an aeroplane both dangerous and difficult.

But perhaps the most curious phenomenon of the air is the "bump" that causes the aeroplane to toss and heave like a boat in a stormy sea, and sends it plunging downward, sometimes as much as 200 feet. These bumps are caused by diverging currents of air. It is not generally known that there are currents in the air, just as there are currents in the sea. The explanation of the cause is simple. The night is always cooler than the day, but the earth retains more of its warmth than does the air. The latter, by the morning, in spring, summer and autumn is quite chilly, in winter icy cold. When the sun rises the rays beat down upon the earth, warming perceptibly the strata of air through which they pass. The earth is more quickly warmed, and the heat which it irradiates warms the layer of air immediately above it.

This hot air commences to expand and rises, forming a vertical column of warm air which, forcing its way upwards, meets with considerable resistance from the cold air which it must traverse, and which is denser and therefore firmer. In order to effect its ascent the warm air begins to work its way spirally, like a drill, or like smoke rising from the funnel of a steamer. Thus, a hot day following a cool night produces a choppy sea of air.

The manner of this current which the airman encounters largely depends upon the physiognomy of the country over which he is flying. Over a forest or wooded country, the flying is quiet and placid, because the leaves, saturated with moisture, are reservoirs of coolness and are warmed very slowly by the sun, and even when warm do not radiate much heat. A sandy beach, on the other hand, or a desert, is warmed very quickly, and in consequence the air above it rises in rapid spirals.

Sandy tracts separating wooded countries are always troublesome. The cool air of the woods pours down upon the hot air of the sandy tracts, the hot air in the meanwhile trying its best to escape to higher regions. The commotion may be imagined. The movement which the aeroplane undergoes over so diversified a surface may be compared to a continuous switchback. Powerless to resist these currents, all the aviator can do is to steer his craft, allowing the winds to carry him up or down.

The little islands of white cloud seen in blue and golden summer days are the lighthouses of the air. They signal danger to the airman. They are the tops of spirally ascending warm columns of air, and, just like a fountain, the cold air pours down on either side of the hot air.

If the airman has been drawn into such a fountain and escapes with his life, he can count his escape as marvellous. Almost invariably if he traverses such a geyser of air his machine turns turtle owing to the fact that the cold air pushes one side of his machine down, while the hot air pushes the other side up.

Bumps, however, are encountered only in the lower altitudes. Higher up they are replaced by clouds if anything more dangerous. In a cloud an aeroplane loses stability, which frequently ends with a nose-dive. These clouds vary at differing altitudes. Up to an altitude of 3,500 feet the most prevalent clouds are *Stratus*, filmy and greyish white in colour. From 3,000 to 6,400 feet are *Nimbus*, or rain clouds. *Cumulo-Nimbus*, or storm clouds, are prevalent between an altitude of 4,500 to 24,000 feet. From 10,000 to 23,000 feet are *Cirro-Cumulus* or "Mackerel Sky," and above 27,000 and up to 50,000 feet are *Cirrus*, or "Mare's Tail."

Above the clouds there is smoother sailing. Normal conditions prevail frequently. The warm air driving upward with uniform strength and wide layers makes an excellent medium for aircraft. If, however, there is a break in the clouds the airman must exercise the utmost prudence. Above such a break in the clouds there is no warm air to uphold the aeroplane. The air has been sucked away from this spot, and the rarefied air that remains cannot carry the machine.

Just as a skater drops through a hole in the ice, the pilot now drops through a hole in the air. The sensation is sickening—the same sensation one experiences in the sudden downward passage of a lift. If the aeroplane strikes a warm current of air in its mad downward rush it is saved. The air checks the dropping of the machine.

Another interesting phenomenon above the clouds is the mirage that often obliterates all landmarks. In hot, tropical countries like Egypt it is particularly noticeable.

After noon, until towards sunset, for this reason, flying is useless. This condition embraces India, East Africa, Salonica, Palestine, and Mesopotamia. From the latter country a noteworthy instance is to hand. An R.F.C. pilot, reconnaissance bound, noticed a detachment of British and Turkish troops, as he thought, sitting watching one another, without an attempt to come to blows. He signalled to them desperately. And it was not until he found his signals entirely ignored that he realised that they likewise were unable to see one another.

A no less unnerving adventure befell a pilot on the Western Front, returning from a patrol, one fine summer's morning, with low, racing clouds. He became aware of the presence of another machine that, in some mysterious fashion, always managed to keep ahead of him despite his accelerated pace. The chase continued for some twenty minutes. The other still retained his distance. He banked left. That tantalising machine followed suit. He turned right: likewise, the other. Until, with his hand already on his Lewis gun, he realised that it was the mirage of his own machine in the clouds.

There is the reverse side of the picture. The almost Arctic conditions that prevailed on the Western Front early this year. "Cold? There's nothing quite like it on earth," remarked one of our muffled heroes in answer to an enquiry. "How I'd bless the man who invented a dug-out that could be carried in an aeroplane fuselage. Of course, you may have the excitement of being shelled, and the possibility of having to dive into chilly space at a moment's notice, to keep you warm. But the atmosphere," he continued, "is about as frigid as any North Pole explorer could wish for."

It is interesting to pass over a high mountain peak in an aeroplane. The air swirls madly about the summit, seemingly attracting the craft like the magnetic mountain in the *Arabian Nights*. Disaster appears imminent, for surely the craft must be dashed to atoms against the walls of the peak. So thinks the inexperienced pilot. To his joy he finds that the aerial current keeps at a uniform distance from the surface of the mountain, rising as it rises, indenting as it indents, and in consequence he is carried in safety over the perilous height.

Having passed over the mountain top, he is confronted with the real danger. We all know how the water descends over the cliffs at Niagara Falls. It describes a huge curve, beneath which it is possible to walk. The air swirls over the mountain in precisely the same way, the airfall also leaving a free space between the mountain and itself. The suction from this hole in the air is terrific, and the unwary aviator who happens into such an empty space is irrevocably lost.

High and low tides of the sea are of extreme importance to seaplane flying. A seaplane pilot setting out for some distant shore, upon arrival there might find the tide out and be unable to land, owing to the distance of the water's edge from the sheds.

The stars are of comparatively small value to the air pilot. Navigation thereby requires numerous heavy instruments, for which there is no space in the limited accommodation of an aeroplane.

The main condition that supplies stability to aircraft is "lift." That is a phenomenon resulting from the motion of a machine relative to the atmosphere, a matter of varying pressures on given surfaces. The greater the lifting power, the more powerful may be the engine. The greater the supply of spare petrol, and the greater the radius of activity. This is important; for where today we calculate in tens of miles, in the future it will be in hundreds.

Now again geographical position comes into force. In a line directly east from Hull there lies no single British possession in this great tract of land, which for purposes of convenience we will name the air continent. Had our statesmen of a decade past been endowed with imagination and foresight they would have realised the supreme importance of the island of Heligoland. With an adequate fleet of aircraft, and Heligoland as a base, we would have dominated Germany, Denmark, Russia, Sweden and Norway. Heligoland would have been an outpost, a first line of defence. As it is, we must devise some other means and that immediately.

Our nearest and most to be dreaded rival in this matter of aerial supremacy is the German Empire. The latter, with her dreams of world domination ashore and afloat finally shattered, will turn her attention to the air. She has already done so in fact. Ten years ago, Herr Martin published in Berlin a remarkable book entitled *Berlin-Baghdad*, in which he stated authoritatively that "the future" of Germany lies in Asia and in the air. Principally he deals with the vast plateau that lies between the Himalayas and the Altai range, that is known as the Gobi Desert. Here is a fine natural aerodrome some hundreds of square miles in area. Strategically this is not a move of vast importance, but it points clearly the working of the German mind. Her designers and constructors are ever busy turning out new craft. Money is unlimited. We hear very little concerning aerial construction, directly; but indirectly neutral visitors tell stories of experiments with gigantic and strange looking craft over the deserted spaces of Lake Constance. Then is Germany's world conquest to be in the air?

Situated in the air continent are several ideal districts of aerial land; between Moscow and the Valdii Hills, which protect the plain from the violent northern winds in Asia, the Gobi and the Roba-el-Khali Deserts, and in Africa the Sahara, Libyan and Kalahari Deserts. And only one of these, the Kalahari, is in British possession, and that far, very far to the south. It must be remembered that now we talk of aerial Powers as apart from Powers making use of aircraft.

In the future each of these spots mentioned will be a controlling point of the world. The early twentieth century found one particular point which controlled the world. Men, matters and craft moved slowly. In time to come it will be a world without distance and without time; a world inhabited throughout, a Lilliputian world, that can hold no darkness, no uncivilization and no surprise.

That world lies entirely within the imagination and capabilities of the designers and constructors. The greater their gifts, the more rapid the realisation.

CHAPTER 3

How the Air Powers Stood

AUGUST, 1914

Flying in the early days of 1914 was somewhat of a gamble. Complaint had been made, and reasonably so, that we in this country did not regard the work of aircraft with due seriousness. Strictly speaking this was not correct, although the British Government neither encouraged the new science nor allowed the military flying services sufficient money for proper development; there were fortunately many far-seeing civilians who stepped into the breach, some with the necessary capital (no small matter where the development of aircraft is concerned) and some with personal services.

These patriots, in the face of all discouragement and official snubs, brought the level of British aviation if not to actually the same as that of the other great Powers, to very little below; thus, when the war broke out, suddenly and unexpectedly, we were not in the difficult position we might have been.

With all the imagination and verve characteristic of their race, the French had already hailed the advent of aircraft as the greatest event in history, and had given of their best, both in the matter of brains and money, to its further development.

GERMANY

With regard to the enemy, it has always been part and portion of the policy of the German War Office to immediately adopt and develop any invention, great or small, which offered in any degree to become a useful engine of destruction. Thus, it was with the aeroplane and the airship. Not with the eager impetuosity of their more emotional neighbours, but steadily, carefully, and at length they produced both craft in a proportion of marvellous degree.

They were in the lists as early as 1900; their champion, one Count

Zeppelin, an indomitable, iron-willed old man, to whom danger and difficulty alike were but items in a strenuous campaign. In spite of lack of necessary funds, numerous accidents and the total absence of public support, he persevered, and by winning the hearts of the latter had no difficulty in obtaining the former. So great an impression eventually did he make on the hearts of the German populace, that when the first aeroplane meeting was held at Johannisthal, the crowd scoffed and jeered openly at the unfruitful efforts of the intrepid airmen, declaring that they were all well content with their more solid and reliable airships; for had not airship L.Z.2 already flown 870 miles in 38 hours?

However, two influential staff-officers followed the Wilbur-Orville-Wright experiments at Auvors and Paris with the greatest interest. But in those early days of flying in the Fatherland, it was always a grim struggle between the lighter-than and the heavier-than air partisans. Then the government came forward with numerous prizes for both machines and engines, and the development of the aeroplane commenced in real earnest.

The principal characteristics of these aeroplanes was a strong adherence to the lines and the shape of a bird, particularly noticeable in the Albatross type; and since German aeroplanes have always retained that gracefulness and slender shape.

In 1913 the public subscribed £350,000 towards a scheme for providing machines and pilots for the Army and Navy. The pilots were to be trained, not at Army schools, but at the factories of the manufacturers. An altogether ideal plan that familiarised a pilot to his craft, from its birth in the shops, its development and up-building, the peculiarities of the engine, and the possibilities of the craft, and enabled him in the case of any emergency to take down his craft and put it together again, an advantage possessed by few pilots of other nations.

At the outbreak of war, the enemy possessed, roughly, 850 serviceable machines. They were divided off into battalions. To Prussia was appointed four, and Bavaria had one other. The total personnel was 84 officers, 493 N.C.O.'s and 1,708 men.

Here a small digression will be necessary to emphasize to a suitable degree that Germany was then and had always been, until recently, more of an airship than an aeroplane Power. The Crown Prince's trip with Zeppelin in the L.Z.3 in 1908 was the first step towards a national movement. From that date the Zeppelin industry grew apace. The L.Z.3 was taken over by the Army and renamed Z.I., and important bases were constructed in the greatest secrecy at Heligoland and

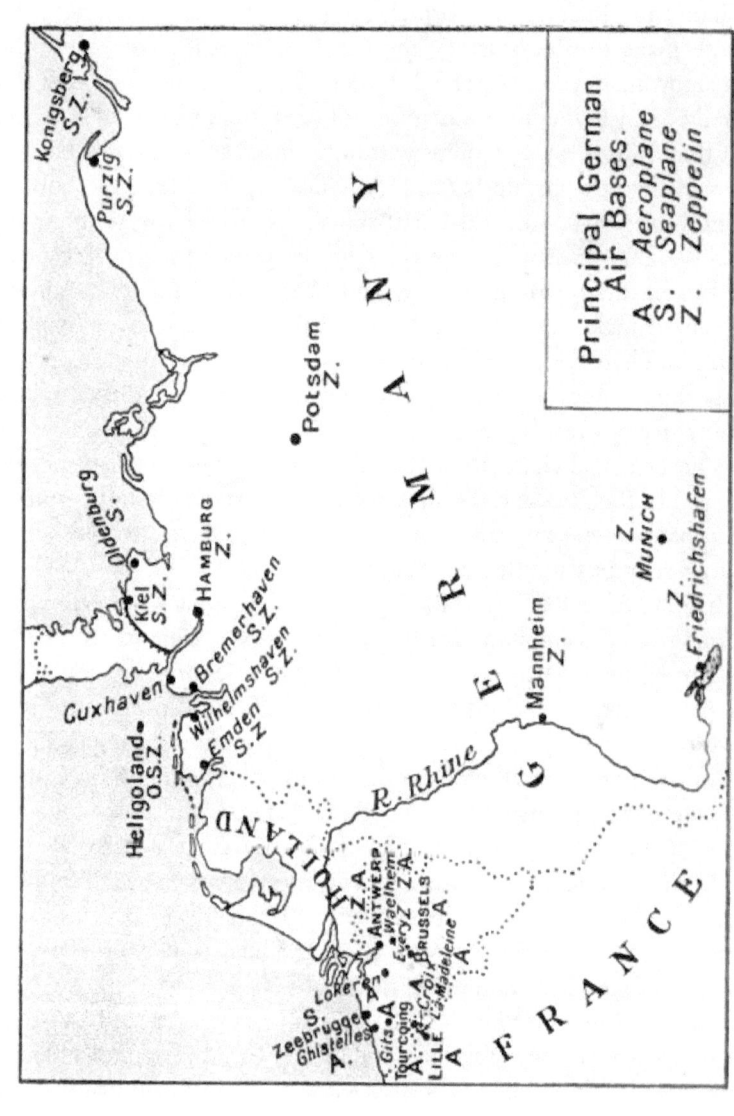

Principal German
Air Bases.

A : Aeroplane
S : Seaplane
Z : Zeppelin

Friedrichshaven.

After the destruction of the L.Z.4 by thunderstorm, August, 1908, the public subscribed 305,000; but disaster followed disaster, and although by 1913 Germany had produced a Zeppelin serviceable and airworthy, it was the most costly experiment that was ever attempted.

The army officials next divided airships into classes, and gave to each class a distinctive lettering. Thus P.L. was the *Parseval Luftschift*; L.Z. *Luftschift* Zeppelin.

To the navy were apportioned two squadrons of four ships and a reserve apiece, and there was a common station possessed of four double revolving sheds. The life of each airship was assumed to be four years, and at the end of that period it was intended that new craft should be substituted.

August, 1914, found Germany possessed of 30 serviceable airships of all kinds.

The navy estimates provided for 50 seaplanes. Six groups of 6 always to be in commission, the remaining 14 to be in reserve. At Cuxhaven a central station was erected; also, six smaller stations, each with accommodation for 10 machines, personnel, fuel, and storage. Putzig, on the Baltic, was converted into a Naval Flying School, and other stations followed rapidly at Kiel, Sonderburg, and Heligoland.

RUSSIA

The air history of our latest and greatest ally will, when it is written, serve to open the eyes of the British public to a more than considerable degree. Choc-a-bloc with interesting incidents, it will make obvious the fact that Russia had not only made great strides with her aircraft, but by August, 1914, was in the foremost rank of aeronautical Powers. Perseverance and practical application of science are the secrets of her success. Owing to State encouragement in the shape of big financial grants, when war broke out Russia had at her disposal about 300 highly trained military pilots, about 100 naval pilots, and more than 250 civilian pilots, while a large number of officers were in course of training at the various schools.

Even the Germans were surprised at the extent of her aerial resources, and Great Britain had no idea whatever of the progress made by her new Ally. In Russian aeronautical circles two names stand out above all others: they are Sikorsky, after whom the world-renowned giant aeroplane is named, and Chessborough, MackenzieKennedy, a young Scotsman, who at the early age of twenty succeeded in attracting the attention of the officials, and by them was entrusted with important experimental work; and at twenty-eight years of age, a stranger in a strange land, became the presiding genius in aeronautical construction. The two men are the closest of friends, and their joint efforts have furnished over a score of different types of aircraft, from the giant "Sikorsky" to the baby scout.

Perhaps the greatest achievement in pre-war Russian aviation was the flight by Sikorsky, flying one of his own machines, 25th April, 1914. He carried 15 passengers to an altitude of 300 metres.

Here it will not be out of place to give a brief comparative table of the various belligerent Powers, the numbers of their aircraft, and of their trained military pilots in August, 1914.

COMPARATIVE TABLES

COUNTRY.	AEROPLANES.		SEAPLANES.		AIRSHIPS.	
	CRAFT.	PILOTS.	CRAFT.	PILOTS.	CRAFT.	PILOTS.
Germany	850	1000	50	50	30	80
Great Britain	126	154	100	120	4	21
France	800	850	*—	—	28	30
Italy	210	200	*—	—	10	20
Russia	800	1000	†50	100	20	35

* Number unknown. † Rough estimation.

These tables naturally do not include either civilian craft or pilots.

FRANCE

France may well be called the birthplace of the modern aeroplane, for it was in that country that Orville and Wilbur Wright first carried out their experiments, that is to say experiments of an important nature. Previously, in America, they had made innumerable essays with simple gliding machines. At first the French Government were inclined to be sceptical, but after being convinced by numerous exhibitions in 1905, through the agency of a private company they purchased the invention for the sum of 40,000, on the condition that a flight should be made that showed a speed of 30 miles an hour. In this manner they gained a considerable advantage over the other Powers; together with an invaluable experience of motor racing, which sport served greatly to develop good engines, the most important asset to successful flying machines.

The first French officer took his certificate in 1909, and at the outbreak of the war there were 850 pilots and 800 machines, which were divided up into field squadrons each of 8 machines. The complete squadron was composed of 7 pilots, one of whom was in command, and 62 N.C.O.'s and men. These were again divided into three groups with headquarters at Versailles, Rheims, and Lyons. Towards the furtherance of this scheme £960,000 was voted in 1912, out of a total of £1,280,000 for military aeronautics.

Public subscriptions yielded a sum of £244,592. A proportionate part of this sum was handed over to the government to buy 208 machines, but only 72 were purchased, and there was a considerable scandal created by the poor quality of these.

The Committee of this National Fund decided to devote £17,000 to the foundation of 75 scholarships for training the military pilots on the condition that the successful candidates signed an agreement to join the military flying corps when the course was completed. In conjunction with the War Office, they selected 32 landing-places. A local committee of three military and three civilians planned the laying out of each new aerodrome. Twenty-five similar sites were under construction, the idea being to cover the entire area of the Northern and Eastern departments. All the aerodromes were joined up by telephone, and there were three alternative routes from Bordeaux to Biarritz, with an aggregate of 123 landing-places.

With seaplane craft the French had not made much headway. The Government at the Monaco meeting had purchased the two best machines for £2,400 and £2,000 respectively. In 1912 they voted £20,000 to this project from the Naval Estimates.

The airships were of the non-rigid type and small of bulk. There were 28 craft of varying sizes, with an average speed of 30 m.p.h. There were 15 airship stations dotted about the coast.

No experiments with anti-aircraft artillery are recorded, but the French pilots very wisely made preparation for future Zeppelin raids by continuous practice in night flying.

ITALY

The war in Tripoli was of immense advantage to the Italians both in the matter of experience and development in aerial warfare. There, 4 officers in six months made an average of 78 flights apiece; but on no single occasion was a passenger carried. Aerial photography was developed to an appreciable and considerable extent, which after proved of value. Two airships carried out 91 flights over the lines.

In Italy the monoplane was the favoured type of craft, and particularly those of Blériot, Nieuport and Bristol manufacture. There were 26 field squadrons in all, each of 7 monoplanes, and 4 squadrons of 7 biplanes, aggregating 210 machines. Each squadron was manned by 4 officer pilots and 4 officer observers and 24 men.

A somewhat curious and unusual difficulty arose in obtaining the necessary pilots, as the parents of the officers objected to their joining the flying services, as they considered such a course both degrading and derogatory. Nowadays they have become somewhat more enlightened.

A national subscription yielded the useful sum of 128,000, the major portion of which went to the purchase of the airship "*Citta di Milano*," afterwards presented to the army.

At the head of the military air service was a director, and under his direct supervision a battalion of specialists manning dirigibles at Lago di Bracciano, Venice, Verona, and Ferrara. Also, two new forms of captive balloon were under their special charge. Again, there was another air battalion, with centres at Turin, Somma, Lombardo, Aviano, and Pordenone, and the great aircraft factory in Rome.

The development of the Italian seaplane was very backward, although there were 15 stations along the coast. Airships were the most successful craft, some 10 in number with an average speed of 65 m.p.h. These were constructed in the aircraft factory in Rome, where 500 men were told off particularly for their construction.

SERBIA

Even little Serbia, in the first of those mischievous and ill-omened Balkan wars, made use of aircraft. Her equipment certainly was not on a very large scale, consisting as it did of 10 machines, 8 of these, together with instructors, being supplied by the French, and 2 others seized on railway transit consigned to the enemy. The majority were shipped from France to Salonika, and there transported to Nish by rail. The latter town constituted the principal aircraft base, where numerous Serbian officers, for the most part cavalrymen, were initiated into the gentle arts of flying, observation and map-making. The difficulties to be overcome were innumerable, particularly those of adverse climatic conditions; and at times the cold was so intense as to bring the tyres rolling off the wheels, and to warp the woodwork of the struts and stays, and even the oil had to be melted in buckets before being fit for application. No mention of Serbian aircraft is made save at the siege of Scutari, but they have rendered excellent service. At least they gained valuable experience for the future uses of aircraft in war.

This, then, was the comparative position of the most important Powers of the belligerents in the opening stages of the 1914 campaign,

CHAPTER 4

What Flying Is

It is not many years ago the brothers Wright essayed a first flight on a frail gliding machine along the sand dunes of the western coast of the U.S.A. and Count Zeppelin experimented over the waters of Lake Constance. Then a flight in the air was an event of worldwide importance. Today it is a more than daily occurrence, and the number of machines and pilots in operation are beyond count. The war has done more to develop flying than would have been possible in twenty years under normal conditions. And it is to be regretted that this, the greatest and most far-reaching invention of all time, should have thrived the most under conditions that savoured largely of death and destruction. However, it's an ill wind that blows nobody any good.

Today we hold the mastery of the air on all fronts. The enemy has been driven back helter-skelter to the safety of his own lines; to the protection of his anti-aircraft artillery. His policy of continuous offensive has been forcibly converted into one of defensive for all time. Yet Germany was better prepared for the war than we, and able to place in the field a numerical superiority in craft and trained pilots. But within six months of the outbreak of hostilities we had them well in hand; within nine, we had wrested from them their much-vaunted superiority.

How was this great feat accomplished? Regarding the personnel at a modest estimate, one may say that only 10 *per cent* of our war pilots had previous experience of flying. For the rest they were drawn indiscriminately from every rank, class and profession. Brought together within three or four months, they formed the nucleus of an efficient fighting unit. The secret is, of course, national characteristics: the calm self-confidence and pronounced sense of superiority of the British egotist. The Air Service needed men, the applicants heeded not when or why or how. The youth left his counting-house, his office-stool, and his chambers; donned leather coat and skull cap, and lo, he was an airman. Better, he was endowed with individuality, a mind of his own, to reason and decide. A stripling youth, he was immediately given sole command on one of His Majesty's latest craft, with power deadly enough to wreck the half of a city; an area to navigate whose limitations knew only the land and the stars. The confidence was not misplaced.

The average Briton—hackneyed phrase—lacks imagination. Therein lies the first quality of the successful airman. To one with too great a sense of the imaginative flying offers cold horrors that would beggar Dante's *Inferno*, or the efforts of the Spanish Inquisition. And last, but not least, he possesses the sporting instinct. The eye to time the ball, the wrist to play the straight bat, the head to take the steep hedge, will not fail him in the air. Flying is a sport! The only sport worthy of the name is flying! Sport quickens the mind, develops the muscles, supplies and develops self-control; each and every quality is necessary in flying.

Aviation is a youth-intoxicated profession. It is of the youth, for the youth and youthful in being, but wise in the inherent lore of the century-old efforts of preceding generations. The successful effort has been built up mainly from the accumulated stores, of experience of the unsuccessful efforts of the past. Our fathers and our grandfathers each and every one were airmen at heart. The hunting squire and the wandering navigator looked up at the birds on the wing and envied. They had the quality within their breasts, but in its most primitive form, that waited only the freedom of inventive faculty to find voice. To the youth of each successive generation, it was the same; it is a calling pertaining exclusively to the cool daring, the iron nerve and the reckless abandon of youth.

The latter is ever bold, yet with the quaint caution that lacks the decision of the older man; it requires that boldness to fling defiance from a frail aeroplane, strung up in the clouds, upon a great city hedged around with anti-aircraft artillery. He loves daring and adventure for the mere joy of it. He may glut himself with both in war-flying. Best of all, he possesses a nervous system unimpaired; to dive a cool hundred feet or so with a curse on his lips, but an unfluttered heart; to pass a shrapnel or H.E. burst at close range and never turn a hair; to sustain a mortal wound in mid-air and carry on.

Typical: there is one callow youngster of my acquaintance, quartered at an aerodrome somewhere on the Western Front. This hardened warrior of eighteen summers has downed more than his brace of enemy machines; made his aerodrome with struts shot away and petrol painfully low. He has nose-dived and spiralled and looped. Now he is pining his young life away with sheer ennui, because there is no new stunt left him to attempt!

There are those who would say he was suffering from air temperament. But does such a condition exist? Opinion is greatly divided. On the one hand, it is said to cause a pilot to become reckless and light-headed; to suddenly discover all rules and regulations irksome. On the other hand, in the delightfully expressive phrasing of the Services, "It is all eye-wash." Such a condition does not and can never exist. Let us consider for a moment the man and his habits.

Placed in a position of great responsibility, participating in a particularly self-centred profession that calls at once for prompt personal decision, foresight and judgment; he is no longer a unit, but a factor. To come to earth both literally and practically, to the status of a unit, in the space of time that his craft needs for descent were almost an impossibility. The individuality of the man is such that it cannot be checked and ordinated by commonplace regulations. But a far-seeing Service has already made allowances for it. He is granted privileges and liberties that the infantry and cavalry man would wonder at.

Perhaps a little of the glamour and the halo of mock heroism of the early days has by now worn off, but the airman yet remains the darling of the gods! We are apt to regard him, and especially on active service a knight errant of the twentieth century, *sans peur et sans reproche*, unmindful of the fact that flying is as much a prosaic business of the everyday as is soldiering or seamanship.

Typical of this view, there arrived one day, unexpectedly, at a well-known naval aerodrome, a captain with a polite request for a flight. The pilot selected was a mere youth little past the blushing schoolboy stage. The senior officer, with a confidence peculiar to our island race, unhesitatingly placed full confidence in his youthful mentor, even to the matter of life and death. The day was ideal. The trip exhilarating. The passenger was profuse in his thanks, terminating with a graceful luncheon invitation for the following day. The invitation was accepted, on the one part at least, with a grateful fluttering of the heart. They lunched *à deux* in a cabin hung about with many a quaint trophy, reminiscent of all quarters of the navigated globe, waited upon by a silent-footed, respectful marine.

When the good things had been cleared away a box of Corona-

Coronas was produced, and over their delightful fragrance they grew confidential. The captain, who wore on his breast a long string of decorations, honours of a grateful country, with an experience of men and matters that dated back many years, devoured the stories of this child of the skies, of another and unknown world, with all the eagerness, impetuosity of a midshipman. They were wonderful stories and matters of the air that were related. And the visit closed with a mutual promise of correspondence which has never lapsed.

From whence spring these youthful Valkyries of the air? The "shop" we know and are familiar with. Its value and efficiency were ably demonstrated in the hard-fought campaign of autumn, 1914. Osborne and Dartmouth are powerful names to conjure with upon the seas. But the airman! His Alma Mater is the British Empire; his university the wise counsellings of hoarse-voiced, capable warrant officers and non-coms., trained in the school of long experience. He is drawn from all ranks in life. A sprinkling of civilian aviators there were before the war, but they in numbers would furnish barely two squadrons; for the rest, they were barristers, clerks, public-school boys, engineers, undergraduates, journalists, motorists, and every other walk and profession in our national life. Unused to the air, within three or four months they have been developed into efficient pilots. How has this great mystery been accomplished?

Let us consider, first, the requisites of the useful airman! First and foremost, our national temperament and characteristics lend themselves easily to this new activity. To the youthful Briton, healthy-tasted, sport-loving, the air offers an irresistible appeal. It brings in its trail a pleasant savour of daring and adventure. The true airman must appreciate both these excellent qualities. Further, he must be possessed of good health. He must not suffer from heart trouble. The rise and descent through the various altitudes of the atmosphere, it has been proved by several very eminent physicians, greatly affect the heart. He must have good eyesight. This is imperative, for the major portion of his work, which will be of an observational nature, will take place at an altitude of 12,000 feet and over. For preference he should be between the ages of nineteen and twenty-four.

The good pilot is born so. He possesses an uncanny sixth sense of intuition. He is ready to the second for the unexpected nose-dive, tail-spin, or side-slip. He flies his craft, not as a machine, but as being one tangible body of which he himself forms part; knowing all its peculiarities—and there are many such faults and tricks; humouring it

A TRAINING AEROPLANE IN MID-AIR

in its every mood, and, incidentally, flying by a sense of touch.

The aspirant to flying honours must be neither too tall nor too short. This is a matter to do with the steering of the machine. Be he the former, he will find himself cramped in the confined space between the pilot's seat and the rudder-bar. Be he the latter, he will find that his legs will not be long enough to reach that most important adjunct.

For preference he should be on the light side.

The aeroplane has only a limited lifting capacity. Therefore, taking into consideration that it is often required to take up two passengers, not to mention bombs, grenades, spare petrol, and a machine-gun, every extra pound of weight is of vital importance. His stomach must be strong. A good sailor usually makes a good pilot. If his stomach be weak, he will be liable to air-sickness.

And the necessary pilots were supplied upon the principle of the organisation depicted in the following diagram:

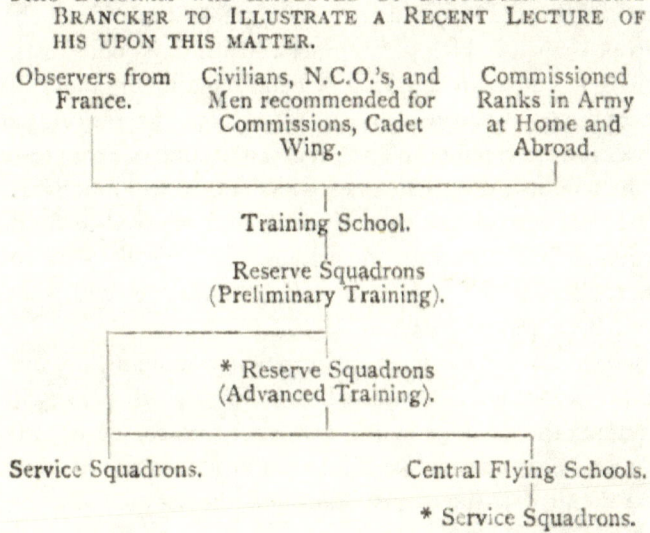

THIS DIAGRAM WAS EMPLOYED BY BRIGADIER-GENERAL BRANCKER TO ILLUSTRATE A RECENT LECTURE OF HIS UPON THIS MATTER.

Observers from France.

Civilians, N.C.O.'s, and Men recommended for Commissions, Cadet Wing.

Commissioned Ranks in Army at Home and Abroad.

Training School.

Reserve Squadrons (Preliminary Training).

* Reserve Squadrons (Advanced Training).

Service Squadrons.

Central Flying Schools.

* Service Squadrons.

* Includes a course at the Aerial Gunnery School.

As to the training, the ethics of good airmanship are not to be found in any text-book. They develop under the hand, emanate to the mouth, and are passed on again from mouth to ear. The new hand is taught that his craft must be humoured, never feared; that the air is always planning and scheming to trap the unwary airman; that gusts of wind will suddenly shriek up from the north or the east, the west

43

or the south, and send him bowling over to destruction.

There are "bumps" that wait, gleefully invisible, his transit through the air, that rock and shake him, then send him upwards to the waiting clouds, that play with aircraft as a cat with a mouse, always ready to send the frail aeroplane diving to the earth. There are fogs that take the air pilot unawares and blot out sea and land, sky and heaven alike, and leave him nerve-racked in an impenetrable gloom; sudden storms through which no aircraft can pass and live.

Solemn-eyed, tobacco-chewing petty officers and old-young, nerve-shattered pilots warn him of these dangers; warn him that the aeroplane is in nature akin to the dog, in that its affections and humours are of the elastic variety, that can be attached at will to each successive master that tends and flies it, that it possesses besides this animal-like affection, personality—a personality that is at once treacherous, sometimes stubborn and wilful, sometimes possessed of a demon of speed, at others of a demon of trickery and rapid movement, sometimes indolent and slow in the uptake.

In the engine shops, where are long grease-covered benches, bare masses of shapeless, lifeless machinery, struts, stays, bolts, bars, cylinders, he will be taught to take down and build up engines of varying shapes and sizes; to satiate their ceaseless appetite for reeking petrol; to remove caps, clean plugs, and polish greasy cylinders. From the engine shops he will be taken to the open air, which he will much prefer, and be treated to several passenger trips up aloft; allowed to fly the machine under part control, and finally under his own. He learns to bank, first to the left, then to the right; to land, sometimes with, sometimes without, his engine.

There follows a short period of practice straights, up and down above the aerodrome. They start him off in the first place with taxiing, running the machine rapidly across the surface of the earth. From taxiing he is allowed to make climbs of thirty to fifty yards, leaping on and off the ground like a great kangaroo, then short flights to gauge height and distance, and by reason of alarming personal experiences he will learn that the movements of the controls when in mid-air must always be slow and deliberate; then the final trip alone, and the gaining of the much-coveted air certificate.

CHAPTER 5

The New Dominion

The war has proved that aircraft has become an indispensable factor of a nation's safety, for the moment the war claims the world's output of its aircraft factories. In this country alone we are producing these machines in thousands, but even that huge out-turn is insufficient to supply the demand.

The military side of the industry alone will always draw heavily upon the aircraft workshops, for we have it on no less an authority than the naval and military chiefs that when hostilities cease, then and then only shall we begin to build up our air services.

Large numbers of aeroplanes will be required to train our flying men, to equip squadrons in all parts of the world, and to defend our island home against the invader. The future that lies before the aircraft industry is obvious, judging it purely from a naval and military point of view, but the military demands will be as naught compared with the civil.

Mother Shipton is credited with having prophesied that "Carriages shall go without horses, and men shall fly." In this Mother Shipton has again been proved to be right. Carriages have long since gone without horses; men have now flown. Since the days of Mother Shipton millions upon millions of money have been invested in railways and "horseless carriages," fame and fortune having been won thereby.

Even railways have their limit; they must confine themselves to their iron track, like the ships of the seas, which can only sail the ocean; and "horseless carriages," which can traverse along our highways and byways but not beyond our coast-line. In the free element of the air, we have none of these delimitations. Illimitable space provides us with a field of operation that knows no boundaries. Aircraft is becoming the greatest of all the industries that human ingenuity has devised for the benefit of mankind. It only remains for us to take advantage of the opportunity.

The uses for which aircraft are forthwith available are legion. Passenger and mail traffic have already become an accomplished fact. Italy today, to evade the submarine menace, sends her mails from the mainland to the island of Sardinia by air. Commercial transport in its many forms awaits only the opportunity for producing the aircraft facilities for bringing the industrial centres of the world into closer touch with one another, by the annihilation of time and distance which it will bring about.

These transformations are the inevitable result of the great strides that have been accomplished in the development of the industry. Aircraft has come into its own, and the future lies with the manufacturer and his supporters. They will "carry on" in the future even more effectively than they have done in the past. The world is ready and waiting for the new industry.

The far-seeing man who at this stage is ready to lend financial assistance to enable the manufacturer to develop the industry must of necessity reap a rich harvest.

While the present great struggle continues the Allied Governments take all the aircraft we can produce. It is not only of the present, however, that we must think, but of the future.

It is only in the preparations now being made for the days of peace that England can hope to gain in aircraft construction that supremacy which she attained in the shipbuilding, textile and other trades. That vast field of enterprise which lies in the sporting, pleasure and commercial spheres of aviation only remains to be developed.

To comprehend adequately the remarkable strides made by aviation during the limited period within which it has become a practical craft, a recital of the principal incidents associated with it must prove interesting to all those who have watched its progress from its infancy and who are keen on its development.

Starting, then, with the year 1900, the Wright brothers built their first glider, and in 1903 made their first free flight with a motor-driven aeroplane.

In 1906 Santos Dumont won the first flight prize.

In 1908 Henri Farman won the Grand Prize with his Voisin biplane, and Wilbur Wright commenced flying in France."

In 1909 Cody began to make successful flights with the British Army biplane; while Bleriot flew the Channel on Sunday, July 25th. In this year (August) the first Gordon-Bennett race took place at

Rheims, and the first British Aviation Meeting at Blackpool (October).

In 1910 the London-Manchester flight was won by Paulhan.

In 1911 the circuit of Britain was won by Lieut. Conneau.

In 1912 the Royal Flying Corps was formed.

Towards the end of 1911 the first practical school of aeronautical engineering was established in this country.

Lieut. C. R. Samson, R.N., made the first flight from a British battleship early in 1912.

In January, 1912, M.Vedrines, on a monoplane, made a speed of 92 miles per hour; and M.Taboteau, also on a monoplane, covered 128 miles in 2 hours.

In 1909, at the first Gordon-Bennett Meeting, the Aviation Cup was won by Glenn-Curtiss (America) at an average speed of 47 miles per hour. In 1910 it was raced for at New York and was won by Grahame-White at a speed of 66½ miles per hour. In 1911 Weymann won it at Eastchurch, Isle of Sheppey, at 78 miles per hour; and in 1912 Vedrines won it at Chicago at 105 miles per hour.

At the latter end of 1912 Legagneux attained an altitude of 18,767 feet in 45 minutes—nearly 400 feet higher than Mont Blanc.

In April, 1913, Gustave Hamel flew, with a passenger, on a Blériot monoplane, over five countries—England, France, Belgium, Holland, and Germany—at a speed of a mile a minute, landing at Cologne, and this without making a single stop *en route*.

Previous to this, M. Pierre d'Aucourt flew from Paris to Berlin—roughly 680 miles—in 7 hours 32 minutes.

In October, 1913, the German aviator Victor Stoeffler, flew 1,343 miles in 22 hours 47 minutes.

In the latter part of 1913, Chevillard toured over Denmark, Sweden, and Norway at a height of 6,000 feet, to clear the mountains, and covered nearly 2,000 miles in very mixed weather, thick fogs abounding.

At the same time, M. d'Aucourt essayed the Paris to Cairo flight, which he would have accomplished save for unexpected difficulties in Asia Minor.

In January, 1914, M. Pourpe flew from Cairo to Khartoum.

The aviator Garros, without a stop, traversed the whole breadth of the Mediterranean, from France to Bizerta.

Jules Vedrines, starting from Nancy, covered the whole of Germany at a bound, and in eight successive flights reached Cairo by way of

Constantinople, Asia Minor, and Palestine, thus emulating Brindejonc des Moulinais, who earlier covered a 3,000 miles journey extending to Berlin, Petrograd, Stockholm, Copenhagen, and back to Paris.

A more remarkable performance was that of Helan, for this French pilot, flying an ordinary Standard monoplane, on 39 successive days covered a distance of 13,000 miles across country, through almost continuous wind and rain. Better testimony to the reliability of the aeroplane it would be difficult to find.

Had the war not occurred, May, 1915, would have seen a round-the-world race in 90 days, starting from San Francisco, for the Aero Club of America had sanctioned it.

Then with regard to large aeroplanes, M. Sikorsky's giant had, before the war, made a series of very successful flights with as many as 16 passengers.

Descending to statistics, the French Aero Club stated at its general meeting in 1914 that in the previous year no fewer than 8,150,000 miles were flown by French airmen, as compared with 1,875,000 miles in 1912. In other words, these Frenchmen alone flew in 1913 a distance equivalent to over 300 journeys round the circumference of the globe.

Enough has been said, however, to illustrate the immense importance of the aircraft industry, and although military and naval needs will ever be growing, commercial necessities will demand a very large output from our factories. The few facts here given amply demonstrate this assertion.

To those able to look into the future it is obvious that the demand for aircraft of all types will continue to increase, and that for a long time demand will be greater than the source of supply.

The genius which the pioneers have so strikingly shown in meeting each situation is ever ready to seize the opportunities presented. The exceedingly interesting history of the industry shows that the pioneers, instead of waiting for opportunities, have made them. Their imagination and foresight, coupled with great powers of organisation and decision, have been the means of establishing on sure foundations the large businesses which, from the early days of the war, have rendered most valuable service to the country.

The experience gained in those early days, and continuously augmented throughout these testing times right up to the present, will be of inestimable value in entering, as soon as Peace is declared, upon the task of helping to equip the Empire in establishing commercial supremacy.

From that severest test of all, the test of war, the Whitehead-built machines have emerged with a solid reputation, and the great adaptability which the Whitehead organisation has always shown will, when the new call comes, prove again its great worth. It is an invaluable asset.

It is very interesting to inspect a well-equipped aircraft factory and to watch the many varied operations in progressive stages until the raw material becomes the finished product and the machine is given its trial flight.

Go, for instance, to the Whitehead Works. Take a look at the mill where the specially selected timber is being prepared for the numerous operations through which it has to pass before finally forming part of the wonderful machine which glides through the air like a gigantic bird. Note, in passing, the method by which the material which would otherwise be wasted is drawn by suction into the power-house, where it is used to produce gas, which in turn is utilized to generate electric current, which drives the machinery and lights the workshops.

In another department the metal parts are prepared. Here, while a large number of skilled men are also employed, women have taken up work to a degree not dreamt of a few years ago. In one section they sit in rows at the drilling machines or lathes, wearing blue overalls and caps; in another, begoggled like motorists with leather aprons, welding metal parts together.

In the large building (which was opened by the then Lord Mayor of London in the presence of some of the most famous men in England and the Colonies) the chief parts of the machines are constructed and the machines themselves assembled. In one of the long galleries the women and girls, in their white overalls, cheerfully apply themselves to the woodwork, while in the other gallery are skilled workmen each concentrated on his particular job.

On the ground floor many employees skilled in various handicrafts are at work assembling the numerous parts which, fitting together with mathematical exactitude, compose the wonderful mechanical birds.

It is always a matter of great interest to the visitor to see the accomplished and highly finished workmanship contained in an aeroplane. Everything is of the best.

During the various stages of manufacture the different parts are tested in a most exacting manner, but it is at the aerodrome that, after careful inspection as a complete machine, the final test is made.

WOMEN WORKERS CONSTRUCTING AEROPLANE PARTS

The pilot sits in the aeroplane, his sharp eyes noting everything, his ears listening intently to the stroke of the engine. At a given signal the blocks are withdrawn from the wheels. The aeroplane "taxies" along the ground, then rises into the air, climbing quickly and easily, as though delighted to demonstrate its power at last.

For a short while it appears to be travelling right away: presently it returns and, under skilful guidance, wheels and darts, climbs and dives, performing every evolution to the great satisfaction of the pilot, who, after light-heartedly "looping the loop," alights and confirms the impression already given to the spectators below.

Such then is a glance over the Whitehead Aircraft Works and Aerodrome, where, ever realising that the best work as well as the best material must be put into aircraft, the founder, whose strong personality permeates the whole establishment, has always made the welfare of his employees a matter of first consideration, and has seen to the provision of modern workshops with up-to-date canteens in close proximity, and, in addition, has established the Whitecraft Club, which is an organisation to bind together the best brain and hand workers for the common good.

Certainly, in peace as it has in war, Whitehead Aircraft is destined to play a great part in the development of the New Dominion.

The cult of flying has already passed into that of a profession, ranking with the best of the older industries. It has attracted the best of our Public School and University men, as well as those qualified by mechanical training to develop into capable engineers. It is a profession for the young, and should be adopted immediately a student has finished his academical career. It offers attractions not possessed by any other calling, and its emoluments are substantial and increasing. But the training must be of a whole-hearted character. It is not sufficient to have a knowledge of controls with deft hands to manipulate them, nor will dare-devil courage compensate for the lack of mechanical tuition.

It is essential for the aviator of the future to possess an intimate knowledge of all the engineering details composing his machine, and practical ability to deal with all contingencies. This can only be acquired by a thorough course of instruction in all the data of aircraft. Consequently, it is incumbent upon the incipient airman to learn his profession under the best of auspices, and to serve his pupillage in an establishment where, step by step, he will learn it thoroughly.

The School of Aviation established by Whitehead's introduces a distinctive method of tuition, inasmuch as a complete knowledge of the science is afforded, including the designing of an aeroplane, the building of it, and then the flying of the finished craft. This curriculum means that a pupil taking a course with this firm acquires all the technical knowledge necessary and then proceeds to the practical side, which includes a course of instruction on engine construction and running; in fact, if desired, the syllabus can be so arranged that when completed the pupil will be an expert.

The facilities at the disposal of anyone desirous of following this exceptional course of training are unequalled in the industry.

A pupil can go through the drawing office, and from there to detail construction, designing, and final erection. He will be instructed upon every item composing a machine. He can observe and take part in all the constructive details of an aircraft engine, and from thence pass on to the pilot in charge of flights, who will add to the knowledge thus acquired by tutoring him how to control a machine in the air.

The works are unsurpassed in this country, and the aerodrome is second to none in the world; in fact, the pupil fortunate enough to pass through this school will acquire a knowledge of his profession that will carry him anywhere.

Every student attending the school will study under such idealistic conditions that success will entirely depend upon himself.

CHAPTER 6

First Flights

There is recorded in some long-forgotten volume the case of the man who proudly asserted that he had experienced every danger that life is heir to, and truly enjoyed each one of them. He had crouched on the extreme crater of Etna when she had been in full eruption. He had escaped with his life from a land-rending earthquake. He had swum in the raging seas for half a day after a shipwreck. He had cheated death in the forefront of a bloody battle. To him danger was danger no longer. It was an event, a dramatic incident in his life in which he played conspicuously before the blinding limelight of publicity. To the small boy just breeched there comes a similar emotion. He feels the eye of the whole world to be upon him. The gawky schoolgirl with the flapping pigtail lately bound round neatly in a bulging bun; the youth at school enjoying a first surreptitious cigarette in some deserted corner of the quadrangle; the airman making his first flight aloft, share equally this feeling.

There is a call in the air that stirs strangely, irresistibly, some hitherto hidden chord in his heart. He is literally longing to try his wings. To see, to learn, to hear, to know, all are insufficient. He wants to do. For in the doing lies realisation; the air is before him, wide, clear, seductive. That vampire voice whispers in his ear. He falls whole-heartedly to such seduction. He does not yet know; that gentle tone is ever waiting to send the blood pulsing through his veins, the riot of madness to his head; his craft and his unwary self to destruction. He does not know, because he has not learnt. That alone is possible in the hard school of experience. But, gently! Caution and prudence are pearls of price to the pilot of the air.

The eventful day at length arrives. He waits impatiently, strangely uncomfortable in his unusual clothing—loose-fitting leather coat and trousers, skull-cap and goggles. He clambers aboard the observer's seat.

53

At last, his dreams are to be realised.

It is the great test, that first venture. Either the pupil will take to the air immediately, and after the first preliminary nervousness be quite at his ease, or, *per contra*, he will never make an airman. Hardly a matter of personal courage this; more of temperament. I knew a man in the Air Service—a quiet, unassuming sort of fellow; an observer by circumstance. He should, by rights, have been directing an army corps. It was his custom during spare moments in the air to chew milk chocolate and munch apples. A pilot glancing round at a strenuous moment would find his observer's head buried over an orange. And once, under a particularly violent bombardment, he had sat at the back and calmly taken photos of the bursting shrapnel.

At the other end of the scale, we have the case of a major of artillery—a man who had fought all through the South African War, and had won a D.S.O. for gallantry in the field. "He had never been up before," he said, "and was anxious to experience the new sensation." Permission was granted. Away he went with an experienced pilot; true, he was known as a daring "stunter." But when they landed his passenger sat like a statue for fully ten minutes without saying a word. Then he clambered out shaking and quivering, and swore a solemn oath that he would never go up in an aeroplane again to the longest day he lived.

But there are so many various craft of the air concerning which the general public are lamentably ignorant. Typical is the now historic instance of the good lady of the suburbs who, chancing to catch sight from her window of a spherical balloon passing overhead at a low altitude, bawled down to her Innamorato: "Come you up, Bill, 'ere's one of them Zeppelins they're talking so much about o' late." Were it not for the conspicuous peculiarities of the craft this would have been pardonable.

But who can mistake the long grey caterpillar-shaped form of the Zeppelin for the squat and graceful aeroplane? The balloon, inflated paper-bag fashion, with the boat-like seaplane? "I thought every air thing (note the delightful feminine vagueness) was a Zeppelin," said a well-educated woman to me recently, and this after two years of war. She would have believed that Nero played a gramophone while Rome was burning, or that William the Conqueror won the Battle of Hastings with his tanks, had it not been for the concise cold print of the history book.

But our budding airman knows. He is inoculated with the fever of the early days; steeped in the lore of the numerous text-books and impressed (sometimes) with the vivid stories in the daily Press. He has already decided which type of craft he will adopt.

As the majority decide upon the heavier-than-air craft, we will deal with the aeroplane immediately. He takes his seat. The braking blocks are withdrawn from the wheels. The engine is started and away they go. They leave the ground, the noise diminishes. They waddle like a lame duck through the "bumps."

The noise of the racing engine is impressive. It stands out above all other feelings. To a degree he is frightened, but such fright is merely due to unusual surroundings. The first view of the side is the marvel of the trip. The perspective is entirely changed.

There far below, the great hangars looking for all the world like a row of tiny boxes beside a long chicken run, lies the aerodrome, that he has so lately set out from. Almost involuntarily he feels a thrill of pride and joy. He, majestically soaring over the earth, and the tiny figures that are its inhabitants, can he be the same down-trodden humble "quirk" at everybody's beck and call in that inconspicuous blot below?

Where the quaint terms of the more experienced men had puzzled him not a little until he had learnt that a "bus" was a more generally understood term than an aeroplane, and that being "all of a doo-dah" was a picturesque way of saying that a pilot had got nervous in mid-air. A "Hun" and a "Quirk," he had discovered, were young gentlemen of about his own accomplishments; a "stunt" or a "joy-ride" indicated a bombing-raid or trick-flying, or a mere trip in the air; the "joy-stick" was that wonderful piece of mechanism that controls both ailerons and elevators; also that no self-respecting airman ever talks of his hat, but rather of his "gadget." His head had soon been filled with such strange terms as "gasbags," "bloaters," "B.E.'s," "glides," "bumps," "stream-lines" and "nose-dives."

Then come the trips up into the air. These first few passenger flights are invaluable to the training of the future pilot. Firstly, it accustoms him to an entirely novel element and sensation. Secondly, it accustoms him to the unexpected drops in the bumps and clouds, and sudden spins or nose-dives. He feels with the pilot. Almost involuntarily the correct moves come to him, and after a few flights he appreciates just the correct moment to climb or to dive, the correct angle to be allowed for banking, and judgment in making a landing.

To meet this need of acquiring the habit of the various movements, an American inventor has gone so far as to construct a balancing machine for amateur airmen. This machine can be fitted with various controlling systems to maintain the equilibrium of this device; so that it requires all the operations necessary in keeping an aeroplane well balanced in a stiff gale. It consists of two long arms that intersect each other at right angles; by means of a universal joint they are mounted on a pyramidal base.

Over the intersection of the arms is an airman's seat, a steering wheel and a foot-brace. According to one control system used on this machine the foot-brace and steering wheel are connected by cables with four weights one of which is suspended from each of the arms, along which it moves back and forth on wheels. By turning the steering wheel and the brake, which is pivoted at its centre, the weights can be shifted and the stability of the operator effected correspondingly; when one weight is drawn toward the centre the opposite one moves away from the centre. Shifting the weights produces effects similar to those obtained by shifting planes in an aeroplane, but of course the danger of a fall is eliminated.

Another method by which the beginner is taught is the dual control machine. With this craft there is a duplicate set of control sticks, steering bars, etc., which it is possible for both men to manipulate at the same time, But, for some mysterious reason, this type of craft, until recent months, has been frowned upon by the powers that be. Naturally it possesses both advantage and fault. For the former, it enables an observer whose pilot had been mortally wounded to bring the craft safely back to earth, whereas, with the old-fashioned machine, both of them would have broken their necks. With a beginner at one control stick is, however, another matter. Losing his head, and making feverish clutches at the stick, it requires all the instructor's skill to get the aeroplane right again.

Without dual controls the passenger, after some few hours' flying, finds himself, unconsciously, following the movements of the pilot, and in thus acclimatising himself, forces half the battle. On this principle many would-be pilots in the R.F.C. were put through a preliminary canter of three months' observational work over the lines before being permitted to fly themselves.

The best of these soldier men to make air pilots are the gunners. One may say without exaggeration that the direction of artillery fire occupies 70 *per cent* of the time of the airman on active service. And gunnery necessitates a knowledge of artillery, great and small, light and heavy, an intricate knowledge of that intricate subject range finding, and a fine judgment of elevation. There is no great difference in studying the battlefield from the surface, or at a varying altitude from eight to fourteen thousand feet.

In this country it is the invariable rule to employ an officer pilot: occasionally an N.C.O. observer. Across the water our gallant Allies reverse the rule. Judged by results, as every factor of war should be, their Air Service is superior to our own. Still, our authorities persist in believing that the rank and file are inferior, both in the matter of courage and mental ability. Which, after all, is nothing more than mere snobbishness.

But to repeat: the new hand has taken his first timorous glance over the side, when the machine lurches in an alarming manner. He finds himself staring up at the sky. For the first time he feels really frightened. However, the machine is not, as he believes, attempting to hurl itself to the ground below, but performing the very usual manoeuvre of banking—turning—though somewhat sharply, in a left-hand direction. He is not reassured until he catches sight of the pilot's face behind him, and then he knows that the angle has been greater than usual for his own particular benefit—to try his nerve.

Apropos to this matter of manoeuvring in mid-air, each movement must be as gentle as possible. A rapid jerk at a critical moment may upset the machine entirely, bringing it into that unpleasant position known as a nose-dive, from which an aeroplane can rarely recover. Also are there "tailspins," "over-banks," "slippings-out," "pancakes," and "stalls." The due avoidance of these ills is all part of this novel curriculum.

However, the worst fright of all is yet to come. The engine suddenly stops. The customary rhythmic roar fades away into coughs and splutters. No longer does he find himself staring vaguely up into the heavens, but cheek by jowl with the earth, that seems, more every second, rushing up to meet him. He is surprised—more, alarmed—at the speed at which the landing is accomplished. He expects a horrifying jolt as the machine first touches the earth, and is pleasantly surprised to find how gracefully the landing has been effected. The machine is driven across to the hangars, where the engine is shut off, and that wonderful craft of might becomes again an inanimate block of metal and wood.

The next few days are busy enough. Wireless, map-reading, gunnery, and then he is sat in a machine in a hangar and put through the various movements. His feet are moved left and right, making an imaginary turn in the clouds. With a reverential touch he pulls back the "joy-stick" to make her rise, and pushes it forward to descend. With other quirks he makes hazardous attempts at distinguishing strange craft in mid-air. It is an amusing pastime, for this art demands months of experience to acquire.

Passenger flights with an instructor follow, perhaps six or maybe ten in number. Until, one fine morning, he is ordered to attempt a solo trip, with a postcripted hint to be careful with his landing.

If only those other grinning idiots would go and bury themselves for the time being, he would feel much happier. Something's bound to happen with that gang jeering and ragging alongside, as he takes his seat. Afraid? Not likely. But, dash it all, what the devil do his aviationable hands mean by trembling in that absurd manner? Was that his voice, that feeble order to the mechanics to let go? If it was—— Possibly he got off in an orthodox manner,

but hardly liable to appeal to the warped understandings of fault detecting instructors. Well, never mind. All aboard. Drat the machine!

So, it goes on. The aeroplane behaves in a really disgusting manner, don't you know. He makes his landing, never more thankful in his life. Was it a good landing? Why can't that fool instructor say something, instead of——Oh! So, it was. Discretion is more congenial than valour.

Fast and slow machines; there is as much difference between a Morane and a B.E.2.C. as between a 40 h.p. and a Ford. From "crocks" he graduates to "buses," "buses" to "scouts," and so on.

He has the undisputed right to negative any machine or weather. But that is not the way of the Quirk. He is an airman of twelve hours' fame, with a strip of pasteboard in his pocket, bearing the magic sesame of the Royal Aero Club. The fall follows pride like a dog after a new bone.

Quite 70 *per cent* of air smashes happen to Quirks and Huns. One youngster, up for his solo trip, was troubled with engine failure at 5,000 feet. He pulled her out of the resulting dive, only to lose his engine again when 400 feet above the ground. By—unconsciously—superb airmanship he got her into the landing ground. But here disaster awaited him in a sudden gust of wind that caught the tail of the aeroplane and, bowling her over sideways, crashed her twenty feet to the ground. Dragged from the midst of the debris, he was a sorry spectacle, with two fractured ribs and broken collar bone. Five months later, to the surprise of all concerned, he was flying better than ever.

Giving a display of excruciating banks and daring downward sweeps over the pier of a once thronged seaside resort on the east coast, a seaplane was seen to crash down on to the shore. It happened so suddenly. One moment the craft had been flying majestically overhead, the next it was a mass of shapeless fabric lying in the edge of the sea. Mechanics hurried to the spot, prepared to find the badly mutilated body of the dead pilot. Instead, there rose slowly from the midst of the wreckage a sorrowful figure, immersed to his shoulders, spluttering salt water, and giving vent to his feelings in true nautical style.

Like the liqueur to a good dinner, as satisfying, as appropriate, the taking of the certificate concludes the preliminary training of the pilot of the skies.

There are several tests, the official rules for which are as follows:

A and B.—Two distance flights, consisting of at least 5 kilometres (3 miles 185 yards), each in a closed circuit, without touching the ground or water: the distance to be measured as described below.

C.—One altitude flight, during which a height of at least 100 metres (328 feet) above the point of departure must be attained: the descent to be made from that height with the motor cut off. The landing must be made in view of the observers, without restarting the motors.

But that is only the first step in his education.

With regard to the other types of craft, one may say that the aeroplane is preliminary to the seaplane. The latter craft is slower and heavier to handle. The balloon, again, is preliminary to the kite, or captive, and the airship. But there we enter upon a class of aircraft opposite in all essentials to the "heavier-than-air."

The motion of the latter craft through the air is, if anything, smoother and more pleasant: but the work accomplished is far in the rear of that of the aeroplane.

CHAPTER 7

Reconnaissance And Photography

I cherish a pleasant memory of the low-lying districts of north-east France, and the Flanders country of Belgium; reminiscent of a walking tour in the happier pre-war days of 1914; a memory of a quiet and peaceful countryside, almost entirely given over to farming and kindred rural professions; of a phlegmatic, somewhat heavy-thinking race of men, who viewed the world no further than the uttermost hedges of their own meadowlands; of a flat un-undulating country of never-ending acres of cultivated land and ploughed fields; of wearyingly straight, tree-bordered high-roads, and a bewildering network of small towns, canals, and railways.

The next view was from over the side of the fuselage of an aeroplane. Other days, other conditions; the country beneath was held tight in the grip of the devouring fiend of war. Yet that self-same country had changed no whit in appearance; the wearying regularity of the contour rendered it the best and easiest air navigable in the world. And the aeroplane from which I peered and its dynamic consorts had introduced an entirely novel element into the science of war.

No longer was possible surprise or sudden sortie. Any unexpected movement of troops on the part of the enemy, any massing together of reserves behind the lines, would be reported by the aeroplane observer in time to render the uses of such movement null and void. From the very first days of the war, aeroplanes took over the work of the cavalry. In a third of the time and at treble the speed the scouting was accomplished. So, it must always be. Warfare of today and of the future is a business of rapid movement, a product of highly scientific inventions and formulas. Motor transports rush troops and reserves from point to point in fewer hours than in previous times had taken days. With the speed of an express train or a high-powered racing motorcar the aerial scout is fluttering over the opposing armies, and the news is flashed back to the wireless to headquarters in an instant of time.

First and foremost, then the business of aircraft is the gleaning of information. This has brought into being a novel issue of warfare, and a strange breed of men whose profession it is to scour and police the skies, as the naval man has been doing for centuries past the seas. And the varying degrees of observation—scouting, call it what you will—all are influenced by the various types of craft.

Of these there are five in number. In order of development, the balloon is a thing of the past. However, it was the balloon that first heralded the uses of aircraft as vessels of war. During the siege of Paris, history tells us that as many as 56 balloons left the city carrying 60 pilots, 102 passengers, 409 carrier pigeons, 9 tons of letters and telegrams, and 6 dogs. In the time of the American Civil War an aeronaut named La Fontaine went up in a balloon over an enemy camp, made his observation, rose higher into the air, and succeeded in getting into a cross-current which carried him back to his point of departure.

In South Africa an observation balloon was in use at Ladysmith for twenty-nine days, doing extremely useful work in the spotting of Boer guns. The observer in an observation balloon reported the enemy's position on Spion Kop to be impregnable, and at Paardeberg disclosed the precise position of Cronje's force, and directed the artillery fire thereon. Today, with the much-improved anti-aircraft defences, the balloon is little better than useless; that is, of course, for flying across the lines.

Of the other craft the seaplane is but in the earliest stages of development, although one of these craft rendered yeoman service in the Jutland battle. The captive or kite balloon is employed on all fronts with excellent results. Here again, however, the craft is stationary and the observation necessarily limited. The airship—including the Zeppelin—is an ideal sea-scout. One Zeppelin will accomplish as much as an entire squadron of light cruisers. It has the advantage of being able to hover over an object at almost any altitude. This advantage, however—to use an Irishism—would be a serious disadvantage over the firing-lines where a stationary object the size of a Zeppelin would make a "sitter" target for the anti-aircraft guns. The aeroplane cannot hover, but is remarkably quick in movement and extremely mobile; a difficult target. This latter craft, then, makes the best scout, and to the uses of the aeroplane we will devote our attention.

First with regard to the personnel that man the craft, the observer is the Admirable Crichton of the air. He is a man of many parts. He must be at one and the same time gunner, photographer, wireless operator, and map-maker. His knowledge of military and naval strategy must be sound, He must know more than a little concerning artillery, both light and heavy. As a man he is abused more than he is valued. He takes the same risks as the pilot; yet when any brilliant feat is accomplished, he is ignored the while the pilot gets all the kudos. The nerve strain for him is greater than it is for the latter. He places his life, unreservedly, in the hands of another man in that most perilous of enterprises. The strain on his nerves may be judged from the fact that many of our best pilots have openly stated that they would not be observers for all the wealth in the world; that they would not have the nerve!

The art of observation is considerably greater than that of pilotage. The latter is purely mechanical, the outcome of practical experience. The pilot is part of the craft, in like manner to a chauffeur hired with a car from a garage. The observer supplies the brains, the head, and the eye. He is virtually in command. The pilot must obey his orders as to course and altitude, but neither is dispensable to the other.

There is a sharp dividing line between the two classes of work. Aerial strategy is concerned for the most part with long distance raids into the enemy's country. On these occasions the pilots invariably fly alone. There is only a limited space in an aeroplane, and with a plentiful supply of bombs and spare ammunition aboard, without which the object could never be attained, there is no room for an observer. Other objects are the destruction of lines of communication, railway junctions, high roads, headquarters, ammunition parks, etc., or the bombardment of fortified towns and areas within the enemy's country. Aerial combat might also be included in this category.

And almost all aircraft work at sea is strategical, as witness the various raids on Cuxhaven and similar ports, which were in nature akin to naval bombardments. The strategical moves, on the other hand, are more local in nature and confined within the limits of the fighting lines and the artillery range. They cover a very wide area. And with them all the observer is practically concerned.

Also, the observer must always try to keep in touch with the military situation, and particularly in the encounter battle be aware of the dispositions of our own troops and the positions of our artillery. Again, there are two distinct classes of reconnaissance—"Line" when observation has to be made along a line between two given points on the map, these points having been marked in previous to leaving the ground, and "Area" when the observation is over an entire area or district—which occupy the best part of the observer's time, and reconnaissance again is a very comprehensive issue. It is so delightfully indefinite, embracing anything from the movement of an army corps to the detection of a trench mortar. No circumstance, however small, but is worthy of note. And when there is no movement, nothing to report, that is the most consequential matter to report of all. It might signify the abandonment of an important position, or, on the other hand, might be merely a "blind" on the part of the enemy.

Decoys and "blinds" must also be allowed for, as the hiding of a gun emplacement, captive balloon, or ammunition park by foliage and branches of trees. Unless closely watched these matters may cause considerable error and misunderstanding. So much depends upon the vision, accuracy, decision, and certainty of the observer.

A railway train under observation becomes a factor of the war. Direction, component parts, freight—when possible—length, position, time, all mean so much to the man who is planning and plotting over his map miles behind the lines. There are trains in the sidings, some goods, some passengers; locomotives waiting with steam up; or the lines are entirely devoid of traffic. There is the sea, with the numerous ships passing to and fro. There, again, their nature is to be considered, direction and position; whether cargo boat, oil ship, steamer, or vessel of war. The condition of the coast-line. The ships lying in harbour; the high-roads leading up to the lines; whether they are congested with troops or the reverse. The position of fresh gun emplacements and headquarters to be noticed. And all these matters have to be entered upon an official observer's sheet; as baffling to the uninitiated as a Greek play.

However, besides discussing the various arts of observation, we must consider the general position. As has already been stated, the advent of aircraft rendered a sudden or surprise movement impossible. The aeroplane hovering over the enemy's lines is cognizant with every movement that takes place therein. Therefore, it behoves the military commander not only to keep his own aircraft constantly scouting over his opponent's positions, but also to keep him from retaliating. It is most necessary to hold and to keep the mastery of the air in the section that he commands; and the only successful policy is that of a constant offensive. This in fact has been the policy of our military commanders throughout the whole of the present campaign. Whereas the enemy has acted, almost invariably, on the defensive. This accounts to a great extent for the higher proportion of the loss of craft on our side as compared with the enemy.

As the war progressed the difficulties of observational work increased. The anti-aircraft gunners became more accurate in their firing, and drove the aircraft up to a higher altitude. This increased the difficulty of clear vision, and the observer was forced in many cases to make use of field-glasses to scan the various necessary objects on the earth. This, with the constant vibration of the machine, was no easy matter. And even at the increased altitude craft were apt to return to their bases, riddled with shot and shell holes. In one particular instance an R.F.C. machine returned from a reconnaissance trip with as many as 365 various holes in the wings and fuselage. Of course, the obvious remedy would appear to be to armour the craft throughout. But here again the difficulty of "lift" manifests itself. The framework of the craft must be constructed as light as possible. Armouring, then, is impossible.

Bomb-dropping is another matter that comes within the scope of the observer, also the direction of artillery fire, and last, but not least, photography.

The main characteristic of aerial photography is the danger involved in getting down to the necessary altitude to obtain the required focus. This altitude varies from 3,000 to 5,000 feet with the old-fashioned cameras, from seven to ten with the later instruments. It is never a very pleasant business, and particularly unpleasant if the anti-aircraft gunners in the district are accurate in their marksmanship. And weather conditions play no small part in obtaining the necessary results. The day must be sunny, clear, and cloudless.

Particularly must there be no clouds. A photo taken from, let us say, 7,200 feet might be blurred and useless, whereas another taken at 7,000 would come out distinct and clearly marked. Between 7,000 and 7,200 feet probably there lay a thin film of mist or cloud. These different *strata* of atmosphere for the air is not one huge void, but is made up of varying layers of air and mist and cloud have always formed one of the main deterrents to obtaining clear negatives with a camera from above.

For aerial photography is by no means a new art. As long since as 1858, Nadar, a Frenchman, made experiments with an ingenious contraption that consisted of a captive spherical balloon, in which there was fixed a small round orange-coloured tent, lined with black. The tent was to be used as a dark room, and in it he proposed to develop the photographs that were to be taken after the balloon had been let up.

From an altitude of about 1,500 feet he obtained some excellent results. Then a leakage of coal gas from the neck of the balloon above the car spoilt the plates. Three years later King and Black, two enterprising New York photographers, flying a free balloon over Boston on a clear day at an altitude of some 800 feet, obtained some excellent panoramic views of that city.

About this time Negretti returned from Italy, where he had been engaged in extensive experiments, to London, and in similar fashion succeeded in obtaining negatives of almost every district and landmark in the vicinity of the metropolis.

The next mention of camera work from above was during the American Civil War, when it proved extremely useful to the Northern States Armies for scouting purposes. An amateur aeronaut named Lowe placed his services unreservedly in the hands of General McLellan. The balloon was captive, and at 1,000 feet he obtained clear results as far as Manchester on the extreme west, and the Chikahominy on the east. After his exposures had been developed the disposition of the enemy cavalry, infantry, and artillery positions stood out in bold relief; likewise trenches and earthmarks.

Lowe invented the principle of map-reading which is used by all observers of the present day, namely, that of dividing the face of the map into a definite number of spaces by means of transverse lines at regular distances. These spaces are then lettered, so the district in the top left-hand corner would be A, that in the top right-hand corner B, in the bottom left-hand corner C, and so forth. The spaces made by the lines were numbered 1, 2, 3, etc. Thus a reading would be given, instead of "Enemy's heavy artillery immediately in rear of Richmond," "Enemy's artillery position A1D67."

However, even with the best maps which could be supplied the results were not as satisfactory as those obtained by the use of the developed negatives. The perspective of the former with regard to the latter was incomparably worse; differences in altitude could not be distinguished with such accuracy, and rivers, woods, buildings, churches, etc., were less easy to define. Therefore, it was determined to combine and to use map and photograph together. The district on the map was covered by the lens of the camera, and the developed negative was compared with the map.

Many plans have been formulated to do away with the human

aerial observer, the most notable of them a complicated idea, in which there figured a camera with a rotating prism. The prism supported the plates and was rotated by means of an electric current controlled by a switch on the ground below. However, it proved impossible to photograph any particular spot, added to which something was always going wrong with some part of the delicate machinery. This idea was abandoned for another and even more complicated scheme that required seven cameras. These seven cameras were placed in a large wicker-work basket in such positions that six of them pointed through specially made openings in the sides, and one pointed downwards through the floor.

Thus, a complete panorama was obtained. This plan was afterwards adopted by the British, French, and German military authorities alike. Later, in the earlier part of the twentieth century, an Italian inventor constructed a camera specially for air reconnaissance work. This was a permanent fixture beneath the under carriage of the machine. It was so designed as to hold 300 negatives, which were released automatically at given periods. A series of views was therefore obtained at regular intervals, giving an absolutely consecutive and complete record of the course of the ground covered in the trip. The pilot regulated the time between each photograph automatically with the altitude of the aeroplane. The higher the altitude the fewer are the exposures required. From a height of 3,000 feet it is estimated that 300 such views would photograph completely an area of the surface of the earth of at least 160 miles long and one mile broad.

With regard to the free balloon and airship, with the former when well under way the passage is smooth, notwithstanding a slight rotary movement, which is replaced by a slight throbbing caused by the engine or engines, for which allowance must be made.

Light and atmosphere, though of great importance for successful photography on the earth, do not there play the important part which they do in aerial work. For instance, the usual negative is obtained by allowing the sun's rays to be reflected off the object to be photographed on to the camera lens, and these

rays from the sun have to pass through a fairly dense atmosphere before reaching the object; and in the case of aircraft, they have to be again reflected through the dense atmosphere, made up of particles which not only reflect but absorb light, back to the shutter of the camera.

It was thought at first to be impossible to operate a camera in an aeroplane or a seaplane owing to the excessive vibration caused by the engine; but this theory proved wrong, for, given a reliable instantaneous shutter, a clear day and agreeable atmospherical conditions, really excellent results can be obtained.

Modern conditions have modernised methods. Today a large camera, remarkable for strength and clearness of its perspective and improvements of all kinds (though what these improvements are one is not permitted to state), is fitted in the base of the fuselage so that the lens will be pointing at right angles with the earth. This is a most important detail, for should the camera be at the slightest angle past 90 deg. the picture will be out of focus in certain parts.

Perhaps the most useful purpose to which the aerial photograph is put is a comparison, day by day, of negatives of certain sectors of the line. Here a new trench will be discovered one day; there a new gun emplacement another. Thus, a constant and careful watch can be kept on the enemy's present and intended movements.

Anent this matter, Mr. H. G. Wells, the greatest authority of the war, wrote recently, in an article in the *Daily Chronicle*:

An air photograph to an inexperienced eye is not a very illuminating thing; one makes out roads, blurs of wood and rather vague buildings. But the examiner has an eye that has been in training; he is a picked man; he has at hand yesterday's photographs, marked maps, and all sorts of aids and records. If he is a Frenchman, he is only too happy to explain his ideas and methods. Here, he will point out, is a little difference between the German trench beyond the wood since yesterday. For a number of reasons, he thinks it will be a new machine-gun emplacement; here at the corner of the farm wall they have been making another. This battery here isn't it plain? Well, it's a dummy. The grass in front of it hasn't scorched, and there's been no serious wear on the road here for a week.

Presently the Germans will send one or two wagons up and down that road and instruct them to make figures of eight to imitate scorching on the grass in front of the gun. We know all about that. The real wear on the road, compare this and this and this, ends here at this spot. It turns off. into the wood. There's a sort of track in the trees. Now look where the trees are just a little displaced! (This lens is rather better for that.) That's one gun. You see? Here, I will show you another.

That process goes on two or three miles behind the front line. Very clean young men in white overalls do it as if it were a labour of love. And the Germans in the trenches, the German gunners, *know it is going on*. They know that in the quickest possible way these observations of the aeroplane that was over them just now will go to the gunners. The careful gunner, firing by the map and correcting by aeroplane, kite balloon, or direct observation, will be getting on to the located guns in another couple of hours. Every day the French print special maps showing the guns, sham guns, trenches, everything of significance behind the German lines, showing everything that has happened in the last four-and-twenty hours. It is pitiless. And, as I say, the German Army knows of this, and knows that it cannot prevent it, because of its aerial weakness. That knowledge is not least among the forces that are crumpling up the German resistance upon the Somme.

Shells. Red and white, black and grey, snap, bark, youf against the clear sky light. Above, the frail speck of an aeroplane—but there, aeroplanes don't hover. More shells, more flame patches. A slight movement—down or up? Neither. A little forward. A mighty sweep. Then, back she goes into her original position. Below, field-glasses are snapped to angry eyes, gunners work at the gun on the grey-green motor trolly vehemently. Range 8,000 feet. Try 8,500. More craning of necks. Loud detonations at hand. Indescribable passages, up and up, up and up into the air—more black and grey patches.

"Thank heaven those damned Huns can't shoot straight," murmurs the pilot. The observer busies himself over his photographic instruments, conjuring up from the depths of his boots resonant curses upon the fool inventor of aerial photography. Lower, he beckons. With a sorry grimace the pilot obeys.

Angry the gunners, louder the guns. Lower! Lower! Ah, splendid! Drat the Archies! Home, Jeames! Like a meteor across the sky the plane turns and dashes for home.

Late afternoon. Early 1916. Battered, weary, glorious lines of British infantry falling back upon shell-shattered Ypres. At their last gasp there comes a Heaven-sent breather from the tornado of bursting shells and hordes of Hun soldiery. Battalions begin to sort themselves out from the *mêlée*. The remainder seize the opportunity for a well-merited doze. To them come that glorious after-glow of victory, splendidly won. When the bombshell bursts.

A morning's aerial photograph, hastily developed, discloses as far as eye can reach, mile upon mile, road by road, field by field, dim, indistinct figures: advancing infantry and cavalry! Never was such a warlike concourse viewed.

"Supports? My personal staff and myself," says the C.-in C., "carry on." And carry on they did to some purpose, saved, at the last moment, by an aerial observer's photo. Later in the war, an Admiralty official, after a series of raids on Zeebrugge, Bruges, and Blankenburghe, informed us that aerial photographic reconnaissance disclosed serious damage to naval and military works.

Among other things, photographic experiments during the war have served to show that if the surface of the earth has been recently disturbed in any way—as a newly constructed trench or gun emplacement, or a footpath across a field—it shows up most distinctly on the camera negative. Such photographs of the "lines" from one end to the other are in the possession of both our own and the enemy commanders alike.

The cinematograph instrument has not been made use of to any great extent; but the few results obtained are highly satisfactory, and point to its continual employment in the near future.

Another ingenious device is the camera *obscura*. This is practically a large camera built upon the ground with its lens pointing upwards. Inside is a table on which a white sheet of paper is stretched at a convenient height for the observers inside to look at and mark with a pencil. An aeroplane flying approximately over this camera *obscura* would naturally throw an image on the paper, and the observers, by following the course of the aeroplane with a pencil, can tell exactly how far from being directly over the camera *obscura* the pilot is, and approximately how fast he is going. Both methods are employed in the training of future pilots.

CHAPTER 8

Tactics and Strategy

To predict upon an uncertainty has always been a dangerous pastime. To predict upon such uncertainty biased by a rather too great element of the unexpected renders the pastime doubly dangerous. Thus, it is with the air. But at least of one thing we can be certain. Aviation is practically akin to sea navigation. The movements of a squadron of aeroplanes in mid-air differ very slightly from those of a squadron of light cruisers at sea. Particularly is this fact noticeable with the airship. The formation of a squadron of Zeppelins going into action is "line." One following the other in ordered and monotonous regularity. A squadron of big ships putting out to sea is surrounded and protected by a host of smaller fry, as torpedo boats. A bomb-raiding expedition in the air is convoyed by smaller and fleeter battleplanes. Will naval policy then be applied to the future strategy and tactics of the air?

Thus far the majority of actual battles up above have been waged between single craft of either side. This condition is greatly to do with the policy adopted by the enemy; which is invariably to remain on the defensive, and seldom to give fight without the radius of their own lines. But the day is not far distant when aerial battles will take place on a greatly extended scale. When squadron will meet squadron, or flight will meet flight, and the fight will continue until either their ammunition has given out, or a sufficient number of machines have been "downed" on either side to necessitate a retreat.

Thus far, then, we may say that aircraft have been merely an adjunct to the military offensive. In the future they will be a factor, and a dominating factor at that. This view-point, of course, with the exception of the Zeppelin raids, and they may be considered more in the light of privateers, with a roving commission to destroy and damage at will. Which brings us to the matter of the various craft.

In all there are three distinct types of aircraft, and of these various types the aeroplane has, thus far, best proved its worth, and therefore it is permissible for us to conclude that the aeroplane has the most promising future.

And the future of the aeroplane depends to a great extent upon the matter of "lift," that depends to a great extent on engine-power. And both craft and engine depend upon the effort of the designer and the construction. The future lies in their hands. The more prolific, the more inventive they become, the more the aeroplane and similar craft will develop.

Theirs is a responsible and enviable task. There are as many different types of aeroplanes as there are ships at sea. Each particular grade of work requires a particular style of craft. A battleplane, for example, must be a craft that is both fast-flying and quick-climbing. That is a matter to do with the ethics of aerial combat. Reconnaissance craft must have ample powers of duration. And a bomb-raiding machine requires every available pound of lift for spare petrol and bombs, and must be as lightly furnished as possible

Another factor that must be taken into consideration regarding war aviation of the future is the anti-aircraft gun. The firing has increased quite 80 *per cent* in accuracy since the opening stages of the war. This is due to constant practice, now covering two and a half years. And the more accurate the anti-aircraft firing the greater must be the altitude of the raiding craft. This again will require a further development in engine power.

So far, we have considered the subject solely from the view-point of trench warfare; when the great push comes and the opposing armies are constantly on the move, what will be the value of aircraft then? Will the work of the airman be rendered useless, or will it become the deciding factor? The majority of experts incline to the latter view. We have only one precedent for comparison.

When the German hordes were overrunning Belgium in the autumn of 1914, what saved our tiny army from annihilation? Principally the dogged tenacity of the British Tommy and the untiring efforts of our, then, mere handful of airmen. The advent of aircraft enabled us to turn an ignominious defeat into a glorious victory. When once we get them on the move again, aircraft will prove their value as never before have they proved it. Then it will be necessary for us to adopt a yet more stringent policy of offence to prevent the enemy divining our new movements, and this policy will ensure tremendously heavy casualties.

Perhaps Germany has realised this fact, and has already made the necessary preparations. Be that as it may, we receive constant reports from neutral visitors of the fact that the enemy is evincing signs of considerable activity in the matter of construction. Today almost every factory and munition works in Germany is working under high pressure, turning out new aeroplanes and Zeppelins. The moral is obvious!

Turning our attention to other craft, the seaplane, we may say, is still in the most elementary stage. Its upholders, however, vouch for it a great and useful future. And as far as this country is concerned, by reason of our geographical position, it behoves us to further the development of the seaplane to the uttermost limits of our power.

For the rest there remains but the Zeppelin for consideration. Allowing for the fortunate results of the last two raids, the Zeppelin as an offensive unit of the air is *non est*. For the present.

It is not today that we need fear these cumbersome craft, but in the future. Germany, beaten on land and on sea, will yet cling to her long-cherished dreams of world domination. To this end she is already preparing a large and powerful fleet of the air. Without a declaration, she could send out under cover of darkness a powerful fleet of Zeppelins, plentifully supplied with bombs, that would be hovering over London before we were even aware of her intentions. Another matter to be taken into consideration is the possible silencing of the engine which experts consider quite feasible and the development of the aerial torpedo, navigable from a distance of as much as five miles, and containing an amount of explosive proportionate to a dozen bombs.

Per contra the Zeppelin is of inestimable value as a naval scout. On no less than three occasions it has been instrumental in saving the enemy High Seas Fleet from annihilation.

On December 16th, 1914, occurred the German naval raid on Scarborough and Whitby. We had enticed the enemy to the open sea and into a trap. By all the rules of warfare their ships were already as good as sunk. Then, as our ships were closing into range, down came the fog. Their Zeppelins hung above and directed the course of the fleet by wireless, convoying them into harbour again without the loss of a single vessel.

On the occasion of the Battle of Jutland Bank our Fleets lay across the North Sea like a great net waiting for the enemy to return. They did not reach harbour again without a serious engagement. But their Zeppelins undoubtedly saved them from further disaster by keeping constantly in touch with the movements of our Fleet.

Again, the audacity of Scheer in making use of the German High Seas Fleet in the raid off Flamborough Head, August 19th, 1916, was warranted by a carefully organised vanguard of Zeppelins—which kept constant watch upon the only routes open to Jellicoe and Beatty, and immediately they were sighted gave warning by wireless, and the enemy retired at full speed. Again, without loss.

CHAPTER 9

Bomb Raids

Vague indeed are the opinions held by the general public as regards aerial bombardment. The very novelty of the affair subscribes to its barbarousness, Zeppelin and aeroplane raids on this country are considered the last word in Teuton Kultur. Yet, looking at the matter from an unbiassed point of view, such raids are perfectly legitimate!

To repeat: aircraft have revolutionized the theories of warfare for all time. Formerly the battle area was confined to the theatre of operations, and the range of artillery fire. Now it has generalized. The entire air-shore within the radius of the long-distance aeroplanes is the battle area. A firing-line is non-existent. The war is carried to the uttermost boundaries of the countries engaged, either by Zeppelin or super-aeroplane.

Of the two craft the former may be said to be the ideal night-raider. It has a decided advantage in the matter of bomb-space aboard. Considerably heavier bombs can be carried. It is also able to hover over its objective. The best type of aeroplane for this class of work is one with good powers of duration and a reliable engine. And usually a one-manned craft to allow sufficient space for spare bombs.

The guns form the most formidable deterrent to successful air-raiding. With regard to the enemy, the majority of his A. A. guns are mobile—that is to say, they are mounted on either motor-lorries or railway-trucks and can be moved quickly and easily from place to place.

Another method is to place them in a stationary position and cross two guns, with the muzzles at some twenty degrees distance, and firing automatically. Thus, the bottom gun would open fire at a range of 7,000 feet. The airman would immediately climb higher, only to find himself within range of the upper gun. Again, for night firing, a searchlight and a gun would be fixed side by side, so that no unneces-

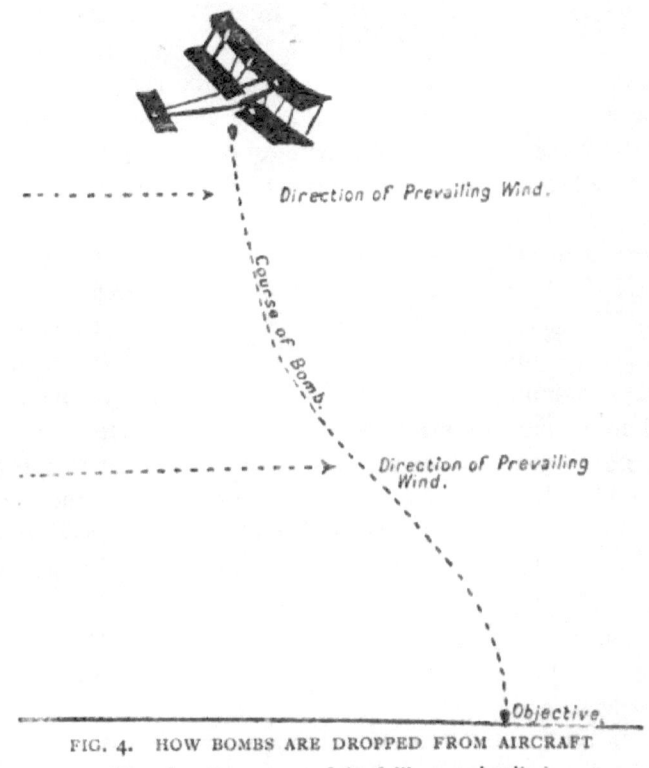

Direction of Prevailing Wind.

Course of Bomb.

Direction of Prevailing Wind.

Objective

FIG. 4. HOW BOMBS ARE DROPPED FROM AIRCRAFT
(Showing the course of the falling projectile.)

sary time would be lost in getting the range once the objective had been picked up by the light.

The matter of bomb-dropping is not an indiscriminate one. Bombs are not taken up haphazard in the body of the craft, and hurled forth, indiscriminately, by hand. A rack is fitted up beneath the under-carriage, with clasps for a limited number of projectiles. It is manipulated by a lever, along the side of the fuselage. To aid in the accuracy of the drop, a special bomb-dropping sight is fitted by the control-lever. This, however, only allows for altitude. For the rest the speed of the craft, the velocity of the wind, the drift in the course, and the direction of the objective must be taken into account. The conditions most favourable are a clear sunny day, with the nose of the aeroplane pointing at the objective, and the craft travelling "down wind"—with the wind at the back of it—as shown in Fig. 4. The French have a somewhat different apparatus for bomb-dropping; a tube, not unlike that in use for torpedoes at sea!

There are two species of bombs, incendiary and explosive. The greatest difficulty experienced with the latter, up to the time of writing, is that the force of the weight of the drop carries them several feet beneath the surface of the earth before the detonator acts, and, as the force of the explosion is for the most part downward and lateral, the projectile loses considerable advantage in the matter of death and destruction.

Other forms of projectiles are the grenade, explosive dart, and, latest of all, the American aerial torpedo. In many respects this torpedo can be compared to the standard field-gun shell. For instance, the airman calculates the distance he is from his target and sets the nose of the torpedo opposite the graduated ring B (see Fig. 5), which corresponds to this distance. The bomb is then released and the momentum of the first 50 feet of descent fires the auxiliary primer N, this being accomplished by the rotary motion of the propeller X, mounted on the shaft C. The method by which this is brought about is ingenious. The propeller shaft, by means of the thread R, frees the spherical end of the stirrup cup-string E, the arms of which have until now been engaged in a recess in the cylinder wall. With nothing to hold it back the spring G forces the plunger F upward, bringing its primer H in contact with the firing-pin I.

The flame that results is carried through the vent W to the cylinder of plaited rope powder composition K. This in turn burns away releasing the plunger stem L, which is forced by the spring P into the chamber below. It is then and for the first time that the picric acid booster charge at V is encased around the detonator N, through the action of the spring P. Meanwhile the primer O has been brought in contact with the firing-pin J, and the flame is carried to the detonator by means of the long or shortened time trains determined by the setting of the nose of the torpedo. The explosion of the main charge follows as soon as the flame reaches the detonator.

Now supposing the pilot misjudged the distance of the target so that the setting of the time fuse would bring the explosion sometime after the torpedo had reached its mark, which would probably mean that the torpedo would fail to accomplish its mission. It is to meet just such a condition that the present torpedo is also equipped with a contact detonator or impact detonator located in the rear of the stem. The firing-pin is seen at Z, the primer at S, the safety-wire at T. The force of the detonator explosion is communicated to the main charge, and so at its worst the torpedo is as effective as the best contact

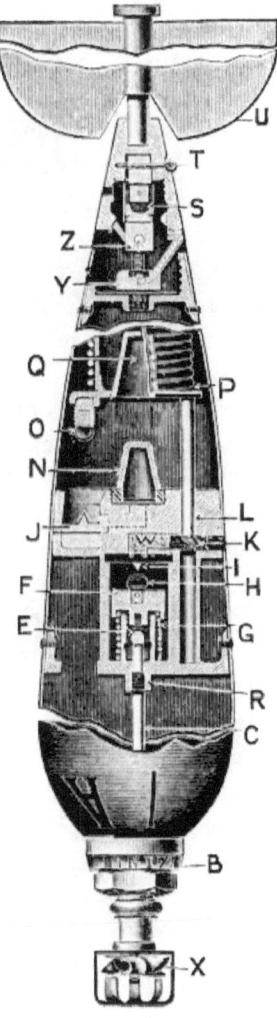

FIG. 5. SECTIONAL VIEW OF AERIAL TORPEDO, SHOWING THE TIME-FUSE AND THE CONTACT DETONATOR

exploding bomb. Lastly, U is a steering vane for guiding the torpedo towards its mark.

These torpedoes, tested by the American Army officials at Mineola, are known as the Barlow torpedo, and are made at the Frankford Arsenal. Quite naturally the details of this torpedo are being carefully guarded, although in its main essentials it probably follows the design of the torpedo described in the foregoing.

It must be understood that bomb-raids for the most part are strategical. The enemy aeroplane, seaplane, and Zeppelin raids are by no means wild eleventh-hour ventures, but part and parcel of the German general offensive. To each effort there accrues more than a small amount of danger; danger alike to craft that cost, in the case of the Zeppelin, roughly £240,000 apiece to construct, and to personnel, who require at least twelve months' preliminary training.

With the use of aircraft in war there are two results that can be attained: the one military, the other moral. Apparently, the enemy hoped and expected to achieve both. Whether or not he was successful in his aim must be judged from the effects of each respective raid.

To a minor degree he did achieve a military result, which requires the bombardment or destruction of some military area, as the dropping of bombs on a dockyard, munition factory, barracks, harbour, fortress, or railway junction; or the serious dislocation of sea, railway, or road traffic. But moral result was entirely lacking.

This moral result is peculiarly adaptable to prevailing circumstances. In the case in point, the enemy was burdened with the idea that he could introduce a state of panic and wholesale fear into the civilian population of this country. Again, he failed miserably in the attempt.

That excellent institution The Hague Convention was thrust upon the world before the day of the aeroplane as a serious factor of war, but nevertheless there are several clauses therein contained which apply peculiarly to aerial bombardment. This code permits of the bombardment of the positions hitherto mentioned, but adds a proviso that notice must be given to allow non-combatants to reach a place of safety.

It should be noted, earlier in the war, in deference to the Convention our Admiralty officials stated in a *communiqué* that:

"Instructions are always issued to confine the attacks to points of military importance, and every effort is made by the flying officer to avoid dropping bombs on any residential portion of the towns."

Again, the question arises, that as London and other large areas are now defended by anti-aircraft artillery, are they still defenceless cities? As to the matter of warning in a Zeppelin or other raid, such a course would be ludicrous from the enemy's point of view, as the primary element of such a manoeuvre is that of surprise.

Now, having discussed the *raison d'être*, let us turn our attention to the craft and the various methods they employ. The principal Zeppelin bases are situated at Heligoland, Kiel, Friedrichshaven, Munich, and Brussels, though it is extremely probable that the latter has long since been abandoned owing to its proximity to the Allied lines, and the Hun's well-merited fear of the Allied airmen. Each town is, roughly, 600 miles distant from Great Britain, and, with one exception, the distance travelled is 90 *per cent* over the sea. This is a great drawback to raids, and until the Zeppelin is further developed, the North Sea will supply a useful natural defence.

Next in order comes the matter of weather. Rain, snow, or sleet obscures landmarks, and thus enhances the difficulties of navigation. With regard to rain particularly. Water is eight hundred times heavier than air, and interferes considerably with the buoyancy of the craft. Fog, for obvious reasons, renders flying impossible. With a moonlit background the Zeppelin is a prominent and easy target for the anti-aircraft gunners. Also, there are various electrical disturbances in the air, extremely dangerous to gas-borne craft; and high winds, those from the south, south-west, and west being particularly dangerous and choppy.

Allowing for this matter of weather, and a comparison of Zeppelin activities of former years, shows us that the most probable Zeppelin periods for 1917 are:—

> April 14th-May 8th.
> August 8th-August 18th.
> September 9th-September 23rd.
> October 7th-October 17th.
> November 7th-November 15th.
> December 7th-December 15th.

Setting out in the late afternoon, with a heavy load of bombs, petrol, etc., aboard, it is some little time before the Zeppelin is able to rise to anything like a decent altitude, although just previous to leaving the ground the ballonets have been pumped almost empty of weight-supplying air. The navigation of the craft is directed across the North Sea by submarines, that keep in contact by means of wireless communication.

Just before dusk, one or the other of the off-coast lightships is sighted, and immediately the craft rises to a great altitude.

Then the real dangers and difficulties of the trip commence. A flight over a darkened enemy country, plentifully supplied with anti-aircraft guns.

Whether the darkening of the towns adds to the difficulty of the navigation is a matter for the authorities to decide. Apparently, they think so! But there are many natural landmarks that cannot be shrouded.

The return journey is a more ticklish enterprise. The North Sea has to be recrossed, this time in the inky blackness, and the Zeppelins have to hover up aloft until day breaks and a landing is possible.

The daylight aeroplane raid is another and considerably more dangerous phase. The latest German machines, and particularly the Halberstadt, with its 240 horse-power Benz engine, are capable of flying at an altitude of 15,000 feet and over. At such a height marks of nationality are extremely hard to distinguish, and a fast moving object makes a difficult target for the anti-aircraft gunners.

Day after day aeroplanes pass safely through anti-aircraft fire at a lesser altitude, with an average 8 *per cent* loss, across the firing-line. Why not over this country?

The solo attempt on London is but preliminary to raids on a larger and more extended scale. It is a prescient danger, and one that can only be avoided by a constant patrol of scouting British craft.

It is impossible to foretell to what limits the enemy may go when smarting under humiliating defeats on land and sea, and a gigantic and devastating aeroplane raid on London is by no means without the limit of his intentions.

But not so much the present war, it is the future we must take into consideration. Germany's air fleets will always remain an unwelcome menace to our national safety.

In the past he did not scruple to send his hordes of soldiers swarming through Belgium without preliminary warning; and in the future he will no less scruple over a sudden and gigantic air raid. For the first and most important element of aerial warfare is surprise.

To guard against this danger, we must destroy Germany's air fleet at the earliest possible opportunity, and by retaliation carry the war into the enemy's country, to keep him there, busily engaged.

CHAPTER 10

Aerial Combat

Two German aeroplanes were brought down yesterday in air fighting," runs the terse, intelligible phrase that occurs almost daily in the British Official, with a possible variety in the number of casualties. The scene of action lies among the grey, racing clouds, across the shell-specked heavens, south to the horizon of the mottled-grey war area, north to the peaceful blue sweep that hides the white cliffs of Dover behind the morning mist. Creeping above the clouds are small, lithe forms, that plunge suddenly downward, like albatrosses, upon their unsuspecting prey; wheeling, turning, diving in that strange, thin air, two and three miles above the surface of the battlefield.

The highway of the air is broad and free; high crawl the powerful twin-engine battleplanes, that scour the skies for enemy craft, the lords of the heavens. Below them ride the slower and more cumbersome reconnaissance and raiding machines, convoyed on either side by strongly armed craft; here a "flight" directing artillery fire, there a squadron of fleet, bombing biplanes. Dawn and twilight the highway is awhirr with adventurous craft.

The highway, for the air is own cousin to the sea. The sinister craft that climb beneath the stars, and the swaying specks of the daylight hours are the privateers of modern war. Their mission? None can say! Only the pilot knows, and he is master of his craft to wander where he will. But in flying logs we come across such quotations as mentioned by Beach Thomas in the *Daily Mail*:

> A general engagement then took place. Two fleets swept up to give battle. Early in the action one of our pilots was severely wounded, but fought on and sunk an enemy ship. Later, when the first squadrons were well in action, the enemy brought up supports, raising the number of first-class vessels from six to

ten, of which four were eventually sunk. The final flight of the enemy occurred upon the arrival of a single supporting ship from our side.

A British pilot watching the sky from harbour saw the battle from afar and hurried his machine out, and, so quickly do these new craft climb, was just in time to take a hand in the fighting, in spite of a long journey of a climb of 12,000 feet. He himself shot down one of these enemy planes almost instantly, whereon the rest scattered and fled.

There must have been a great breath from the sea when aircraft first took the skies that swept rampant all the customs and traditions of the older Service into this prodigy of the war. For it was thoroughly human, typically British, and delightfully sporting. It was the code of the football field and of the cricket ground. A code from which the word defeat was entirely eliminated; where the mind shunned fear, and the will was hardened to all kind of mishap and adventure. In a word, it was to always fight clean and fair.

This untrained body—the Flying Corps—was developed with a thoroughness and rapidity that outdid even the magic Kitchener Armies. Resultingly, Britain very soon held the supremacy of the air. This necessitates maintaining a ceaseless photographic reconnaissance far behind the enemy's trenches, to spot for the heavy guns along an extended front, and to "keep the wind up" the Boche so that for every ten British aeroplanes that crossed the German lines barely one of his would dare to cross ours.

The future pilot was instructed by young, seasoned warriors of the early days, trained upon the fascinatingly narrated personal encounter and adventure. That training today is as comprehensive as beforetime it was haphazard.

A school of aerial gunnery has been established where practice from the air takes place against every form of target, both on the ground and in the air.

This matter of aerial gunnery is the most important of all to the aerial fighter. And the possibilities of gunfire vary greatly with the type of craft. With some, an automatic control of the engine regulates the gun to firing between the revolving propeller blades. With others, again—with the engine at the rear—a yet greater field of fire is possible. This is best indicated in Fig. 6, where we discover

(A) has a restricted area of fire, while that of (B) is entirely unre-

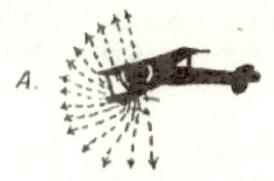

FIG. 6. RANGE OF MACHINE-GUN FIRE FROM AEROPLANES
(a) Limited.   (b) Unlimited.

stricted. The advantage of (A) over
(B) can hardly be imagined.

Fighting is also practised by various methods; two machines may
be sent up to manoeuvre one against another, both trying to attack,
or the pupil is sent up while the instructor tries to attack him, or *vice
versa*, or an instructor goes out and attacks a group of pupils returning from a cross-country flight, and so on. The air fighter, when fully
trained, is a specialist, and confines his attention to this type of work
alone.

Apart from being a useful pilot he must be able to read maps,
fire machine-guns, and send wireless messages accurately. Risks and
adventures he will encounter in plenty, against which he must be endowed with imperturbable courage and great initiative. It is the unexpected that invariably carries the aerial combat; the manoeuvre for
which one's opponent is unprepared.

A naval pilot flying a Nieuport—the terrible "baby" of the skies—
ten miles out from the shores of the North Sea, and when approaching Ostend, at about 12,000 feet, encountered a German seaplane. The
latter had glimpsed him from afar, and manoeuvred into a position
behind and below his course. Too late the British airman was aware
of his proximity, and, in an endeavour to retrieve himself, executed a
steep glide over the enemy, who passed underneath. Thus, he gained

the desired position and opened fire at a range of 100 yards, The enemy machine burst into flames, falling headlong to the ground. By unexpectedly looping he was able to convert a possible defeat into a certain victory.

A brother pilot, on six different occasions in one flight, attacked and drove off hostile aircraft which threatened the bombing machines that he was escorting, one enemy machine going down.

On another occasion a British airman, unable to reach his opponent by any other method, charged him direct from a short distance. The German, who must have been a cool fellow, kept a perfect bee-line to the end, apparently seeking mutual destruction. Our pilot turned at the last moment and rammed, not the centre, but the right wing of the opposing craft, which he carried away, and the German plane fell, helpless, to the ground. The British machine was badly damaged, but still airworthy, and the engines carried it wobbling but safely into harbour.

Aerial combat requires a special class of aeroplane, with a powerful engine, rapid in its movements, and fast to climb. The best types are either a fast single-seater fighting plane, a double-engine battleplane, or, latest of all, a triplane—triple-decker aeroplane.

It must be realised that one of these craft, whether British or German, can do what it pleases with most of the planes designed for observation or photography. They are like destroyers as compared with merchant vessels. The air being the big place it is, a good number of these more cumbrous craft must necessarily fall victims to the fighting ships whosoever rules the air. Most of our losses are among this unwarlike flotilla. Of course, these slower, clumsier craft can give an account of themselves, but they have little chance at the best against the pace and climbing power of a heavily armed vessel.

The ethics of aerial combat are the simplest and oldest in the world. For as many centuries as there is history, the winged denizens of the skies have been giving valuable demonstrations. Watch two common or garden sparrows; the fight develops, upward—upward—upward. All the time both opponents are struggling for the upper berth. An air fight differs in no respect. The back is the human's most defenceless spot. Above and behind is the best position in aerial combat. An air pilot with a rakish machine gunfire pouring into his nethermost parts is helpless. He might well, as a Hun humourist did recently, hold aloft his arms, with a despairing "*Kamerad.*" It is his only chance to escape a drop of some thousand feet and death.

OLD TYPE FIGHTING CRAFT

The air fight is the sole relic of old-time romantic warfare. It is a matter of wits and courage, strength and endurance to the end. Those modern knights ride their petrol steeds, with their gun-lances atilt their shoulders, in the lists of the clouds and boundless eternity, with the smiling Queen of Victory awaiting their victorious return below. Her name is no commonplace feminine equivalent, but the proud cognomen Duty.

Of these graceful duels one cannot forbear to mention the affair of Rouzier Dorcières, a personality famous in two continents; a composite of Cyrano de Bergerac and d'Artagnan. Dorcières was premier duellist of the great Republic across the Channel. More than a score of victorious duels could he claim. But the greatest was in the clouds, the last—fought not for self-glory, but for the honour of his beloved France. The story was quoted in a recent number of the *Weekly Dispatch*.

Wherever Dorcières travelled, his reputation preceded him. At Zurich, in 1910, he was publicly insulted by an officer of the Prussian Guards. The latter approached him after dinner, as Dorcières was sipping his coffee in the lounge.

"So, you are Rouzier Dorcières?" he said sneeringly. "I recognise you. And they say you have never been touched in a duel. Well, I am sorry I have never had the good fortune to meet you in one."

"But you will have the chance to meet me," replied Dorcières heatedly.

The Prussian's expression grew dark. "*Monsieur*," he said, "I shall meet you here before ten o'clock with my seconds and the swords. We will settle this affair before I depart. Will you await me?"

The duellist waited, but no Prussian appeared. He had departed hurriedly. And from that evening he registered a mental vow to obtain satisfaction from his cowardly assailant, somewhere, sometime, somehow.

With this object he enlisted in the French Air Service on the outbreak of war. Said his pilot of Rouzier Dorcières:—

He was the strangest machine gunner I ever had. Unlike other gunners, he always carried binoculars, and when we sighted and approached a Boche he spent his time in peering intently at the occupants of the enemy machine instead of preparing his *mitrailleuse* anxiously as most gunners do.

As we circled near the German machine in his last fight, Dorcières passed me a scrap of paper. On it he had scrawled a request that I swoop past the German as near as I could. Instantly I divined his reason—and his reason for always carrying and using his high-power glasses. He thought he recognised one of the occupants of the other aeroplane.

Our fuselage cracked and splintered as the leaden hail perforated the car, and the choking gasps that I heard behind me were the positive indications that my gunner had been hit. I turned upward, as my motor was undamaged, and climbed with the German. Then we both planed and approached each other, and the test was which of the two machine-gunners would prove to be the better man.

Dorcières's first shot at the new elevation must have killed the enemy gunner. And his torrent of bullets ripped off the tail of the Fokker and it dived into our lines like a stone, nose down.

I piqued down, too, and landed within fifty yards of the broken Boche car and its occupants. Two stretchers were waiting there for us, but I was unhurt, miraculously. We put Dorcières in one, tenderly as a baby, and then started off. But he had seen the wreck of the Fokker there and he begged that we stop beside it. Beside the German machine were the pilot and the gunner, both dead. By a superhuman effort my dying gunner raised himself on his elbow. He gazed at the battered dead face of the enemy machine-gunner.

'It is he,' was all he said. And we carried him to the field hospital.

The principal methods of aerial attack are the dropping of incendiary and explosive bombs, the use of firearms, as a Remington or Winchester repeater—now almost extinct—the dropping of hand-grenades, and, more effective than any, the use of the Lewis machine-gun.

This gun fires through the blades of the propeller, which deflect at least 5 *per cent* of the bullets; thus, firing is a one-man job, The difficulty for a man to pilot and fire at the same time is beyond comprehension; two men at least are required, the one to direct the course of the craft on to the object, the other to fire the gun.

Another important matter is to obtain a suitable mounting for the gun, namely, one that allows the largest possible angle of elevation and depression. The advantage accruing to a machine with an area of gunfire that includes every position and angle is enormous. The best direction to fire the gun depends largely on the type of machine. Suiting the machine to the gun, the "pusher," with propeller in the rear, offers a clear bow. The "tractor" is impeded by the propeller blades and the limited space in which the gunner has to work.

Next in importance is the matter of manoeuvring. When giving chase to another machine the pilot must always keep his enemy in view; his own machine, as much as possible, out of sight. Once he takes his eyes off the enemy in mid-air, he is apt to lose sight of him altogether. He must always endeavour to place himself between the enemy and the sun, and always keep him on the gunner's left hand. Finally, he must always turn toward the enemy, never away from him.

Entering into the actual combat is, by nature, more of a tactical manoeuvre. As yet it is on too minor a scale to be classed as strategical. That is with the exception of the one great fight of March, 1917, when five British aeroplanes fought twenty-seven Germans, and sent eight to earth, crippled or in flames.

It was a day of great heat. There was a haze so thick that the ground was barely visible. Our men started late in the afternoon, and at five o'clock were well over the enemy country when, with the sun at their backs, they saw two enemy machines ahead. They endeavoured to close, the enemy making some show of fighting. However, it was only a show, for as our leading machines drew near the Germans turned and made with all speed for home. Our machines gave chase and were led into a decoy. Out of the haze and void on all sides new fleets came closing in. The new arrivals flew in three formations, two of which contained eight machines, the other nine, making twenty-five craft in all, to whom the other two, which now ceased to run away, joined themselves, making a minimum of twenty-seven machines in all.

One of the enemy fleets, taking advantage of the thick air, had passed behind our little squadron and came at it, as from the direction of our own lines, straight between it and the sun an awkward direction. The other fleets came from the north and south-east. As they approached, they spread out so that our men were ringed around with enemies on every side.

The order to attack, though given, was hardly needed. Each one of our five turned at once for the enemy who was nearest. The fight began at about 11,000 feet, but in the course of the things that followed it ranged anywhere from 3,000 to 12,000 up and down the ladders of heaven. And an extraordinary fact is that, all the while that it went on, the German anti-aircraft guns below kept at work. Usually, as soon as aeroplanes engage overhead, the "Archies" are silent for fear of hitting the wrong man.

Such a general *mêlée* inevitably breaks up into a series of individual fights. "Formation," as it is technically known, breaks up, but nothing could have surpassed the way in which our men fought. Not one of them ever allowed himself to be cut off and isolated from the rest. Not one failed to be ready when a friend was in imminent danger to turn to his assistance. This is the more remarkable as, with the exception of the Flight Leader, all the pilots were practically new men, with little experience of fighting. Some had only been in France a fortnight. Yet no veterans could have exceeded these youngsters in coolness and fighting judgment. As for the Flight Commander himself, he, still a youth, may fairly be called a veteran, for in that battle he reached his seventeenth German victim.

During the course of the fight, one of our machines plunged down with flames bursting from its reserve petrol tank. An enemy, glimpsing an easy quarry, dived for the flaming ruin as it fell, but, quicker than he, a comrade plunged down to his aid. And while our crippled machine, still belching flames, slid off, with its nose set for home, the German, mortally hit, dropped like a stone.

Strangely enough, our burning aeroplane got home. The wreckage was a pitiful sight to view; with the reserve petrol tank on the roof bearing two bullet holes on one side, and great ragged tears on the other where the bullets passed out. The whole tank was scorched and crumpled. The flames had burnt away the whole central span of the upper plane. Yet, like a great blazing meteor, it crossed our lines and came to earth, not indeed at its own home, but on safe and friendly ground; and as another airman said in admiration, "He made a topping landing."

The "Archie"—anti-aircraft shell—is the worst enemy a fighting airman has to face. There is a natural and not to be wondered at enmity between our aeroplanes and the anti-aircraft guns of the Germans. Though one must not imagine that a British aeroplane takes a straffing from Archie as a matter of course. Time after time they have shown their resentment by diving at the presumptuous batteries and scattering their crews with rapid bursts of machine-gun bullets, just as by night they have dived at searchlights behind the German lines. Here the simile ends, however, for instead of being singed the planes have shot and bombed the lights to darkness.

Dawn is breaking when No. 4 returns, tired-eyed and more mono-syllabic than ever. It came off all right, but No. 3 had seemed to lose control and slide down the beam of a searchlight with shell and balls of red fire (some new stunt, he supposed) bursting all about her. How-ever, she got her bombs off first, and touched up something that sent a flame 200 feet into the air. He himself bombed a group of searchlights that were annoying him, and some trucks in a railway siding. The speaker has an ugly shrapnel wound in the thigh, and observes with grave humour that his boots are full of blood—this is a Navy joke by the way. Also, that he could do with a drink.

But it came off all right.

Since our aerial offensive began the Germans have rushed many anti-aircraft batteries to the Western Front in an effort to check the care-free manner with which we cross their line. They are barking all through the day and often far into the night. One of these new bat-teries, larger and noisier than most of its truculent brothers, incurred the special disfavour of a certain squadron a short time ago; not that it was doing any particular damage to anything or anybody, but it was just deemed too blatant and noisy to exist any longer. So, the squadron flew up one bright afternoon, drew the fire of the battery, then closed in upon it, and let go with 124 bombs.

British pilots, when they get peevish, rather like having a go at the guns. When they get tossed about by a too-familiar big howitzer shell hurling by in the air, it is not an uncommon thing for them to hunt down the annoying gun and admonish it to better manners in the convincing lexicon of the Lewis gun.

The most thrilling combat of the war occurred between six British scouts and eight Germans. It was an affair of wits as well as machines.

In the evening, towards sunset—about eight o'clock, to be pre-cise—skirting the low-lying, dark grey clouds, there crept the British patrol, like a covey of wild ducks winging home to roost. Over the firing lines they passed, almost unnoticed. When well into the enemy's country they encountered the German craft. The latter fled hurriedly. Our machines gave chase, eventually overtaking them.

The battle closed in, growing furious. Wings scraped wings, and the fighting pilots could look each other squarely in the eyes. The leading British machine dived at the nearest German. The latter went down 4,000 feet, in a spin, hopelessly out of control.

Out of the *mêlée* there plunged two craft, one above the other, driving him down. The harassed machine was British. Immediately one of his comrades, having despatched the machine with which he had been engaged, dived down to his rescue. The enemy was too intent on his prey to notice the British machine at the back of him. With a single tray of ammunition, he went down, falling over and over.

Another pilot of the patrol, meantime, had attacked two enemy planes that were in the downward procession started by the leader. The first one of these soon cried enough, and cleared away to the east, and having got on to the second aircraft's tail, he drove him down with a spin, but later he seemed to flatten out and, in the language of the corps, "was apparently all O.K." The British pilot was pretty close to the ground now, so he turned and climbed to 9,000 feet, where he attacked another German, and the two fought all the way down to 4,000 feet, when the German, with a riddled machine, went plunging downward to an inevitable crash.

The greatest of all British fighting airmen was the late Captain Ball, V.C., D.S.O., M.C., a short, lithe, monosyllabic youth in the early twenties. This splendid pilot had brought down no fewer than forty-three enemy aeroplanes and one captive balloon, and figured in countless adventures. He was the "Scarlet Pimpernel" of the air, always waiting, waiting above the clouds and mist, over the enemy's country. Below, British aeroplanes would suddenly be attacked in overwhelming numbers. Down would come the avenger with a mighty sweep, and the enemy would clear off, pell-mell. For his craft and manner of handling it were known and respected by friend and foe alike.

Captain Ball first achieved fame when on escort duty to a bombing raid. Returning, after a useful morning's work, they encountered four enemy battleplanes in formation. His was the only fighting craft of the patrol, but he immediately dashed forward to give battle. The enemy waited the onslaught with dignified self-assurance. When, suddenly, they found this "mad" Britisher was performing the most unusual manoeuvres over their heads. Flying by a rapid mental calculation—as was invariably his rule—he had realised that, hopelessly outnumbered though he was, he could yet save himself, and the machines in his charge, if he could climb to a certain position. This he proceeded to do, first baffling the enemy with a series of most unusual turns and dives.

At last, he had climbed to the necessary altitude, and diving down on them broke up their formation in hopeless disorder, engaging hotly with the nearest enemy craft. The latter plunged earthward, wreathed in smoke and flame. Ball followed to within 500 feet of the mouth of the German guns, to make sure it was wrecked.

Further on they encountered a large patrol of twelve German machines. Before giving the enemy time to think out a possible offensive, he repeated his former tactics, again breaking them up, and driving one down. One against twelve! Enemy reinforcements came speeding up. Turning, climbing, wheeling, diving suddenly this way, suddenly that, the tiny British machine kept them all at bay, and drove another, flaming, to the ground.

On another occasion he attacked a group of seven enemy machines single-handed. The leading machine he shot down, and went after the others, which were retiring hastily. Within ten yards of another enemy machine, he opened rapid fire and brought him down on to the roof of a house in a village in our lines. He then returned to his aerodrome for more ammunition, and encountered three more fighting planes. These he drove to the ground in rapid succession. When, finally, his day's work was completed, he glided home, his craft riddled from nose to tail with over three hundred bullet holes.

Towards the end, the enemy, who both feared and respected this daring airman, laid many traps for his destruction. Far from avoiding them, however, he deliberately went out of his way to match his wits against theirs, always returning unscathed, and, from being the victim, added further victims to his own ever-growing total.

Almost the last aerial battle in which Captain Ball took part occurred when he was out with a patrol squadron, which encountered a German machine, and riddling it with bullets, drove it down.

Described by the correspondent of the *Evening Standard*, it read as follows:

Four red Albatross machines then came up, and a brother officer of Captain Ball, who may be called Captain X——, engaged one of them at close range.

The German manoeuvred for a favourable position, and his opponent dived and shook him off. Climbing again, Captain X—— pursued another of the red enemy squadron, and fought it for a considerable time, the German machine being outmanoeuvred and sent crashing to earth.

Then Captain X—— engaged a third machine, but he was shot through the wrist, and the top of his control lever was carried away. Although suffering great pain and further handicapped by the damage to his aeroplane, he succeeded in landing in the

British lines without further injury, and then fainted.

Captain Ball had many thrilling fights during those last few days, bringing down three enemy machines and putting many others to flight. One day, while patrolling, he sighted two hostile craft, and as he was fairly low, he flew away from them, climbing steadily. When the German aeroplanes were quite near his tail he swerved sharply, slid underneath one of his opponents, and turned on his machine-gun. The German fell out of control.

He then manoeuvred in order to attack the second enemy machine, but it flew straight at him, firing steadily. Captain Ball returned the fire as the German came full tilt at him, and a collision seemed inevitable, when the hostile machine suddenly went down. The engine of Captain Ball's machine was hit and the pilot drenched with oil.

No other hostile aircraft were in sight, so he dropped and saw both German aeroplanes lying completely wrecked within four hundred yards of each other.

As he came home, he fell in with two other hostile aircraft, but as his ammunition was exhausted and his sights covered with oil, he reluctantly "put his nose down" and returned to his aerodrome.

Last seen, Captain Ball was disappearing over the Hun lines in the fading light.

CHAPTER 11

Wireless and Direction of Artillery Fire

The value of aerial artillery direction may best be judged by the value of artillery in the war. The latter has invariably paved the way for the infantry and cavalry attack. To make a forward movement with infantry in these days of highly developed scientific weapons without a preliminary artillery bombardment would be to court disaster.

The accuracy of such bombardment is essential; thus, it was at Mons and the Marne, where the hordes of German soldiery failed to force back our thin, exhausted lines; the latter gave way, step by step, in face of a murderous artillery fire. Back and back until our aircraft began to make themselves felt, and the French airmen became largely responsible by reason of the wonderful work of the famous .75's.

Principally this matter must be judged from the point of view of the gunner on the ground, and the difficulties and disadvantages that he must contend with. In all previous wars it was the custom with guns with a range of above three miles, the target of which was not visible from the firing position, to send an observer, or observers, up to some point of vantage, preferably a church tower, or the roof of a tall building as near the object to be fired upon as safety would permit. This task of observation was often both dangerous and difficult, and, when no suitable observation post could be discovered, impossible.

Thus, the firing of the guns became purely a matter of mathematics and judgment; the gunner being unable to discern whether the shells fired were near or wide of the mark, a thoroughly unsatisfactory arrangement to all concerned. It was then suggested that aeroplanes should be utilized for the purposes of observation. This has since become the main duty of aircraft along the battle front, and the direction of artillery has been a veritable triumph for the "Fourth Arm," employing daily countless pilots and machines.

For the direction of artillery, the observer is generally responsible. Following the shell bursts on the map, he wirelesses their positions back to the gun-post and corrects the range. Together with the direction may be classed the observation of artillery. While out directing our own fire, an airman might very possibly spot one or a group of enemy heavy guns. Then it is a simple matter for him, knowing his own altitude, to gauge, by geometrical bearings, their position, and control the range of fire upon them.

On the Western Front the victory or defeat, the good or bad day fluctuates with the command of the air. This passes from one side to the other with a pendulum-like regularity; now the enemy, now ourselves; then the enemy, then ourselves. Immediately the enemy has lost the command his aircraft are conspicuous by their absence. Regaining that command, they come swarming overhead in droves. Then is an anxious time for the men in the trenches. If a Hun aeroplane appears overhead that is to say, over an important or vulnerable spot—it is followed almost immediately by a violent artillery bombardment. The advent of enemy aircraft necessitates the immediate taking of cover. Of course, many of the more important positions are hidden or distorted out of their original appearance; and at this art again the enemy excels. His subterfuges are as numerous as they are ingenious. And not alone hidden positions, but false markings and dummy guns, also traps of anti-aircraft guns for the unwary airman. For this purpose, a dummy battery of heavy guns or an ammunition dump is rigged up. Down comes the airman, thinking he has made a coup, to find himself, often too late, within a barrage fire of A.A. guns.

This class of work is confined for the most part to daylight. Occasionally a night stunt does take place, but the matter of observation and of communication is rendered doubly difficult. The only practicable way of communicating is by means of a Very's pistol. Several of the later craft have small searchlights aboard; which brings us to the matter of aerial signalling.

Of these there are two methods. The one we may say is audible, the other visible. Under these two categories come flags, which can only be read from a very short distance, telephones in captive balloons, smoke-bombs which leave a trail of black or white smoke, according to climatic conditions and, with the enemy, a handful of tinsel, which in falling glitters in the sunlight. The smoke signal is the most reliable.

Again, the enemy have a method of signalling with a powerful horn similar to the one in use on a motor-car, worked upon the siren principle. And last, and most important, there is the wireless instrument.

A wireless transmitting apparatus with a Morse sending key attached is fitted in each machine. An observer is shipped, and away goes the pilot to "sit" over the target. This sitting business is a matter of first attaining a great altitude, then gradually spiralling down with wide circles over the object or area to be shelled. Meanwhile the battery opens fire, and the observer, after each shell has burst, signals to the wireless receiving station by the gun: Hit, over, under, left or right as the case may be.

The results thus obtained are little short of marvellous, both in regard to the prevention of the wastage of shells and the development of greater accuracy in firing. On a good clear morning it is no uncommon sight to see as many as ten aeroplanes all hovering over various points on the Front, target registering, and it speaks volumes for the efficiency of the wireless operators and erectors that, although so many machines would be in the air at the same time, they never jammed each other's signals.

The extreme advantage of this method of communication may well be judged from a cutting of a recent number of the *Wireless World*. Said that excellent journal:—

One very excellent way of learning what one owes to a certain instrument is to do without it for a while. We get a good insight into the utility of aeroplane wireless from an account recently sent home by a newspaper correspondent. It is concerned with the adventures of a subaltern in the Flying Corps who was serving in Mesopotamia at a time when he was 'monarch of all he surveyed' (*i.e.* when his was the only plane available). He was scouting on a machine unfitted with radio apparatus, and, as soon as he went up, noticed how at a certain height he ceased to be troubled by the shimmering mirage which in hot climates confuses the human eye and judgment of distance so long as the observer is located on the earth level. From his vantage point in the sky everything was 'clear as a bell.'

"Yonder go our cavalry and the enemy's, nearing each other in the haze totally unawares! . . . What's ——'s brigade wheeling round for now? A mile further advance would turn the enemy's flank. . . . The Turks are leaving their front trenches; they're fully

3,000 strong: oh, if only I could get our gunners to shell them from across the river. . . . Now's the time; if only the cavalry would go for them! . . .What a chance they've missed!

Matters have been amended now, and the British air ascendancy in Mesopotamia is at present as complete as it is in France. The machines are of the latest pattern, and aeroplane wireless keeps the pilots and observers in the sky in close touch with the artillery commanders and army leaders beneath them. The erection of hangars has reduced the wastage of aircraft by giving protection against the alternate sun-baking and rain-drenching to which the machines were subjected in the earlier stages of the campaign.

The scraps of the flying man's remarks, from which we have just quoted, speak eloquently of missed opportunities which would not have been let slip had wireless been available.

By the gun position a special operator is always waiting at the receiving station, also an officer to take the range.

The receiving station?

Imagine, if you can, a peaceful group of farmhouses and outbuildings; on either side are the grazing meadows and, perhaps, a duck-pond or so. Slovenly, unkempt-looking women are lounging in the doorways of the cottages, stolidly regarding the movements of the artillerymen gathered round that black, ugly-looking barrel that rears itself from amidst a pile of screening tree-branches and foliage in a near-by meadow. An aeroplane passes swiftly overhead. Immediately half a hundred pairs of eyes are focussed thereon. A hasty consultation, then the gun is laid, the range gauged, and the wireless operator ordered to stand by! He assembles his set among the bales of straw in a barn, claps on the head-receivers—and waits.

The signal is not long in coming. *Birr—birr—birr; Siz—siz—siz* go the 'phones over his ears. He informs the officer by the gun that the attendant aircraft is ready and waiting. Boom! goes the gun. One of the gunners hurries across to the wireless man. *Birr—birr—birr* go the 'phones again. "Last shot over," he translates. The gun fires again and again. This is a matter of extreme importance; the gun must be fired as rapidly as possible in order to enable the airman to give the correct range.

So, they go on. Now the wireless signal is over the target. Now short of the target; now to the left, now to the right—and at last correct. The gunners have got the range, and proceed forthwith to pound shells into the unsuspecting Boches for all they're worth.

Despite this extreme usefulness of wireless in aircraft, it has at present one serious disadvantage. The earth for the set has to be obtained from the metal of the engine, and does not permit of too large a radius. Thus, though it is a comparatively simple matter to send signals over a distance of twenty miles from the aeroplane, it is usually impossible to receive signals over distances of over two miles. Such signals as are employed can be picked up with equal facility by friend and foe alike. That is to say, if the receiving instrument is "tuned up" to the same range. Again, with so many different instruments working, at one and the same time, in a small area, it is very possible that "jamming" will occur.

The noise of the constantly running engine is another difficulty to be contended with. This renders it exceedingly difficult to hear the signals in the telephones.

The aerial of the set is stowed away upon a large round wheel at the side of the fuselage, from which it is paid out in similar fashion to an anchor. But it has to be all rewound within 200 feet of the ground, as with the then tilted altitude of the craft there is a constant danger of its fouling the propeller.

The weight of the entire set is limited to 100 lbs. Necessarily this entails very little power and an extremely limited radius; per contra a great radius requires considerable power, and considerable power requires a large and weighty wireless set, which would be impossible in an aeroplane.

The wireless receiving stations are situated either on large and powerful motor-lorries, with a mast for the aerial, or in dips and hollows in the ground, so that they may be sheltered from the enemy.

Wireless is most important in Zeppelins. But the instrument must be well protected, owing to the danger of the spark igniting the gas. The entire instrument is more satisfactory, as it is possible to obtain a good earth from the huge metal framework of the craft. But this framework, which is, for the most part, constructed of aluminium, presents another danger, as it is a great collector of electricity. The value of wireless work with these lighter–than–air craft is dealt with to some extent in another chapter.

Finally, aviation has done a lot to help forward and develop wireless experimental work, in that it has introduced it into an entirely novel and hitherto undeveloped sphere.

Chapter 12

Kite-Balloons and Parachutes

The observation balloon—today an ungainly creature that sits always tailwise in mid-air—is not a product of this war. Its history dates back to the late eighteenth century. In 1794 Coulette presented the first war balloon to the French Government, and it was employed against the Austrians, who considered it an insidious form of attack, and declared that all balloonists who fell into their hands would be treated as spies forthwith.

Aircraft played a more than important part in the Franco-Prussian war of 1870-1. Jansen, the celebrated astronomer, who was interned in Paris, was desirous of reaching Algiers by December 22 to witness a phenomenal eclipse of the sun. The English offered to procure for him a safety permit through the German lines, but this he declined, and elected to effect his escape by balloon. He accomplished this feat on December 2, landing the next day some sixty-five miles south-west of the capital.

Subsequently numerous balloon sorties through the air greatly annoyed the German military commanders, and orders were given forthwith to Krupp to construct the first "Archibald" gun. This weapon was mounted on a specially constructed gun-carriage, and was capable of being tilted to almost any angle; but no instance is on record of a target being registered.

The original captive balloons were spherical in shape. The present-day craft, the kite-balloon, is more useful than ornamental. It was proposed by a Scotsman, Archibald Douglas, as far back as 1845, but two Germans, Colonel von Parseval and Dr. Kriegsfeld, first constructed one of these strange craft in Augsburg. The captive spherical was soon discovered to be impracticable for war purposes. In any wind of over twenty miles an hour it rolled about to such a degree as to make accurate observation impossible. Thus, we have the present peculiar shape.

The two main portions of the craft are the envelope and the car. The former is the balloon portion which is filled with gas and provides the necessary lifting power. The latter, strung below the envelope by means of the rigging, is a large basket capable of housing a crew of two, with maps and other necessary paraphernalia. The main idea of the craft is that it sets itself diagonally like a kite to the direction of the breeze. It is serviceable in a wind of up to a velocity of forty miles an hour.

The only remaining portion of the craft is the steering-bag, a strange excrescence under the hinder lower parts. The function of this bag is to keep the balloon head on to the wind. The air enters the steering-bag and passes by means of another valve into the air-bag whenever the pressure in the latter falls below normal. Thus, the air-bag is constantly kept tight, and so solidifies the whole balloon.

To hold it in captivity the balloon is connected by a light and durable steel cable to a steam winch on the ground below. This cable was originally attached to only one point of the rigging. With the later kite balloons, however, it was found more expedient to connect it at two different points, thus always holding the craft at an angle of between thirty and forty degrees to the horizontal.

Behind and below the main body there hangs a long ungainly tail of six small parachutes. The purpose of this tail is to anchor the craft against any sudden gust of wind, which would be extremely dangerous to the observers in the basket and liable to tilt them out.

The military function of the balloon is observation. In the car are two observers. Before them are two specially prepared, squared maps of the district under observation. The car is connected to the winch by telephone, which passes down through insulated wires in the strands of the cable. From the winch, again, connection is made across country by the usual telephone wires to the group of heavy guns for which the balloon is spotting.

Thus, the gunner, by his battery, will telephone to the spotter above, and often four or five miles away, when he is ready to start. The observer gives the required signal. The gun is fired. The smoke clears away; through his glasses the observer has noticed the position of the burst. He gets through to the gun again. "Your last shot was over," he says, or under, or so much to the left, or so much to the right, as the case may be. The gunner remedies his error and fires. Again, he inquires of the observer. Then possibly the reply may come. "Dead on that time. Go ahead."

At sea, observation balloons are, if anything, more useful. When not in use they are stowed away in the hold of the parent ship. Then they are let up in precisely the same manner as their brethren ashore. In the Dardanelles they were in commission continuously: one "sausage" spotting for the *Queen Elizabeth* when she was firing from one side of the peninsula to the other.

The K.B., however, is the most harmless and easily attacked of aircraft. The gas in the envelope prevents the employment of arms of any description. When the enemy aeroplane flies up overhead with intent to bomb, there are two courses open to the crew. Either to have the craft rewound on to the winch on the ground; the other, to take to the parachutes. A parachute drop is generally the last resource. When all other means have failed, the pilot, in desperation, takes to those few closely-folded feet of silk and cord. It is by no means a pleasant experience! One feels that the plane or, as the case is, the kite-balloon one is about to leave is endowed with all the safety of *terra-firma* when compared with the bottomless void into which one plunges down— down to where?

Will the parachute open, or has the cording got entangled, or the body jammed? Those few seconds are a lifetime. With the assurance that it would open, a parachute drop would be no more terrifying than an ordinary flight through the air. With nothing below and very little above, a pilot could well appreciate the situation if the sides and bottom of the body of his machine had been cut away, likewise the cowl, the engine, the undercarriage, and the wings, and nothing but his seat remained.

However, with all its terrors the war has necessitated the revival of the parachute. And, from the occasional Press accounts that are allowed to filter through, it is apparently doing excellent service on the other side. But the parachute is no modern invention. In the history of its development are numbered such prominent pioneers as Leonardo da Vinci, Fauste, also Joseph Montgolfier: prior to his balloon experiments Lenormand made a descent from a tree as long since as 1783, but confined his further experiments to animals. Blanchard was the first to take the matter up as a profession, and made a very considerable sum of money thereby. And Garnerin, on October 22, 1797, made a drop of 3,000 feet from a balloon. Since those days the parachute drop has usually featured as the *pièce de résistance* of the country fair or the public exhibition.

When leaving the craft, the aviator drops like a stone a distance of some sixty or eighty feet before the parachute opens. And, curious to relate, the greater his weight, the sooner the parachute unfolds. Then its course follows the fashion of the bend in the letter L.

It is the rush of the upward currents of air that is responsible for the action, and the strength thereof, as may be judged, is tremendous. The speed of the drop, on a general estimation, is four feet nine inches per second. Thus, Robertson took thirty-five minutes to drop 10,000 feet. But, on the other hand, Frau Poitevin, a German parachutist, made a drop of only 6,000 feet in over forty-five minutes. This depends, to a very great extent, on the weather conditions prevailing.

The feelings experienced are varied. Some say there is a sort of numbness: a blank in the mind from the second that the parachute leaves the craft until the time when it opens: others, that after it is all over nothing but a horrible nightmare remains; and yet others, the feelings experienced are similar to those in a high dive.

Talking to one of the best known of our pilots, and one who has made many drops, he explained that the feeling was composed half of horror, half of joy: horror at the entirely novel sensation of the dead drop, joy to think of what one had accomplished. But, he confessed, he never made a drop from any sense of pleasure. And whether one fears it or no depends largely on the mood one is experiencing at the time as well as on the temperamental fitness on the whole of the one making the experiment.

The highest drop recorded in this country was one of 10,500 feet made by Wing-Commander Maitland over London: the lowest, and incidentally the world's record, one of 350 feet made by Sir Bryan Leighton.

There is a considerable difference in dropping out of a balloon and an aeroplane. With the former it is a comparatively simple matter of stepping over the side. With the latter, however, one has perforce to scramble out of one's seat in the body, and gingerly, very gingerly, climb out on to the wing, there to be blown off by the backward current of air. An airship, having a moderately steady motion, and possessing the property of being able to hover in mid-air, renders parachuting the simplest of matters.

Of the three forms of craft, drops have rarely been made from aeroplanes, a few only from airships, but quite a number from kite-balloons. As a matter of fact, with the latter craft it is almost an every-day occurrence on the other side. A good example occurred only a few days ago.

Imagine, if you can, a gaunt, forbidding-looking shape, rising from the shelter of a dense wood some five miles behind the British lines. The day is clear and sunny. The craft is up directing artillery fire. After some two hours' observation two tiny, dark shapes are observed nearing overhead. Instantly all is consternation. An attempt is made to wind in the kite-balloon. Too late, the enemy planes are now well overhead. They dive steeply, and circle round the craft, dropping bombs, luckily without registering a hit, at least not on the kite-balloon. The two observers leap out in their parachutes, two tiny black specks that sink like stones to the earth, gradually growing larger as the parachutes open. They land safely. And, at an opportune moment, one of our fighting planes arrives upon the scene, and routs the enemy within only a hundred yards of his target.

But to return to the matter of K.B.'s. I do not think that I am overstating my case by saying that our kite-balloon service is the most efficient and best organised of any of the belligerent nations. For this we have to thank the untiring efforts of Squadron Commander Delacombe, of the R.N.A.S., and, later, Lieut.-Colonel Bovill, R.F.C.

During the last few months, another and more perfect captive balloon has come into use. It was invented by Captain Cacquou, of the French Army. The principal characteristics of the craft are its triple-bag appendage and the increased stability that permits the craft to be flown even in a full gale of wind.

CHAPTER 13

Airships

A comparison between the histories of the lighter-than-air and the heavier-than-air aircraft serves to show us, firstly, that the former is by far the older craft; and secondly, that the principles and construction of the two species are not altogether dissimilar. The natural gifts possessed by the lighter-than-air type would obviously be sooner apparent than the scientifically developed properties of the other craft. And as long since as 1852 a dirigible made a really successful trip in France. This airship was constructed by Henri Gliffard, and made several flights at an average speed of six miles per hour.

Previous to this date, however, experiments had been carried out by the brothers Robert, two Frenchmen, in 1784, in an oblong-shaped craft, 52 feet long and 32 feet in diameter, buoyed up by pure oxygen. A flight of over a kilometre was accomplished in this craft.

The Duc de Chartres made a flight in another of the Roberts' craft. And on this occasion the dirigible encountered a strong cross-current that tore the airbag from the envelope covering the neck and preventing the necessary escape of the hydrogen. Just in time the duke averted the danger by plunging his sword into and rending asunder the envelope.

The next recorded flight was that made by Dupuy de Lome. And ten years later Tissandier made a flight at an average speed of 10 miles an hour.

In 1872 Hanlein, a German, constructed an airship propelled by a 6 h. p. Lenoir gas-engine that touched a speed of 10 miles. And in 1879 Baumgarten and Wolfert constructed an airship which, unfortunately, was burnt in its first attempt at flight.

But it was not until 1884 that the dirigible developed true airworthiness. In that year Captain Renard flew round Paris at a speed of 14½ miles an hour.

Schwartz, an Austrian engineer, in 1897 built the first rigid airship fitted with a petrol motor. And after this came the period of Santos Dumont, the best known of aeronautical pioneers, and of Count Zeppelin.

These earlier types of dirigibles were, in reality, balloons fitted with mechanical propulsion. Several of the foremost types were driven by hand propulsion, by means of oars. The Zeppelin, or the super-Zeppelin of today, and the old-fashioned spherical balloon of the past consisted alike of two similar main portions, the envelope and the car. The envelope was always spherical in shape, and was inflated with hydrogen gas, which is the lightest gas known, being only 7 *per cent* as heavy as air, of which 1,000 cubic feet weighs 50 lb. Thus 1,000 cubic feet of hydrogen will give a lift of 74 lb., or practically, 35,000 cubic feet will lift one ton. It must not be forgotten, however, that that "lift" must include the weight of the balloon and gear.

Thus, if a 35,000 cubic feet hydrogen balloon weighs half a ton, it will only lift another half a ton besides its own weight. A modern Zeppelin has a "lift" varying from 20 to 28 tons.

Once in the air, there are many factors that must be taken into consideration. Chief among them are the natures and properties of the gas, and for that matter of all gases. The effect of heat upon gas is to make it expand, which expansion causes the balloon or airship to rise. *Per contra*, cold causes the gas to contract, and incidentally causes the craft to descend. It will be seen, therefore, that on a fine sunny day the craft will rise with greater ease than when the elements are dull and cold. Air pressure is another factor which must be considered, and this is greatest at sea-level.

The greater the altitude the less the pressure becomes, and the less pressure on the outside surface of the envelope the easier it is for the gas to expand; but this is compensated for by the fact that the atmosphere is considerably cooler at a high altitude. Practically these are the only factors governing the science of aerostatics, and we may state briefly that to make a balloon or airship rise it is necessary to allow the gas to expand.

This feat is accomplished by throwing ballast overboard in the form of sand; and to make it descend, gas must be dispensed with by allowing it to escape, thus reducing the "lifting" forces.

Airships, of which Zeppelins are the largest and most perfect type, are nothing more than huge balloons, driven in a forward direction by mechanical propulsion. The shape differs materially, being rather like that of a long cigar, but this is by reason of offering less head resistance. Altogether there are three types of airships: the "non-rigid," in which the two portions, the car and the envelope, are entirely separate portions, being held together by means of rigging—most British airships are of this class; "semi-rigid," in which the car is partly attached to the envelope, a type greatly favoured by the French and the Italians; and the "rigid airship," of which both car and envelope are in the same framework. The Zeppelin is of the latter class.

Now, we discover that the airship is composed of a long wasplike body, known as the envelope, and containing the hydrogen gas, by which it obtains its lifting forces, and a car or cars.

Lighter-than-air craft were none too popular in this country in former years; but now at last we are beginning to realise their great advantage, and are constructing airships, both large and small, as fast as we are able. Concerning which construction, it premises some extremely pleasant surprises for the public in the near future.

As long since as 1900, however, a Dr. Barton constructed an airship with which he made a successful flight over London. Mr. Willows, of Cardiff, experimented up to 1904, and produced the first British craft that was thoroughly airworthy. It was 74 feet in length, 18 feet in diameter, and was fitted with a 7 h.p. Peugot motor. Of the semi-rigid type, it had a single seat and a capacity of 22,000 cubic feet of gas. From Cardiff a flight was made to London, over a distance of 140 miles. Every few miles the pilot, Mr. Willows in person, came down near the ground and inquired his whereabouts by means of a large and powerful megaphone.

It is needless to add that this method of procedure would hardly commend itself today, with the apparent hostility of the German peoples.

He accomplished the journey in under ten hours. In November, 1910, he made another flight from Wormwood Scrubs to Douai, in France. The airship passed over the French coast at an altitude of 5,500 feet, but in landing in the dark was severely injured.

The Government Balloon Factory at Farnborough was next in the field, in 1907, with a crude form of craft, constructed with the aid and under the personal supervision of "Colonel" Cody. It was sausage-shaped and named the "*Nulli Secundus.*"

Unhappily it wasn't! And the next craft produced had an envelope of 42 feet diameter. It was fitted with a 100 h.p. engine, and registered a speed of 40 miles per hour. It was named the "*Nulli Secundus II.*" It justified the appellation!

After this craft came the *"Baby"* in 1910, and the *"Beta"* in June, 1910. The latter was fitted with a 30 h.p. Gnome engine, made several successful flights over London, and took part in the autumn manoeuvres of that year.

In September of the same year the *Morning Post*, as the result of a public subscription, presented the *"Lebaudy"* airship to the nation. This vessel was in length 337 feet, fitted with two 135 h.p. engines, and flew from Moisson to Aldershot, a distance of 197 miles, in 5 hours and 28 minutes, or at an average speed of 36 m.p.h.

Vickers turned out their first airship on the 24th of the same month, the *"Mayfly."* She was 510 feet long, 48 feet in diameter, and fitted with two 200 h.p. Wolseley engines. Immediately after leaving her shed for the first trip a gale of wind sprang up and she was totally destroyed.

After the *"Mayfly"* were the *"Gamma," "Delta,"* and *"Eta,"* neither of which achieved any very great success.

At the beginning of 1914 we possessed only two really reliable airships. They were a *Parseval*, bought from the German Government, and an *"Astra Torres,"* purchased in France. However, these craft rendered yeoman service in scouring the seas for enemy submarines; thus, aiding materially the convoying of the British Expeditionary Force to France.

The Naval Authorities, some time before the war commenced, took over all the lighter-than-air, and are today responsible for these craft, which consist for the most part of "Baby's" or "Blimps," or "S.S.'s" and "C.P.'s."

FRANCE

Our neighbours across the Channel have made considerably more progress with lighter-than-air vessels than we have ourselves. This is not at all to be wondered at! The psychology of the two peoples is as far apart as the two poles. Where we, in this country, regarded the advent of aircraft in a stolid, unemotional manner, coldly reasoning that if a few hardy adventurers were willing to risk their necks beneath the all-enveloping cloak of sport, that was entirely their affair, but as a practical enterprise it was absurd, and such a thing "wasn't done"; the French, with all the verve and impetuousness of the Latin races, hailed the event as one of the most important and far-reaching events in history, and forthwith devoted the best brains and ample finance to experiment with and develop the airship.

As the pioneer ballooning country of the world, they held a very great advantage from the start. For, as has been already pointed out in this chapter, the balloon and the airship are almost kindred craft.

The Lebaudy Brothers were the pioneers. In 1899 they constructed the "*Jaune*," a vessel 183 feet long, 30 feet in diameter, and of 80,000 cubic feet capacity. The engine was a 40 h.p. Daimler, and gave a speed of 26 m.p.h. In 1902 she made 29 flights and was successful upon 28 of these occasions in returning to her starting-point. In November of that year, she hit a tree when landing and became a total wreck.

In 1904 the Lebaudys produced their next craft, the "*Lebaudy*." This vessel was possessed of a triple airbag or ballonet, was 190 feet long, and had a capacity of 94,000 cubic feet. She was a most successful ship, and after 76 flights had been made their "rights" were acquired by the French Government, who therewith commenced to construct Lebaudys—they were of the semi-rigid type, with a spar running along the entire length of the envelope, thus evenly distributing the weight—at Moisson.

In 1906 there followed, by the same firm, the "*Patrie*," and in 1909 the "*République*." They were larger and improved types of the "Lebaudy" ship, with an average speed of 28 m.p.h., a radius of 280 miles, and accommodation for a crew of nine. In 1907, while the "*Patrie*" was anchored outside Verdun, she was torn from her moorings in a violent gale, and trailed off over Northern France and the British Isles, and finally disappeared in the direction of the Atlantic Ocean.

The "*République*," which possessed an engine of some 80 h.p., made successful flights over a period extending from July, 1908, to September, 1909. Then a propeller breaking in mid-air, a blade thereof flew upwards, tore a large gash in the envelope and killed 2 officers and 2 N.C.O.'s. Similar airships of the same type were the "*Russie*" and "*La Liberté*."

The first craft of the "*Clement-Bayard*" type was the "*Ville de Paris*." In length it was 200 feet, fitted with a 70 h.p. motor, giving a speed of 25 m.p.h. and having a capacity of 120,487 feet. In 1909 came the "*Clement-Bayard*," a larger ship but built on similar lines. Her engine was 100 h.p. and gave a speed of 30 m.p.h. On August 23rd, 1909, the "*Clement-Bayard*" flew for two hours at an altitude of 5,000 feet, but finished her career by depositing herself in the Seine. Other ships of this class were:—

The "Ville de Bordeaux"	3,200 cubic metres.
The "Ville de Nancy"	3,200 " "
The "Colonel Renard"	4,000 " "
The "España"	4,000 " "
The "Clement Bayard II"	6,500 " "
The "TransAerienne I"	6,500 " "
The "Flandre"	6,500 " "

Several of these latter craft were "Astra-Torres," designed by a Spanish engineer, Señor Torres.

ITALY

It has been said by many aeronautical experts that the Italian semi-rigids are the finest in the world. This may or may not be. We are not open to discuss such matters in these few pages, further than to say the Italian Government has always specialized in this type of airship.

The first, the P1—P, "Piccolo," small size—was constructed in 1908. The P1 was 200 feet long, of 40 feet diameter, had a motor of 100 h.p., and possessed a speed of 35 m.p.h. She was not very successful in her trials, and in 1912 the government purchased a "Parseval" from Germany.

The next home-constructed product was the M Class—M, medium size—with engines of 500 h.p. and a speed of 48 m.p.h. She was 250 feet long and 55 feet in diameter; the largest semi-rigid ever constructed. The next class, but of the same type, was the Forlanni, and the "Città di Ferrara" was the first ship of the class. She had a capacity of 424,000 feet, a length of 233 feet, a diameter of 59 feet, and three 85-100 Isotta-Fraschini engines.

The Italian airships have accomplished many remarkably useful flights during the war.

GERMANY

And by no means least, but last, there is the German Empire. And here again psychology plays no unimportant part. The Teuton is notoriously methodical, invariably a plodder. His inventions are never the outcome of a flash of genius, but generally an idea from some other source, worked and improved upon gradually, painstakingly, until the object of consideration assumes unrecognisable proportions. Germany, then, took a considerably greater time to construct her aircraft, but when finally completed they were perfect in every degree. And she did not, as most people imagine, confine her attentions solely to the

Zeppelin.

Among her other accomplishments was the *"Parseval,"* a type of "semi-rigid" airship, the principal feature of which was the arrangement by which the suspension cables allowed the hull to be canted in relation to the angle of the car, in order to enable her to climb at a much-increased speed. The first *"Parseval"* was produced in 1906, but was not a very great success. The second was 190 feet long, 35½ feet in diameter, 113,000 cubic feet capacity, possessed of two 120 h.p. engines, and fitted with the same system of suspension as number one. She made many voyages, with sometimes as many as twelve passengers aboard.

Another type was the wooden *"Schütte-Lanz."* An attempt by a firm at Mannheim in 1912 to produce a rigid airship constructed of wood braced with wire. It was cigar-like in shape, and approximately the same size as a Zeppelin. However, the wooden structure rendered her considerably heavier than the latter craft. And no very successful flights were then made, though it is thought that several of the *Schütte-Lanz* craft have participated with the Zeppelins in raids on this country.

THE ZEPPELIN

The Zeppelin is due to one man, and one man alone. The greyhaired, bent old Count, formerly an officer in the German Army, who lived to find himself, a once much-despised, impoverished inventor, acclaimed the saviour of his country, loaded with honours and riches, the personal friend of the most autocratic of autocracies, and a notorious figure in the history of the world. His iron will and determination triumphed over poverty, adverse circumstance, and disbelief alike, until finally he forced the very people, who had formerly regarded his invention as a waste of time and of money, to clamour in a wailing hell-chorus for that same craft.

Zeppelin commenced his experiments at Friedrichshaven, on the shores of Lake Constance, in 1900. The first ship was 400,000 cubic feet in capacity, possessed two 16 h.p. motors, weighed 9 tons, and carried 5 men. It made only one flight, but during the course of that, remained in the air for one and a quarter hours, and touched an altitude of 1,000 feet.

Encouraged by this success, the old man constructed, with the aid of influential friends, in 1906, a second craft. This ship was more powerful than her predecessor, and possessed two 85 h.p. Daimler engines.

A trial flight was made in November of that year, but the craft was wrecked shortly afterwards in a violent gale of wind. Undeterred by these added misfortunes he persevered, constructing fresh ships as year succeeded year. Until eventually he received royal patronage and the aid of the State; and at the outbreak of hostilities was able to place at the disposal of the authorities some thirty airworthy ships.

Cuxhaven had already been selected as the headquarters of the German Air Fleet, with air harbours at Heligoland, Tondern, Emden, Wilhelmshaven, Hamburg, Kiel, Wismar, Rostock, and Konigsberg. These stations had been stipulated for in the four years' building programme of the Reichstag of October I3th, 1913. This programme provided for 10 rigid airships, for several first and second class air harbours, the majority fitted with revolving sheds, and for maintenance of material; the total to be completed by January 1st, 1918.

Of the Zeppelins there were, or rather are, six several types. The which, for purposes of convenience, we will refer to by numbers, from 1 to 6. The first type was the Super-Zeppelin class, that contained products both of the Zeppelin and the *Schütte-Lanz* ships.

It was constructed at the Zeppelin works, Friedrichshaven, and Mannheim:

Length	630 feet.
Capacity	1,906,200 cubic feet.
Useful lift	19 tons.
Engines	Six 250 h.p. 6-cylinder Maybach.
Maximum speed	65 m.p.h.
Endurance	35 hours.
Maximum altitude	16,500 feet.
Complement	22
Armament	6 maxim guns

Class 2 are constructed at Friedrichshaven and Rheinau:—

Length	775 feet.
Capacity	2,471,000 cubic feet.
Useful lift	28 tons
Engines	Seven 250 h.p. Maybach
Maximum speed	68 miles
Endurance	40 hours.
Complement	22
Maximum altitude	16,500 feet
Armament	6 maxim guns, 4 tons explosives

Class 3 are constructed at Friedrichshaven and Potsdam:—

Length	528 feet.
Capacity	1,059,000 cubic feet
Useful lift	10 tons.
Engines	Five 210 h.p. 6-cylinder Maybach
Maximum speed	53 m.p.h
Endurance	26 hours.
Complement	16
Maximum altitude	11,550 feet.
Armament	4 maxims, 2 tons bombs.

Class 4 are constructed at Friedrichshaven and Rheinau:—

Length 5	60 feet
Capacity	1,235,000 cubic feet.
Useful lift	13 tons.
Engines	Six 210 h.p. 6-cylinder Maybach.
Maximum speed	59 m.p.h.
Endurance	30 hours.
Maximum altitude	13,200 feet
Complement	18
Armament	6 maxims, 2½ tons of bombs.

Class 5 are constructed at *Schütte-Lanz* factory at Rheinau:—

Length	544 feet.
Capacity	1,059,000 cubic feet.
Useful lift	14 tons.
Engines	Four 240 h.p. Mercédès.
Maximum speed	53 m.p.h.
Endurance	26 hours.
Maximum altitude	8,250 feet.
Complement	16.
Armament	5 maxims, 1½ tons of bombs.

And lastly, class 6, the latest of all, are constructed at the Zeppelin works at Friedrichshaven:—

Length	521 feet.
Capacity	953,000 cubic feet.
Useful lift	8 tons.
Engines	Four 210 h.p. 6-cylinder Maybach.
Maximum speed	50 m.p.h.
Endurance	26 hours.

Maximum altitude	8,250 feet.
Complement	16.
Armament	4 maxims, 1½ tons of bombs.

CHAPTER 14

Fighting the Zeppelin

The novelty of Zeppelin fighting is the main reason for the bitter criticism levelled thereat. It is new, strange, and to a certain degree unexpected. The British public (those that have never been on the other side) have alternately howled, gasped, cheered, and reviled thereat. Because such a thing had never occurred before, because it was a departure from all precedent, it was condemned. The Zeppelin crews were deemed baby-killers and murderers, and one of our own country-women threw wood at the coffin of a dead German airman as it passed her in the street! For this we must thank the foolish, screaming headlines of the daily Press.

But Zeppelin raids are legitimate! I advance this most unpopular view unhesitatingly. War is war, whether fought on land or sea or in the air. The enemy, previous to 1914, gave us a pretty good idea why he was constructing his great Zeppelin fleet, also to what purpose they would be put. It was up to us to take the necessary precautionary measures. What did we do? A cabinet minister, with more lung power than veracity, informed us that, should the enemy ever venture to send his aerial fleet over these islands, they would encounter a swarm of defending "Hornets." But the "Hornets" never found their wings.

To these novel circumstances we must immediately adapt our perspective. No evil is without its remedy, and judging by the excellent performances put up by our anti-aircraft gunners on the occasions of the last few raids—it leads us to believe that that remedy has already been discovered. But, not content with this alone, the best brains in the country must be devoted to this problem of the skies, for the Zeppelin raid is but the pin-prick in the ocean to what the future holds in store.

War in the air has already taken a powerful hold on the public imagination. The spectacular effect has dazzled their eyes, the fascination of the thing has seized upon their senses, and the crudity of their methods of offensive has roused them to the heights of wrath and anger. It will be wise to sweep away these trimmings of romance, novelty, and fascination. Therein is constituted a very grave danger. Treated simply as a vessel of war the Zeppelin is for the time being a failure; but the age of a Zeppelin as a craft is just over seventeen years. Aircraft have unlimited scope. The future may hold a more powerful Zeppelin, able to climb with ease above the range of the A.A. guns, a combination of Zeppelin and aeroplane, or a heavily armoured form of aircraft, shell-proof against all form of artillery.

The game of the air is like a mammoth game of chess, the opponents sit, unseen and unseeing; the one somewhere in these islands, the other beneath the mantle of the All-Highest of Potsdam. We move, a new and powerful aeroplane is invented. Immediately after they move, with a yet more powerful craft. The German engineers construct a powerful engine, we go one better. Ours is yet more powerful! And thus, we will go on. But there! Are not international politics altogether and entirely a gigantic game, a strange jumble of kings, queens, and bishops?

However, this chapter is primarily intended to be devoted to the matter of defence against raiding aircraft. First it must be well realised that it would be a matter of utter impossibility to guard each and every townlet and hamlet from attack from above. Such a course would require a multitudinous number of guns, searchlights, men and craft alike, and particularly today they cannot be spared. It will only be possible to guard the more important positions. And in the meantime, it will be a comparatively easy matter for the pilots of the raiding craft to pick out the least defended districts by a simple study of the map.

How are these raiding Zeppelins to be met? Obviously, the best method is with similar craft. With Zeppelins of our own, the best defensive policy would be to take the offensive. To raid and bomb the enemy craft in their sheds and air harbours would indeed be carrying the war into the enemy's country, as they have carried it into ours. And it would serve the further purpose of preventing any possible raid. As an alternative, our craft could scout over the North Sea somewhere off the German coast and either give them battle at their weakest moment—*i.e.,* with a heavy load of bombs and spare petrol aboard— or give ample warning by wireless to our fleet and home defences.

As our Zeppelins have not yet materialised (?) we must consider our present possible methods of defence, and they consist principally of anti-aircraft guns and aeroplanes. With these it would surely be reasonable to establish, somewhere along the east coast, a definite line of defence; or rather shall we call it an air-board similar to the sea-board supplied by the North Sea? Here concentrate all our aerial defences!

Of them all, the anti-aircraft gun is most effective, but even that is useless without a good searchlight. Neither is dispensable to the other. The *modus operandi* is for the distant listening post to give warning of the approach of the Zepp, as will also the incessant barkings, or rather whimperings, of the dogs of the neighbourhood over which the Zepp may happen to be. The searchlight will then first locate the craft, and following it incessantly with the light, put it within easy view of the gunner. The gunner, having the craft in view, proceeds to find the range as follows:—

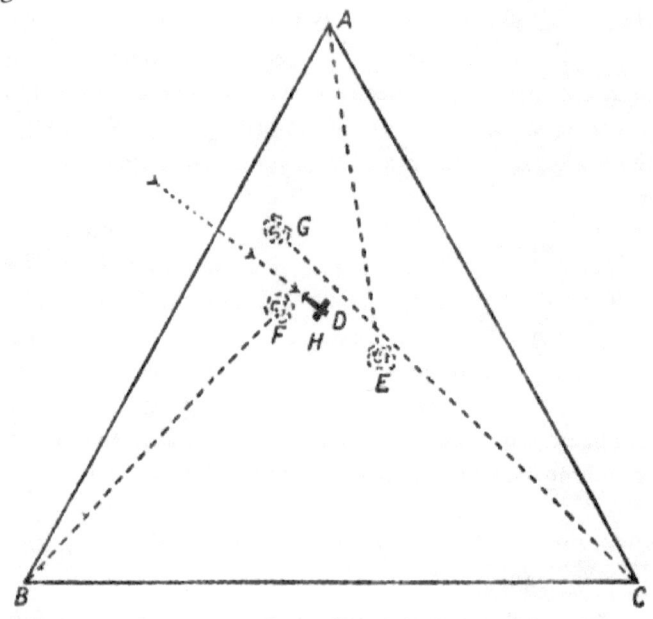

FIG. 7. TRIANGULAR METHOD OF OBTAINING RANGE AND
ALTITUDE OF HOSTILE AIRCRAFT

Thus far we have confined our attention to stationary guns alone. Many of the A. A. guns, and practically all those of the enemy, are mobile—that is to say, they are mounted either on motor-lorries or on railway trucks. Being able to move the guns quickly from place to place makes the matter of range-finding and accurate firing easier and less complicated for the gunners. But the Zeppelin, despite its great bulk, is a most elusive target.

In the first place, we will suppose that the shell has burst on or in close proximity to the aircraft. Had the envelope been in one single piece, as was the case in former days, the craft would crash down to earth immediately. Nowadays, however, the envelope is merely the outer covering to some thirty odd smaller ballonets. If only one or two of these are pierced the craft can still continue on its way without any really serious disadvantage. Again, a Zeppelin, by reason of the gas in the ballonets, can climb at an enormously rapid pace, and so completely alter the altitude of the range in a very short space of time.

It was owing principally to these reasons, and also to the fact that the matter was so novel, and that no practice whatsoever had been obtained in firing at moving objects in the air, that our anti-aircraft gunners failed so dismally in their earlier attempts. The improvement was in no manner of means due, as they would have us believe, to the agitation of the *Daily Mail*—which latter journal always makes capital by agitating for reforms which they are fully aware are already well under way—but to continuous practice; practice that ensured both experience and accuracy; practice that rendered it possible for them to bring down the Zeppelins at Cuffley and Potter's Bar.

For without good gunnery it would be impossible, save in exceptional circumstances, for an aeroplane to bring down a Zepp unaided. The latter are the *matadors* of the air, which, after the Zepps have been crippled or disabled, perform the necessary finishing strokes. Which brings us to the third means of defence, namely, the aeroplane.

The discussion between the relative values of the airship and aeroplane is the most difficult and delicate matter connected with aviation. The aviation world has always been, and will always be, divided into two camps, the one that swears by the lighter-than-air, the other by the heavier-than-air craft.

A comparison between the two craft serves to show us that "lift" is the main property that most stringently divides the merits and the demerits of the two. The weight of the aeroplane body, wings, engine, fittings, etc., takes up at least 50 *per cent* of the total "lift." The weight of the pilot, observer and accessories takes up another 25 *per cent*, which allows only twenty-five for "war lift," by which I mean that necessary for bombs, ammunition, machine-gun, and spare petrol. The Zeppelin, on the other hand, has two sources of "lift," namely, the natural "lift" of the envelope and the "lift" supplied by the motive power, and almost double the "lift" in aggregate. And "lift" effects speed in climbing, also allows for greater engine power aboard. Climbing is essential, for the aerial combat is always fought out in the upward direction, and the

117

best strategic position is to be well over the enemy craft. Also, greater "lift" allows more space aboard for supplies of bombs, ammunition, and spare petrol. Therefore, in the all-important matter of "lift" the Zeppelin has a distinct advantage.

The aeroplane, however, has a distinct advantage over the Zeppelin in the matter of speed in a lateral direction. But the latter is becoming faster every day. The aeroplane, again, is essentially a craft of the daylight. The danger of landing the heavier-than-air machine, always a tricky operation, is trebled in the darkness of the night. The supply of petrol aboard is extremely limited, and the duration power at the outside is six hours. That of the Zeppelin is somewhere in the neighbourhood of twenty-six.

In the darkness, and even in daylight, the aeroplane pilot rarely sights a Zeppelin, the meeting being entirely a matter of luck and circumstance. The Zeppelin pilot can shut off his engines, and by ballasting can proceed unimpeded at his original altitude which the aeroplane can never do and be able to listen for the approach of the aeroplane by the sound of the engine, and manoeuvre accordingly.

The aeroplane can only bring a Zeppelin down once it has climbed above it; and it must be admitted that in that position the latter craft is entirely at its mercy. Several of the Zeppelins have a machine-gun mounted on top of the envelope, but this weapon is little better than useless against bombs. Again, however, for the aeroplane pilot the danger arises; in bombing he may miss the enemy craft, and the bomb drop down to the land below. Should engine-failure occur while in mid-air the aeroplane must come down immediately, but the Zepp can continue on its way.

Although the altitude record of the aeroplane is considerably higher than that of the Zeppelin, the average flying level is considerably less; being with the former some 12,000 feet, with the latter some 16,000.

The aeroplane, as a craft, is comparatively inexpensive to construct, the landing-ground required not extremely extensive; neither the personnel to maintain the craft on the ground. The aeroplane hangar is no mammoth erection. The Zeppelin, on the other hand, is extremely expensive to construct. The personnel aboard require at least twelve months' preliminary training. The landing-ground required is enormous, likewise the personnel to house the craft, also the shed to contain it.

The Zeppelin is much more the victim of adverse climatic conditions and thus less airworthy. There have been considerably more craft lost that way than by casualties.

Finally, it must be an extremely fast aeroplane with great climbing powers to successfully tackle a Zeppelin in mid-air; and, again, the aeroplane must be well up before the Zeppelin arrives overhead. The Zeppelins, it is known, have on several occasions been convoyed by powerful-engined aeroplanes; and this fact leads me to observe immediately the similarity between this manoeuvre and that of the large type of warship convoyed by a skirt of torpedo-boats at sea.

Entering upon the actual combat, the Zeppelin is more heavily armed, and the steadiness of its gun-platform allows it a great advantage in the matter of accuracy of firing. It is, however, when compared with the aeroplane, a slow and clumsy craft to manipulate. It is preferable for two or three aeroplanes to attack a Zepp at one and the same time, as was recently the case off Norfolk.

An American paper said recently, with reference to our latest anti-Zepp aeroplanes:—

In spite of the tendency to exaggeration in the reports of the new war material which is being developed in Europe, it is possible to sift out the true from the false, and there is good reason to believe that the British, in their latest aeroplanes, have found an effective answer to the Zeppelin.

When the first raids on London were made, the British possessed neither the guns nor the aircraft in sufficient numbers or quality to meet, destroy, or drive back the latest Zeppelins. The anti-aircraft guns could not reach effectively the great heights to which the Zeppelin could rise, nor could the aircraft rise in time to attack. Since that time both guns and aircraft have become thoroughly efficient for the work. Just in what numbers and of what calibre are the anti-aircraft batteries with which London is now so well defended, is not known; but, because of the great value of high velocity and a straight trajectory for anti-aircraft gunfire, it is a pretty safe guess that there are many batteries of guns larger than the 3-inch. The 50-calibre 47and 6-inch gun, if fired at high angles of elevation, have a trajectory of slight curvature and the time of flight is small, elements which simplify the task of the gunner in finding and keeping on a moving target.

Information is now available as to the new anti-Zepp aeroplanes, and Lieut. —— of the Royal Flying Corps, who recently landed in New York on furlough, has given some details which agree with information we have received from another source. The problem has been to build an aeroplane with climbing powers sufficient to enable it to reach Zeppelin altitudes in time to meet the raiders and bring them down. The latest machines are of comparatively small wing surface, and are driven by unusually powerful engines, capable of making speeds of 120 to 140 miles per hour. The increase in climbing speed in the past few months has been truly astonishing, having progressed from an ascent of 10,000 feet in 6 minutes to 15,000 feet in 7½ minutes. The scouting service, both on the North Sea and along the east coast, is now so effective that London is warned of the approach of the Zeppelins in time to permit the Zeppelin chasers to take the air and be in position for an attack before the raiders reach their objective.

An invention which promises a decided usefulness in this matter is a 3-inch aeroplane gun, that hurls a shell at a velocity of 1,000 feet a second, but has no recoil. *Popular Mechanics* describes it as:—

Designed particularly as offensive armament for aeroplanes, a high-power 3-inch gun of the quick-fire type has been developed which does not recoil when discharged. This distinctively new feature enables the instrument to be installed on a light machine of almost any size and fired freely without danger of shattering or capsizing the craft. The piece is unlike all other guns, and is apparently suited solely for aerial purposes. Its bore is uniform throughout and has no surface upon which pressure can act longitudinally. The barrel, instead of being open only at the muzzle, is open at both ends. This permits the propulsion charge to act in two directions, thus obviating the recoil. The projectile is hurled from the muzzle toward its target at the same instant that a quantity of metal filings or fine shot is discharged from the breech. After travelling a short distance, the latter loses its velocity, so that it cannot injure soldiers below at the rear, although it closely resembles that ordinarily used in pieces of the same calibre; the ammunition is specially made for the gun. The projectile travels at a speed of about 1,000 feet per second. Light process steel reduces the weight of the gun to the minimum.

Finally, and from what is considered a wholly dependable source,

A "PUSHER" BIPLANE WITH PROPELLER TO THE REAR

information comes concerning a most unusual aeronautical experiment being carried out by German aerial experts. It deals with the development of a powerful flying boat which carries, for both defensive and offensive purposes, a swift, mosquito-like aeroplane on its back. The idea is almost analogous to the Dreadnought and destroyer of naval use. The machine, when last heard of, was being put through test flights, but had not at that time been sufficiently refined to warrant its actual use.

The new machine has such remarkable stability, carrying capacity, and cruising radius that its engineers think it can be made to replace the more bulky and highly-expensive Zeppelins. If this actually comes to pass it will mark the recognised triumph of the heavier-than-air machine over the much lauded dirigible, for war purposes at least.

It is a heavily built triplane mounting three motors. The wings, which are staunchly built and of a design that gives the craft great inherent stability, have a total spread of approximately 146 feet. The body is entirely enclosed and its windows fitted with reinforced glass that will not fall apart when subjected to heavy impacts. The panes are made by gluing two thin pieces of glass to the opposite surfaces of a heavy sheet of transparent celluloid. When struck with a hammer, for instance, the shattered part of the glass remains fast to its backing.

Although it is to be supposed that a craft of this size would be difficult to manoeuvre, as compared with the lighter and more agile machines, it is said to have unusual qualities of stability, because of its design, and to be capable of battling successfully against heavy, fickle air currents that would swamp most flying boats. It mounts two quick-fire guns of small calibre, carries a crew of five men, a cargo of half a ton of bombs, and a sufficient supply of fuel and oil to keep it in the air for forty-eight hours.

The auxiliary aeroplane which it supports on its back is equipped with bomb-dropping devices and a machine-gun. It is provided in order to ward off the attacks of enemy craft and to drop low and hurl high-explosive projectiles upon particular objects of attack, such as arsenals, forts, docks, and naval vessels. The chief difficulty standing in the way of its perfection has been the problem of providing some practical means of enabling the small craft to return to the mother machine after executing its mission. No trouble has been encountered in carrying the tiny machine, nor in launching it in mid-air, but it has been found quite another thing to pick it up again. And this is necessary to render the unit efficient for the part it is intended to play.

CHAPTER 15

The Airman's Point of View

There was a look about him that was distinctly of the air; good, clear-cut features, hair that tended to curl, a thick-set figure, supple and muscular. But about the eyes one noticed particularly a not unpleasing steely look; a slight contraction about the temples. The indefinable expression of the man to whom danger is fraught with full meaning but small fear.

"I can't understand it," he said, "this feeling that our work; in the air is so daring and so heroic. What about the poor devils in the trenches? Personally, and for that matter, almost every airman I know entertains a wholesome dread of paddling about waist-deep in a muddy trench. And, strange to say, the infantryman reciprocates the feeling—the admiration, I mean. I met a man only the other day: 'You beggars must have nerve,' he said. 'I couldn't do it myself.' Why not?"

"Perhaps it is because flying is so novel; so little understood," I suggested.

"Bah! There's not the least thing unusual about it. It's a much more prosaic and matter-of-fact business than submarining, for instance. There's a cold-blooded calling if you like. That's the man for my hero. Besides, you never hear anything said about the man who creeps out of a trench in the dead of night, under heavy shell fire all the time, to bomb an enemy dug-out, or the man who dashes across No Man's Land in a tank, or a sailor who's patrolling the lonely seas through every vile wind that blows."

"But the air——"

"Ah, yes, the first trip, it shakes you up a bit, I admit, but you soon get accustomed to it. You rock about when you get into the bumps—cross-currents of air—and feel that you want to grasp the sides of the machine for mental support. Then when she starts coming down, and the nose of the aeroplane sinks down in front of you, you feel your stomach edging up towards your mouth, but that is all. Afterwards it's just a matter of experience and plain common-sense.

"Then? Oh, then you just knock around getting the hang of things, as it were, learning how to take down and build up an engine, to box a compass and set a course, and to operate your wireless and machine-gun. Several passenger trips in an aeroplane follow on. That's to accustom one to the new sensation. After that you go up for a few flights in a dual-control machine, to acquire the correct movements of the rudder-bar which you operate with your feet, and the joy-stick that manoeuvres the craft up and down, to the left and to the right.

"About that period, you're what's known as a 'Hun.' Oh! just a youth who's learning to fly, you know. We've got a quaint slang, peculiarly our own conception. A 'bus' now is an aeroplane. A 'stunt' doing some unusual trick in the air. A 'bump' you know already. 'Getting the wind up you,' a not very picturesque way of saying that a fellow is feeling extremely nervous. And a 'gasbag' is one of those ugly brutes they use for observation, that sit like diseased and fallen angels in mid-air. By the way, the Naval Air Service vary 'Hun' with 'Quirk,' and they've got a pet name for every stranger they meet—'George' I think it is.

"No; getting your aeroplane ticket's not a very difficult matter—a distance flight of about 547 yards, turning round two posts, once to the left and once to the right, a landing without your engine, and a landing made on a given mark. But in the R.F.C. that is only half the battle won. You've still got a lot to learn before you get your wings.

"Practically, you may say then the new hand is taught to regard the air as a bad master but an obedient servant. It must never be feared, always humoured, and never taken liberties with. Every movement up there must be gentle, not sudden, and never violent. For the craft is one of moods. For in this the aeroplane is akin to a child, now sulky and petulant, now happy and obedient, now unruly and violent. To know these humours and to master them is all part of the pilot's education."

I asked, "What are the feelings experienced on the first trip across the firing-lines?"

"Feelings!" he replied. "They are a strange mixture of pride and fear, a certain feeling of satisfaction in something achieved, something done—a nervousness bordering on curiosity with regard to any unusual happening that may occur.

"Below, the earth is very similar in appearance to what it is at

124

home—a jumbled medley of green and blue and grey. Here and there are little white puffs of smoke that spring up suddenly and die away again in the same mysterious fashion. It is by the time you are over the trenches that your real business as an airman commences. Before, it has been merely a matter of 'joy-rides' over peaceful meadows and rivers and fields. Here you realise that you have the greatest battle in history beneath you, and somehow you feel that you are only a spectator.

"Though," he added hastily, "they say that the onlooker sees most of the game. This is certainly the case in the air. It is like watching two eager opponents making their moves in a gigantic game of chess. At last, you reach the trenches, looking like two great cracks that run zigzag fashion across the surface of the earth. They open fire with their anti-aircraft guns. An unpleasant moment. Shrapnel's never very pleasant, but high explosive, ugh! that's beyond words. Then, of course, it's all a matter of luck. Some fellows get through all right, again and again, others get pipped the very first time across. And you finish your reconnaissance, or your bomb raid, or whatever it is, and go home again," he finished naively.

"Fighting?"

"Well, the first fight in particular."

He pondered hard for a few seconds. "Well," he said, "you'll have to use your imagination a bit."

I smiled acquiescence.

"You are," he continued, "8,000 feet up on a clear summer's morning.

"Northwards to the sea, southwards to where the earth is lost in the mist and cloud, stretches the grim battle area. Down below the roads are thronged with traffic—motor transports, gun-limbers, supply columns, a regiment on the march, a battery of artillery. A little group of white-roofed huts indicates a field hospital; behind the woods groups of old-fashioned bell-tents mark an infantry rest camp.

"As we climb higher the view extends, now taking in the misty English coast-line and then the occasional flash and smoke-burst of a big gun somewhere in front. A kite-balloon, unearthed from a sheltered declivity, rises ponderous and ugly from the ground. Aeroplanes seem to come creeping up from all quarters. Every moment we are climbing higher and drawing nearer to the battle area. Now the winding lines of trench are visible, the smoke clouds of the big guns. The enemy is putting some 'heavy stuff' into the little town immediately below, which commands two main roads and a railway junction. We get our first dose of 'Archies,' but are far out of range.

"Who can describe one's true feelings in that first flight across the lines? Fear and bravado, nervousness, desperation, hope and despair, all are experienced. Before the next 'dose' we climb higher; the latter may have been a chance shot, but the next attention, when they have us under observation and have gauged the range, will be more methodical.

"Now the earth is Lilliputian—a toy world, where men crawl like ants, and there are tiny pinpricks that deal out death and destruction. Whole armies are crowded into spaces that appear to be only a few square yards. Can this be the greatest war in history, this pigmy affair, this scattered collection of darkish shapes, units of the two greatest armies in Christendom? Convincing proof is not long in coming; two shrapnel shells burst in unpleasant proximity, and high explosive jolts and jars the machine in nerve-racking fashion.

"Down below the most prominent landmarks are the trenches—winding, turning lines of grey and white, serried across the deep grey surface of the earth. It is a curious phenomenon this—that when the surface of the earth has been disturbed in any way it should always show up so prominently from above.

"Over the lines and well into the enemy country, we are not long in finding our objective. From behind a bank of cloud a great Albatross appears coming 'downwind' at a rapid pace. Now for it!

"An analysis of one's feelings would shatter every recognised theory of psychology. First, one measures the opponent with his eye and gauges, always incorrectly, his capabilities. What is his speed? Is he higher or lower in altitude? A mad joy, a wild impetuosity seizes the pilot. He wants to get at close grips, but that is impossible in the air, and there is something unsatisfying, something disappointing in 'potting' at a man from a distance, wheeling by him at sixty miles an hour without even a glimpse of his face. What is he thinking of? What will he do?

"Then there comes a feverish anxiety to know whether the observer is ready. Why is he fumbling with the Lewis gun like that? Can't he fix the tray? At last, all is ready. He turns with a smile.

"Still half a mile away, the enemy appears to be slightly above us. We open out the engine and climb as fast as we can. Now we are level with him, but a quarter of a mile to the right. A few passing shots and he has flashed by. We wheel back and turn slightly inwards, very close this time. The machine-gun at his nose spits red, and ours replies; the fight resolves itself into a machine-gun duel between the observers.

"A few bullets flash past the wings, one ripping the fabric, but no harm is done. Again, we wheel, again plunge into the fight, again engage in the machine-gun duel. The foe is wheeling and climbing until he gets above us, and our danger is very real when his observer turns his machine-gun on us. It is a tense moment, for a few seconds will decide whether we live or die, return home again in comfort or go spinning down broken and uncontrollable to a hideous death beneath.

"The observer has been hit in the arm and the blood shows through his thick tan coat. Must we give in and go? No; the observer is a plucky chap and, tying up the wound as best he can, he signals smilingly to go on. We climb gradually until at last, we are rising above the enemy, and ours is proving the more powerful machine.

"At last, the moment arrives when we almost hover over him. *Zipp-zipp-zipp*, goes the machine-gun. He staggers, recovers himself, staggers again, and then begins to climb rapidly. It is his last chance to live. We 'open out' as fast as we can and follow him, the machine-gun yapping in the prow. Earth and sky, danger and safety, everything is forgotten in this mad rush through the air, with the wind whistling by, and our ears deadened by the roar of the racing engine. All that is most primitive, most savage, rises in a man's breast at a moment like this. The only desire is to kill, kill, kill.

"Now the enemy is struggling on as only a man can when it is a matter of life or death. Now! But the machine-gun tray has run out. Another tray! Quick, or we shall miss him. . . . Just in time! The other staggers. His machine begins to plunge and lurch, then suddenly it noses down, and falls with a sickening speed towards the earth.

"The glow of victory, the feeling that cannot be equalled in this world, seizes one—but with it a feeling of genuine sorrow for an opponent who has fought like a sportsman and a man.

"So, you see, it's all really so matter of fact and commonplace. There's nothing that savours of heroism, nothing at all," he concluded naively.

CHAPTER 16

How A Battle Looks from the Air

Imagine," he said—and he was an authority upon such matters—
"imagine a sweeping, animated *vista* of land and sea, valley and hill,
city and meadow. The world at your feet! A landscape limited alone by
distance and oblivion. Imagine, again, that you are gazing into one of
those strange contraptions that house themselves on piers and prome-
nades of popular seaside resorts, in which may be seen for the humble
sum of one penny a varied panorama of the world, and you have the
airman's outlook. Well, perhaps, not quite!

"We, that is to say, my observer and myself—nowadays it is becoming more and more the unpleasant duty of the pilot, like an aerial
chauffeur, to merely fly the machine, while the observer directs the
course and laps up the brainwork had received orders to proceed
forthwith over X—— to direct artillery bombardment, preparatory
to an infantry advance on a large scale.

"The day was well advanced, moderately clear with milky thin
racing clouds that hung low. These we skirted after the manner of a
steamer hugging a friendly coast-line. Our orders were positive; direction of artillery fire, fighting disallowed.

"Yes! That is a hard-and-fast rule. Fighting for the likes of battle-
planes. Reconnaissance for special craft told off. The latter never to
enter combat unless defensive."

"The various types different in character?" I ventured mildly.

"Mostly as regard engine-power," he replied briefly. "For reconnaissance an engine with duration; for fighting—speed and climbing-
powers.

★★★★★★★★★★★★★★★★

"Prominent below, a long, straight high-road, tree-lined on either
side, pointing with the directness of a signpost to the firing-line. We
are low enough to distinguish the crawling streams of traffic in either

direction. From the level of the ground this road appears packed to extremis. From above, at the same hour, large patches of white road surface can be seen between—a heavy gun, drawn by a smoking 'Puffing Billy' on a limber; a string of supply lorries returning from their bi-diurnal trip to the trenches; a company, or is it a battalion, of infantry toiling linewards to relieve; motor-buses, motorbikes, ambulances, farm-wagons, and motorcars.

"Only from above can one gauge the vastness, the complication of this world campaign. On the fore-front of the stage, well in the limelight, the marionettes, the gallant infantry who hold the trenches. They are worked and moved back and fro by the orderly jumble of live wires that reach to a back-distance apex, some fifteen miles. The base is C.H.Q., from whence, in triangular formation, the wires extend to divisional H.Q., thence to brigade, thence to battalion, immediately in rear of the scene of action.

"And the motive power that supplies the current to work the marionette, the plain word of command.

"For the rest, a three-belted panorama of earth surface, the green, fresh look of the peaceful country-side; the green, tinged with brown, of the districts adjoining to the mud-brown waste, from which rise, here and there, a column of smoke which needs no definition. Standing back from the highroad a frowning *château*, timbered around, with a large sheet of blue water before. Slightly incongruous, it strikes one, in such surroundings. But apparently it has its uses. Aside of it there rears itself a gaunt and ugly wireless pole, a fringe of white-domed bell tents, a fairly continuous crawl of motor traffic, up and down the broad drive; evidently an H.Q. of some description.

"On again, over a town of ample proportions, evidently convalescing after a severe bout of bombardment. The scene of action draws near. Now we have to discover our own particular sector for observation.

"Oh, yes! By map, marked out preliminary to leaving the ground.

"Now we are over shell-fire. The observer is busy wirelessing to the guns. The continuous series of white-grey bursts reveal the results of their fell business. But we hear nothing! Only the continuous grunt of that infernal engine. It is an eerie, blood-chilling sensation, to know that down there, somewhere below, the air is rent with the shriek and whine of the great shells in their transit, and the roars of the resulting bursts.

★★★★★★★★★★★★★★★★★

129

"It is getting near the time now for the signal to advance. Seven o'clock was the hour decided.

"At ten to, the white shell-bursts cease and fade away. By rights we should be turning for home now. But this is the finest spectacle of all. The anti-aircraft bombardment has long since ceased, for a most excellent reason, the guns are *non est*. We can sink to a lower altitude with perfect safety.

"Eight minutes to seven! Six! Four! Will it never come? At last! Even in the air, thousands of feet above, we get the atmosphere, the second of hesitation, the quiet before the storm. Then the dull waste of No Man's Land is alive with moving ant-like figures, that appear, almost miraculously in swarms, from those hidden ruts in the surface of the earth.

"Now a similar body makes itself manifest from the opposing trenches. The two lines meet. They intermingle into a bewildering jumble. For one brief moment the line is taut and rigid. Then it wavers, solidifies, wavers again, and breaks. But which is it? The line farthest from our own trenches!

"It lasts for but ten minutes. Above it seems a lifetime. We turn for home leaving behind a charred and burning earth, from which the smoke and dust rise in mournful and never-ending clouds."

CHAPTER 17

Airfare of the Future

We are at last beginning to realise that in aircraft we have a hitherto uncontrolled factor of war that will alter entirely every condition of the modern civilized world.

No one dare predict exactly what the future holds in store for aviation: but it may safely be deduced that warfare will be to all purposes instantaneous. The belligerent fleets of aircraft will set out with the dawn or darkness as the case may be, and within twelve hours the conflict must be finished one way or the other. For the airman there is no falling back on a reserve line of trenches, no preliminary skirmishing and no quarter: the fight must be to a definite finish.

But war is only one side of the matter. On the one hand we have the use of air machines as craft of war. On the other, the numerous uses to which aircraft can be put as vessels of commerce. Which will be considered the more important— to develop aircraft for war or for commerce?

The answer is obvious. We must have air vessels for both purposes. And the latter is by far the more important. We may not think so to-day amid the turmoil and anxiety of war, when our thoughts are all alike, devoted to the same purpose: but the fact remains. The war has revolutionized the social status of the world. In the near future, when socialism and the labour movement have further developed, war will be non-existent. This war, provided that democracy gains the upper hand, will be the last. But human nature is human nature, and there will always remain the turbulent spirits in our midst, and to keep these people in order it will be necessary to display a certain amount of armed force.

However, aircraft, and particularly the airship, of all the weapons employed in warfare, will prove itself to be the only one that will serve a satisfactory purpose after peace has been declared.

Of what use are the 1.5-inch shell or the trench mortar, or the torpedo or the .75 to humanity when war is finished? But the services of aircraft in the future will be inestimable. Likewise, the Zeppelin has been considerably developed, but will serve a somewhat different purpose.

As there have been entirely different types of sea vessels for war and commerce in the past, so in the future there will be widely differing classes of aircraft. For a craft of war, every unnecessary frill is stripped away. She enters the combat, like a battleship, with her decks cleared; every available inch of space being required for powerful engines, and spare petrol to give her the necessary high turn of speed and climbing power. The altitude at which she flies must be well over twelve thousand feet. And great powers of duration are unnecessary. On the other hand, the commercial aircraft will need greater powers of duration, a greater "lift," more space aboard, less speed to climb, and an altitude of between five and six thousand feet will be all that will be necessary.

It is practically impossible to construct an aeroplane possessing speed, duration and climbing powers alike. For the former, as also the latter, a highly powerful engine is required. This requires weight. Weight reduces "lift" and, necessarily, available space aboard. Loss of space requires the cutting down of the supply of spare petrol. And this means loss of duration. An altitude of over five thousand must always be maintained, in case of engine failure, to give the pilot time to recover himself, and to pick out a suitable landing-place.

How greatly aircraft of all descriptions have already developed it is impossible for the general public to judge. Very necessarily the details of aerial construction have been, and will be kept extremely secret. However, to give a slight comprehension it will only be necessary to add that the average speed has increased from that of 1914, of 70 m.p.h., to that of today of somewhere in the neighbourhood of 120. Powers of duration—average—has increased from two and a half to six hours. Climbing power from 5,000 feet in three minutes to 2,000 per minute. And average altitude has increased from 8,000 to 14,000 feet.

With every combat in mid-air some new theory is set up, some new conclusion arrived at, and as yet nothing can be definite. We may say for practical purposes that the strategical work is confined to seaplane and airship scouting with the fleets at sea and long-distance aeroplane raids into the enemy's country; tactical work to reconnaissance trips over the neighbourhood of the lines and the direction of artillery fire. The battle formation of the aeroplane squadron is now and will in the future be similar to that of a fleet at sea. Even now the two methods of battle are closely akin.

The future fleets of the air will be composed more of a number of vessels of uniform size, than of a few vessels of enormous bulk. However much aircraft will be developed, there is always the matter of "lift" to be contended with, and thus necessarily the personnel and war accoutrements aboard will be limited.

There are three distinct phases of aerial combat to be considered— aeroplane versus aeroplane, airship against airship, and aeroplane against airship. Which is the most useful as a fighting unit is a difficult matter to decide. Thus far one is inclined to say the high-powered aeroplane. Zeppelins and airships are for the most part clumsy and unwieldy beasts. Seaplanes, again, for the most part are heavy and slow to answer to their controls.

The important factors are the lifting power of the machine and weather conditions.

Good pilotage is of supreme importance; the pilot who is able to get the most out of his machine and knows it best will almost invariably gain the day.

Clouds are often made great use of by pilots. Almost every day we read of a machine dashing out from behind a bank of cloud and taking another by surprise. On the other hand, clouds may prove disastrous to both combatants, owing to the peculiar property they possess of influencing the stability of the machine, often causing it to nosedive suddenly towards the earth.

Lift, however, is still the great factor, since the fight always develops into a struggle for the upper berth, and is usually fought out in an upward direction. It is climb, climb, climb, then, with the wind at his back, a last swoop down on the back of the enemy's craft—his most vulnerable position—and the fight is over. Various expedients are made use of to gain this end, such as getting between an opponent and the sun, "diving" suddenly, and "looping." With either aeroplane or airship it is the uppermost position that counts.

The type of craft most useful for this class of work is the high-engined biplane of the "tractor" —propeller to the fore—type, the machine-gun firing through the blades of the propeller. The essentials of these machines are speed and ability to climb quickly. The slower machines, with greater powers of endurance, are more useful for bomb-raiding and reconnaissance purposes.

Airship combat has yet to materialise. Many opinions and theories, often widely conflicting, have been put forward concerning the possibilities and probabilities of such conflicts, but nothing definite can be advanced until a battle between airships has taken place. The opinion of the majority of the experts is that an airship would be little better than useless to meet an airship, and for our own particular requirements—that is, the repelling of Zeppelin raids—aeroplanes are of more use; which brings us to the combat between aeroplane and airship.

Considering first their main qualities, the airship has greater "lifting" powers, is more heavily armed, can climb at a much faster rate, and has greater powers of endurance; whereas the aeroplane has a faster turn of speed, is more easily manoeuvred, and is less unwieldy. With the Zeppelin at a greater altitude than the aeroplane, the latter is powerless. At the same altitude the odds are greatly in favour of the airship, its one vulnerable point being the stern—the Zeppelin guns only firing in fore and amidship directions, leaving the stern unprotected. With the aeroplane on top the airship is entirely at its mercy, and its broad back presents a target that cannot easily be missed.

The tendency of the Zeppelin commanders, however, is to increase rather than decrease this altitude with every raid, which renders attack by aeroplane more difficult; but, on the other hand, aeroplanes are being developed at so remarkable a speed that they will soon be able to climb above any Zeppelin altitude. When that occurs the Zeppelin menace will end for ever.

Manoeuvres in the air, the more they are developed and the more extended they become, the more they evidence a similarity to manoeuvres at sea. And, regarding aerial warfare from our own point of view, everything points to the necessity of forming an entirely separate Air Service, built up on the principles and methods of the navy. For the latter service is, in reality, the defensive arm of our units of warfare, whereas the army is invariably the offensive arm.

This Air Service must be controlled by one commander, who preferably has had practical experience of aviation. It must be represented in the Cabinet by an air minister, to voice its requirements and obtain necessary financial grants. Adequate training-schools must be established all over the country. A certain proportion of the pilots and observers must be devoted exclusively to naval aviation, and a similar proportion exclusively to army aviation. And the main objects of the aerial policy must be one Aerial Offensive, and the other Aerial Defensive.

Allowing for the development of the aircraft of all belligerent powers, the aggregate today must be well up into the tens of thousands. This aggregate should prove a more than useful basis on which to build up the after-war commercial air fleets. But to develop the commercial aircraft at a profit, it must be done on a most extensive scale. The construction of the craft, exclusive of the training of the necessary pilots, is a highly expensive item. The wrecking of a machine is all too frequent and too possible. The cost of the upkeep, housing maintenance, and personnel is extremely heavy. Spare parts of the craft must always be to hand, and in large numbers. Standardization of parts would save a considerable amount of money in this respect. And the necessary landing grounds will have to be laid down.

The aerial commercial system is no novel idea. Already, previous to the war, it had been attempted successfully in Germany with a service of passenger-bearing Zeppelins. Commander Usborne, R.N.—since killed in carrying out an extremely difficult and plucky experiment in the air—had well under way a scheme for a passenger service over Great Britain. This scheme had a financial backing of over eleven million pounds. The commander estimated that the average cost—allowing for all expenses—would be 1½d., and when further developed would be reduced to ¾d. per mile.

Several similar schemes are now in existence, and in the U.S.A. the American Aircraft Company has been formed to establish a transatlantic service of rigid airships between England and America; while aerial mail services are already in existence between San Francisco and Sacramento, and several other large cities, and the U.S.A. within a year or so will be linked together with innumerable routes in the air.

The cargoes of commercial goods that come within the scope of aircraft are wheat, flax, wines, tobacco, silk, flowers, vegetables, dates, feathers, wool, hides, ebony, wax, fish, fruits, carpets, hemp, spices, cork, cotton, indigo, opium, rice, tea, ermine, sealskins, sable, otter, pearls, coffee, sugar, and ivory. Neither of these commodities, in reasonable quantities, should prove too bulky for transportation by aeroplane or airship. On the other hand, heavier burdens as metals, manufactured goods, and minerals will follow the old-fashioned route of the sea and the railway.

The principal aerial trade routes will, most probably, be two main tracks leading south and two main tracks leading east. The first southern track will follow the route: London-Paris-Bordeaux-Gibraltar Fez-Lagos-Loango-Johannesburg-Capetown. Allowing a minimum average of 110 miles per hour, with little wind, and allowing half an hour for each landing, an aeroplane leaving London at eight on a Monday morning would keep the following time-table:—

London	8 a.m.	Monday.
Paris	10 a.m.	"
Bordeaux	1 p.m.	"
Gibraltar	8 p.m.	"
Fez	9 p.m.	"
Lagos	5.30 p.m.	Tuesday.
Loango	2 a.m.	Wednesday.
Johannesburg	8 p.m.	"
Capetown	4 a.m.	Thursday.

Total: London–Capetown, 2 days 20 hours.

By steamer, *via* Funchal, the time taken is three weeks, which gives an advantage of two and a half weeks. Another route to Capetown would be: London-Paris-Lyons-Rome-Alexandria-AnkobarMombasa-Zanzibar-Bulawayo-Johannesburg-Capetown.

The "Far East" routes would be: London-Petrograd-Moscow-Samara-Omsk-Tomsk-Irkutsk Pekin-Tokio, and London-Berlin-Warsaw-Odessa-Astrakhan-Merv-Delhi-Calcutta-Canton-Shanghai-Yokohama-Tokio. The Australian route would follow the latter as far as Calcutta, and branch off there, *via* Singapore-Surabaya-Port Darwin and Adelaide to Melbourne.

Finally, we have been introduced to the aeroplane and the airship in all their numerous spheres of activity. The Zeppelin we have discussed at great length, the *Parseval*, the *Schütte-Lanz*, the triplane, and the "Baby" monoplane. We have dabbled with the past, in the early days of aviation. We have lingered with the present, and timidly peeped into the future. We stand now like a swimmer on the fringe of the great ocean, hesitating to plunge into a sea of uncertainty, that may hold for us only the calmest of pleasures, or on the other hand, the most gruesome of dangers.

As I write, the news of a great air battle is to hand:

Germans lose 46 machines, British lose 28 machines. Intensest fighting between large squadrons of aeroplanes.

It is the writing on the wall—the herald of the gigantic matters that are to come; when the aerial navies will be maintaining peace and

A CORNER OF THE WHITEHEAD AIRCRAFT CO.'S AERODROME

goodwill not on, but over the surface of the earth.

The handling and ordering of these multitudinous craft will be no small matter. Every reader who has sailed down Channel in the piping times of peace has some idea of the ever dangerously congested state of that waterway. That will be as nothing when compared with the numerous craft that will throng the aerial routes both south and east. Aircraft, we know, when meeting under way, must pass each other always to the right, and at a distance of over 100 metres. This indicates, then, that the rule of the air, as of the road, will be to the right. The traffic will be divided into two continuous streams by floating aerial lightships that will serve the double purpose of landmarks by day and lightships by night. There will be two tracks, the one above the other, the higher for lighter-than-air, the lower for heavier-than-air craft.

The matter of entering the territorial limits of a country has already been allowed for in the Aerial Navigation Act of 1913, which prohibits certain areas to foreign craft, also the carrying of goods chargeable upon importation into the United Kingdom with any duty of customs. It will be practically impossible to make the necessary examination of incoming craft in mid-air. And it is possible that a large open space as Salisbury Plain will be utilised for this purpose; with Government boats always patrolling on the look-out for suspicious craft and smugglers. The other regulations will be similar to those of the present day applying to merchant vessels.

The actual flying conditions will be far less dangerous, more airworthy, and considerably more pleasant and healthy than those appertaining to sea voyages. The aerial voyage will be a God-send to those passengers liable to *mal de mer*. The spherical world will be enlarged from the level of the sea and the land to that of mid-air.

It will be interesting to note how a developed and general aviation will influence our everyday life. For some eight hundred years, until the advent of the Zeppelin raids, the British race had been immune from enemy attacks. It was always possible to escape the ravages of enemy ships and guns, by the simple expedient of living without their range. But is it possible to find a spot without the range of aircraft? Does this mean that for the sake of peace and comfort we will perforce resort to the methods of the prehistoric tribes, and develop again into a race of cave-dwellers?

With houses burrowed into the sides of the hills, or in underground cavities, far beneath the surface of the earth, is safety alone possible. With the advent of the "Zeppelin cellar" one may almost imagine the leading theatres, museums, and restaurants, and the places of amusement, on a level with and leading off from the underground railways. A long line of dwelling-houses along either side of the lines, and an extensive system of underground ways, distancing from as far as London to Manchester, Glasgow to London or Plymouth. Who can say? The idea is of the farcical-humorous order judged from the standpoints of today. But then, so was the aeroplane and the airship to the peoples of the early nineteenth century period; the submarine and the oil-fuelled battleship to their sons and grandsons of the later half of the century; and the tank and the gas-shell to the majority of our own generation as late as 1914.

A flight in the air, once a matter of world event, is today a matter of the uninteresting commonplace. In the future it will be even more so. Even the most timorous of women will take to it, with the ease that they took to sea-voyaging in the past. For flying is no longer dangerous! The price has been paid, and dearly paid. The very novelty of aviation served to furnish fifty *per cent* of the assumed dangers. That novelty has passed away entirely and for good.

Where a man in former days employed a motorcar as means of personal transit, he will, in the future, make use of an aeroplane. The landing in London will be accomplished on wide, flat roofs. And aeroplanes constructed on the ornithoptic principle will be able to effect a landing in a confined space about the area of Leicester Square.

In time, probably, the unpleasing roar of the engine will be silenced, or at least diminished. The steadiness of the flying will be greatly increased. And the lines and construction of the machine will follow the principles employed in the construction of the ocean-going liners of today. By means of improved wireless telegraphic and telephonic systems, constant communication will be maintained with the earth from any altitude and from any distance.

Aircraft will prove of immense value in exploration. No corner of the earth, however hidden away, will be inaccessible from above. Supervision and police patrolling of out-of-the-way districts will be aided materially, and a certain amount of surveying will be possible from the air.

The psychology of the peoples will play no small part in the future development of aviation, as also in the future mastery of the air. And it has been demonstrated in a previous chapter that our own race in this respect shows more than usual promise. As it was the race of soldiers who dominated the world in the early days of continents alone, and later after the discovery of America and the more general usage of the seas the race of sailors, so in the future it will be the race of airmen that will dominate the world.

But each and every nation is made up of types of manhood. There is the "land-lubber"; the self-centred individual; the materialist with never a thought beyond his own profit and loss; the frontiersman, or the colonist, the greatest patriot of all, who gives his life unasking, and unthoughtful of reward, on some out-of-the-way frontier, manfully pushing on the development of civilization. There are the men from the hills, hardy and independent, seeking advancement by labour and strength alone, and the sleeker men of the plains, who substitute cunning for labour.

Previous to 1914, we people of Great Britain were notorious for our egotism and overbearing arrogance. 'How many are there even of our great men who have been stupid and foolish enough to state, as the case may have been, that an Englishman was more than a match for three Spaniards, or two Frenchman, or two Germans? This was due largely to our insular position. Our politics and policies were of the fireside order, that grasped only borough councils and city corporations. In the future we will obtain our true ideals of empire and imperialism. Our policy will be turned to nations and empires and continents.

We, the greatest sea-power that the history of the world has ever known, were made up of a population, at least fifty *per cent* of whom had never seen the sea, and were so lamentably ignorant as to be unable to distinguish a battleship from a liner, whilst a further large percentage had never forsaken the safety of their own shores. Of these many suffered under the delusion that every Australian must be an Aborigine, that gold was to be found in the streets of Africa, the inhabitants of which country were notable for their advanced epicurean taste for missionaries, and that America was overrun with whooping cowboys and war-lusting Red Indians. This, of course, previous to the war.

This latter, and the greatest of all evils, ignorance, aviation will cure, and cure effectively. It will enable the people to travel rapidly, comfortably, and cheaply, and share with the previous chosen few the beauty, the wonder, and the wisdom of the world without, and more particularly that of the air.

Aviation will affect the psychology of every nation in that it will develop an entirely new race of men. It will eradicate the decadent side of human nature, and will build up the better side, the hunger for beauty and peace, and ever natural and wonderful phenomena of a wonderful creation. The air can never be petty or small or mean, so neither can the beings that navigate it. This view has already been proved by the chivalrous conduct of the airmen of every belligerent power.

This new race of men will be quite a race apart; the legitimate descendants of those bold sailors the Vikings, those splendid soldiers the Romans, the Drake privateers, the Wellingtonian Bill Adams, and the men of Mons and the Marne.

They will be the missionaries throughout the world of light and hope, friendship and good feeling, education and health; and more than all of everlasting peace and democracy. For in the air the heart of every man is the heart of a king. He is "monarch of all he surveys."

CHAPTER 18

The Diary of an Aeroplane

The prospect certainly wasn't exhilarating, unless one can find matter to rejoice over in a prison forty by forty, that's as dark as blazes, cold as the arctic regions, and through the roof of which the rain percolates like a shower-bath. But I've grown used to it all now, so used that I can tell you the number of cobwebs to each corner, the exact moment the rats and mice creep out of their holes and come ambling around the shed; almost imitate the waltzing arrogant gait of the long-bearded grandfather rats or the coy frisking of the lady mice. I can tell to a second the exact number of raindrops to each hole, and where it will drop. Ugh! And then it collects in pools all round my frame. No wonder the poor old B.E.'s got rheumatics in every joint. Sometimes they will slide back the great front gate, but that event becomes rarer and rarer as the days go by.

Luckily for myself, I am of a philosophical turn of mind; had I been of a nature like that cynical engine of mine, that groans at earth and sky, man and beast alike, there's no knowing what might have happened. I might have shed a wing in sheer ennui or collapsed at the under-carriage from sheer exhaustion. Instead! But there, I wander from my story.

The last few days the most extraordinary events have taken place. Two days ago, a young man, I am sure he was young, for he did not pause to stroke his beard and hum and haw, and say: "This is my theory, and it is on this calculus that I base so and so and so." Instead, he came right over to where I was standing, and passing a cool hand down my wings, said to the blue-overalled, oil-grimed mechanic at his side, "Better give her a thorough overhauling, Simmonds, she's a bit shaky in the limbs."

And then through the open door of the hangar I caught sight of the great wide expanse of blue sky! My sky! It hadn't changed to any

142

appreciable amount during all these months; it was still as fresh and as lovely and as interminable as ever. "Soon, very soon, I will be up there again," I said to myself; "my home!" I will be fighting and struggling with that vampire spirit of the air, with the blades of my propeller smiting the clear atmosphere, and the cool fresh air fanning my sides, and blowing the cobwebs from my engine.

Meanwhile, the examination over, the mechanic was busily rubbing my sides down with some cooling preparation, the technical name for which is, I believe, dope. How can I describe that sensation to a human being? I think it must be a cross between a shampoo and a shower-bath.

Day after day this was continued, until at last one morning I was dragged out gently from the shed and squatted on the cool, fresh grass. How excited I felt. I heard again the loud huzzas of the crowd; the rippling melody of laughter and excitement. The air was full of colours and flags and bunting. There were long, long rows of motorcars that stretched as far as the eye could reach behind the aerodrome, and ant-like men, women and children that thronged the enclosures and roads and sheds. But no! This was a beautiful sunlit morning; an ideal day for a crowd. Yet the old place was very nearly deserted, save that now and then a grimy mechanic or hideously goggled pilot would pass by, or an occasional motorcar would roll up; but there were no pretty frocks, no pink cheeks and sparkling eyes, no merry happy laughter to greet me this morning. Instead, everything was grim and stern and business-like.

"You'll be thinking of the old days, and wondering where the crowd is?" asked a blunt-nosed Vickers by my side. I drew myself up haughtily, for even a crock is not without a certain sense of dignity; even he can be particular of the company he keeps. And a gun-bus of all things! But he was a quiet, good-natured old fellow this, and ignoring my sneer, he went on in reminiscent fashion: "I know you, they've just brought you out of that shed there. It was a scandal to have kept you bottled up so long." I explained somewhat stiffly that I had been very happy and contented, though bottled up, as he called it. "You know what it is, I suppose?" he continued. "It's this new man-power board, they don't want any of us fellers to be wasted." He cast a critical eye over my parts. "You'll be grouped B.III, I expect."

"What's that?" I enquired, feeling piqued.

"Only fit for sedentary work abroad," he explained. "They'll use you to carry pilots back and fro across the Channel; no joke, I can tell you."

Just at that moment our conversation was put to an end by the arrival of a tall young pilot, with fair curly hair and blue eyes. He looked at me hard for a moment or so, then burst out with a merry peal of laughter. "So, this is the old bus they expect me to fly, is it?" he exclaimed. "May as well say *au revoir* now." I felt very hurt, and must have looked it, for he added in a more conciliatory tone, "Well, I suppose it might have been worse." There and then I registered a mental vow that I would show him that all the good qualities weren't devoted entirely to the new-fangled type of aeroplanes, and that an old crock could do its share with the rest.

Then he started my engine, and in a few minutes, we were skimming over hill and valley, village and town. At first everything went wrong. That vile engine coughed and spluttered and sneezed, as only engines can. The controls were stiff. The wings wouldn't bank properly, and once we nearly nosedived. The fair-haired boy cursed profusely, bringing down all manner of dire dangers upon my person.

That first flight wasn't really a great success, but he stuck to me, and I did my level best to please him. So very soon I had got back my form of the old days, and then we got on famously together.

At last came the day when I was to leave my old home for good. The Vickers gun-bus told me about it first of all. "You're going away today," he said, "to D——. The mechanics were talking about it in my shed this morning. As you're going so well, you're to be sent over to fly on the other side." My feelings may be imagined. I was proud to think that no longer was I considered an old crock, but sorry, very sorry to leave my old home. It was the only home I had known. Sometimes I had spent an odd night or so, or a weekend at Salisbury or Brooklands or Eastchurch, or someplace like that, but that was all.

I will never forget the pangs of remorse I suffered at that last sight of the dear old place, with its cluster of low-roofed sheds. The wide, gently sloping aerodrome, with the straight, sun-glinted railway lines at the base. The clustering roof-tops, and the wide, winding roadway that disappeared in the direction of the blue, mist-hidden, fog-bound city. Then it all disappeared behind a bank of cloud, and I was clattering on to the unknown, the new life.

Now and then I caught glimpses of old familiar landmarks, of sand-splashed golf links and blue-lined rivers, the glittering roof-top of the Crystal Palace. Then another aerodrome, wide and circular in appearance, round which my fellow craft squatted like broody hens.

Suddenly, coming up from the south, I could hear the approach of another machine. Oh! why do they call us machines, these un-understanding humans? We, that are beings of grace and rhythm and life. There was something familiar in that regular and rapid tap-tap, something that sent my mind flashing back to the old days. Nearer and nearer, it crept, and then—I threw my nose up joyfully—a movement that caused my fair-haired pilot to tremble and curse alternately.

I sang out joyfully, "What! Don't you know me, can't you remember?"

"Why! If it isn't the old Hendon exhibition-bus," interrupted the other, joyfully.

"Not so much of the old, please," I replied with dignity; "remember you're getting on yourself."

"Suppose I am," he called back over his shoulder. "My! How the time does fly to be sure. Now I come to think of it, I'm even six months older than you."

"Age lends wisdom to the craft," I quoted, and would have followed him, had it not been for the inexorable wrist of my pilot. So, we quietly wished each other goodbye and good luck, and went our respective ways.

Towards noon I had my first glimpse of the sea. I had never seen it before, that wonderful interminable stretch of moveless shimmering blue. The land I knew and understood, with all its varying moods. How often—how very often had my feet slipped safely past its numerous traps, death-dealing bumps, treacherous clouds, and mist-hidden altitudes, until with the familiarity that breedeth contempt I had laughed softly to myself, and gone out of my way to meet cunning with cunning, and passed on unscathed. But there was something in this wide, voiceless void that held me spellbound, that filled my heart with apprehension. If it has this effect on me in the sunshine, I argued to myself, what must it be like when the sky is hidden with dark clouds, and the wind comes howling along to whip up that placid surface into a terrifying wilderness of mountainous seas?

Then I felt the pilot's hand tugging gently at my control-stick, and obediently I turned my nose downwards towards the earth. Now I could see the aerodrome we were making for. Perched like an eagle's nest on the crest of the white towering cliffs, it was neither so large nor so pleasant looking as my late home, but nevertheless it looked very comfortable and cosy, tucked away inside a semi-circular line of metal-roofed hangars.

I remained in this place for three days, and there said farewell to

145

my cheery, blue-eyed pilot. On the third morning he came into my shed with a surly-looking, dark-haired individual with an ugly briar pipe stuck at an aggressive angle in his mouth. "Not much to look at, is she?" said briar pipe. I felt I could have slain him on the spot, and took an intuitive dislike to him there and then.

"But she's a good 'un to climb," said the other; "bit moody, but all right if you humour her."

"I know the kind," replied briar pipe; "their humours usually end in a nose-dive at about 3,000 feet, and then——" He shrugged his shoulders expressively. They both laughed. Like their impudence!

I wasn't far out in my conjecture. My new master was a wild, erratic individual, that first sent me rushing through the air with the speed of an express train, then plunged me down earthward like a bolt from the blue; and banked and switch-backed me until my old—here, in the privacy of my diary, I own to the soft impeachment—ribs creaked and groaned and creaked again, until it seemed as if every moment they must fly asunder in sheer protest.

Then he landed me with a nerve-trying bump, and with a "Have her ready by this afternoon, petrolled and oiled up," to the mechanic, he disappeared to his lunch, and left me standing, cold and shivering, in the fresh sea-breeze, with my mind full of apprehension concerning my approaching flight.

He was more gentle with me in the afternoon. Perhaps he had lunched well, perhaps he had begun at last to appreciate my good qualities; or perhaps, and what was more than likely, the sea held as many terrors for him as it did for me. Whatever may have been the reason, he no longer persisted in swinging me about, left and right, up and down, but moved the controls easily and gently. The fascination of the sea must have got into my brain, for the next hour or so I was moving as in a dream. I could feel my pilot pulling savagely away, but I did not move an inch. All I wanted to do was to get down, down to the sea. In fact, I behaved altogether most disgracefully. A point my pilot did not miss, not that that troubled me much.

I was too intent on watching the vast blue waste beneath and the queer shapes that inhabited it. Northwards, to where the Kentish coast thrust nose-fashion into the sea, and a few miles distant from the shore, were the high-piled Goodwins. A lone sentinel, stiff and upright, in the blue coast mist stood the Lightship at the Knock. The fairway was thronged with shipping of all kinds. White and slim looking the cross-Channel boat slipped by beneath. Racing up Channel like a school of porpoises were a dozen or so dark, rakish-looking destroyers. Here and there dotted about a squat, ungainly tramp, a larger and more graceful liner, or a monitor, broad-beamed as a pancake. At last, the French coast came in sight!

I knew what was coming before he landed me; my pilot was furious, perfectly furious, at my cross-Channel performance. Landing with a jerk, he sprang out of my body, and catching my ribs with a flying kick, until they shook again and again, he stalked off towards the sheds. Soon he returned with two mechanics that rubbed me down, and after feeding me up with oil and petrol, pushed me gently into my shed. "Don't trouble to cover her up, Bill," said the taller of the two.

"Not cover her up?" demanded the other man.

"No, she'll be going back tomorrow, she's a dud," was the reply.

Then I knew my fate. I was to be sent home! In an instant all my fond, happy dreams were shattered, I was disgraced and humiliated. I was an old crock, and would, now, never be able to join my brave comrades in the battle. I nearly wept my heart out that night, and when at last the dawn broke, I was long past caring. I determined to throw myself to the earth at the first opportunity, and die. But the sun had risen far into the heavens before they roused me. I struggled violently, but it was useless. I was dragged out into the aerodrome amidst a lot of young and self-opinionated neighbours who either deigned not to say a word to me, or passed sneering remarks about my old-fashioned shape.

You can guess then how pleased I was to catch sight of my old-young friend, the fair-haired pilot, coming across the ground, arm in arm with my late master. I felt so excited that I began to shiver with sheer joy, so that the mechanic began to think I was going to fall on top of him, and savagely kicked me again. Then the two pilots came up and stopped in front of my nose, making the sharp-eared Moranes and Nieuports throw up their noses with rage.

"I don't care what you say," exclaimed blue-eyes, "I flew her for over two hours yesterday, and she was top-hole."

"Pity you didn't fly her across Channel then," said briar-pipe, clenching his teeth from sheer annoyance. "She not only refused to climb, but made at least three distinct attempts to nose-dive into the water."

Alas! It was only too true, and I knew it; it must have been when I was suffering from a touch of the I-don't-know-what-you-call-its. I felt very sorry, very humble; not that I minded in the least what briar-pipe thought, but I was upset to think the fair-haired boy might agree with him.

But no! The latter told briar-pipe that it must have been due to his mediocre pilotage, and then they fell upon a violent argument concerning their respective qualities and failings as air-pilots. This much to the amusement of the other planes, who, despite their 'igh and 'aughty demeanour, plumped solid for my champion. "Well, I tell you how well decide," the latter went on, "I'll take her up when I go to strafe that big gun at Z—— this afternoon."

How my heart throbbed within me. At last, my fondest dreams were to be realised, and I was to take part in a glorious raid. My day-dreaming was interrupted by the savage voice of briar-pipe. "Very well, you do so at your own risk," he said, "and don't forget I warned you. What's it to be? Two quid—that's a bet, isn't it?"

Never had I felt so fit in my life as I did that afternoon. The weather was sunny and clear. I had been thoroughly overhauled and petrolled. A squat, ugly Lewis gun had been installed over my nose, and my engine was working with the regularity of a piece of clockwork.

At last, he came; looking strangely grotesque in brown leather coat and trousers, close-fitting skull cap, and over it a woollen Balaclava and a pair of hideous goggles. "Everything ready, Bates?" he enquired.

"Everything, sir," replied the mechanic.

As we began to rise into the air it took me some considerable time to grow accustomed to the unusual weight of bombs beneath the prow. I must confess I felt a wee bit afraid of them. With these murderous implements of death, I, and of course my pilot also, were to slaughter helpless but, saving grace, not harmless human beings, thousands of feet on the ground below.

Up and up, we climbed, up and up. Now it began to get cold and still. The earth was almost blotted out from sight, and now ran on all sides to the dim haze of the horizon, a mad riot of blue and white, green and grey. I had never been up so high in my life before. Desperately hard though I tried to hide my true feelings, that confounded engine began to splutter and cough. I shook it and remonstrated with it, but all persuasion was useless. It persisted with its uncanny groans. I think my pilot must have guessed, for he leant over my side, and gently caressing me with a cool, steady hand, whispered in my ear, "Steady, old girl, steady, we'll need all your energy this trip." My heart swelled with pride, until it seemed as if it must burst. At least he believed in me!

And then we turned eastward and clung to the edge of the low-lying coast. Now the country grew strangely unfamiliar in appearance. Fields and meadows that should have been fresh and green were earth-pocked and cut about as though a giant plough had been passed over them, carrying away with it, in its mad career, crop and hedge, road and river-bank alike; stripping the trees of young foliage and scarring the earth with repulsive furrows. And round and about it all there flashed murderous pin-pricks of red flame. Tiny, crawling, ant-like figures, hurrying now this way, now that, and then a strange hissing noise filled the air. An unaccountable feeling of fright and terror crept over me. I felt the grip of the pilot tighten on the control-stick. Then in a flash of smoke and flame it burst beside me. I trembled in every plane. Gently, very gently, we climbed higher, followed everywhere by those awesome bursts of flame.

I expected the pilot to turn back, but no, he kept on and on. Now the bombardment had ceased, save for an occasional burst.

Still, we keep on. The country on this side of the lines is very similar to that we have just left, scarred and earth-marked with shell-holes. A seemingly peaceful country town looms into view through the mist. A large cluster of houses, from which run roadways in all directions, north, south, east, and west; a gleaming railway line and a sluggish, winding river. To the south of the town, half a dozen tall chimney-stacks—evidently the manufacturing quarter—from which the smoke curls discolouringly and thickly heavenwards. Before the town is a dense, green wood. No more peaceful view could be imagined. Can this be Z——, where the great foundries work incessantly, where thousands of workmen labour night and day, shaping and forming every deadly implement of war?

Suddenly the green wood is cleft apart as if by an earthquake. There is a terrifying explosion, a cloud of dense smoke, followed immediately by a long-drawn shriek and a mass of masonry and torn earthworks that goes flying heavenwards at a point far to the rear.

This is the gun we have come to demolish. We! mark you.

Everything is quiet and peaceful again now. Lower we come; lower and lower, in wide sweeping circles. Now the enemy anti-aircraft begin to open fire, now here, now there. Now on all sides the air is filled with picric smoke and bursting shells. How can we pass through it all? We bank and climb and dive, and bank again; coming lower all the time. Momentarily we are out of range, but only momentarily. Then the firing reopens with renewed intensity. Suddenly there is a sharp, stinging pain in my left wing, as if someone had suddenly plunged a red-hot knife therethrough. I lurch, only in time and with a sharp intake of breath the pilot pulls me up.

Now we sight the dull gleaming form of the gun through the trees. Down go the bombs, one, two, three, exploding on all sides, but never near the gun. Again, we wheel. The bombardment grows terrifying in its intensity. We bomb again and again.

Again, I feel those sharp stabs left and right. It is the most trying moment of my life. With his sixth my pilot hits the gun-emplacement. There is an explosion louder than all the rest; where the forest had shown a moment or so before green and restful, the earth is distorted with up-blown trees and strange towering piles of fresh earth.

We sneak off, like a dog with its tail between its legs, fearful, yet hoping, leaving in our wake, in place of the peaceful country town, an armed fortress, the guns of which fill the heavens with wailing, bursting shells.

Will we ever get back? I try to climb, but fail miserably in the attempt. We are winged, hopelessly winged. For a moment it seems that my pilot must give way and land in their country to be made prisoner. This is the psychological moment, now or never. With a desperate effort I climb another thousand that leaves me throbbing and panting for breath. I feel the rich, warm blood of the pilot trickling down my body. Suddenly he falls inanimate in his seat. He has been hit and has fainted. Now I can show my appreciation for his kindness. I keep as steady as a rock. Thank heaven I do not possess any infantile, sudden tricks like those skittish Nieuports.

Presently he recovers, and now my own wounds agonise with a dumb, gnawing pain. We are near the lines, we must, we shall go up. Desperately, helplessly I try to climb. The effort almost brings me crashing to the ground. There is now only one thing for it; the pilot opens the engine out to her fullest extent, we dash on as we have never done before, through a fusillade of rifle bullets, anti-aircraft and other bursting shells. I feel that I am hit in a hundred different places. Ah! can we ever reach our aerodrome again?

We are across, as if by a miracle. The next twenty minutes seems a lifetime. Can we—will we ever get there? Ah! At last!

★★★★★★★★★★★★★★★★★

I am back in the old dark and draughty shed again, a broken, helpless crock, fit only for the wood-broker or the old iron merchant; brought back ignominiously they tell me, by rail and steamer, for all the world like a bar of iron or a mousetrap. But then these silly, thoughtless humans still persist in regarding me as a soulless machine. I have put up a good fight, I have done my duty and all that was expected of me. I can do no more; hence I must be scrapped. It is the way of the world, and the world can be at times, ah, so cruel!

The cobwebs are still there, more numerous if anything. And when the twilight falls the old familiar rats and mice creep out of their holes and sit round in wondering circles to listen to the stories of my great adventure, or potter round my wings to examine my honourable scars.

Now probably they will nail a brass plate on my fuselage, with an account cut prosaically in prosaic letters thereon of the great deed. More probably I will become the *pièce de résistance* of the local Red-Cross show, or be wheeled through the streets, drawn by a donkey or a decrepit horse on a flag day. Perhaps cut up and made into blacklead pencils. Ah, me! It's a strange world!

Events in the Air

By E. W. Walters

THE BIRTH OF THE AIRSHIP

Progress in the construction of aircraft has been rapid of recent years, but there was a long period of experiment and preparation. It is a long flight from the aircraft of today back to the efforts of the Robert brothers in 1784.

The Robert brothers' experiments took the form of a balloon shaped like a melon, made of silk carefully proved, and measuring 52 feet in length and 32 feet in diameter. The gas employed was pure hydrogen. Underneath the envelope was suspended a long, narrow car, in general idea not unlike that used on some modern airships, and three pairs of oars with blades made like a racquet-frame, covered with silk, and a rudder of similar material.

The two brothers, accompanied by a third person, went up in this early dirigible and succeeded in describing a curve of one kilometre radius, thus showing that, at any rate, they could deviate in some measure from the wind then prevailing. But at the time of the ascent there seems to have been very little opposition in the way of wind pressure. Favourable weather was naturally chosen. Nevertheless, something was attempted and something done, paving the way for further efforts.

Another airship, which led to a thrilling adventure, was built in due course. This was fitted with an internal air ballonet. An ascent was bravely attempted, but the ship got into a strong air eddy, which tore away the oars and rudder and detached the air-bag from its sustaining cords. This airship, however, is said to have reached a remarkable height for those days—no less than 16,000 feet! This, however, was *not* intentional.

Another airship worthy of note was the dirigible built in France by Henri Giffard. This took a spindle shape, measuring 143 feet in length and 39 feet in diameter. It had a 3 h.-p. steam engine and an 11-foot screw propeller. The first trip was made in September, 1852. Six miles were covered in conditions not entirely favourable, and it is recorded that several further journeys were made. Ten years, however, passed before marked progress was shown in the construction of this type of dirigible.

Tissandier was the next in the field. His dirigible was not unlike previous efforts in shape and construction; but now an electric motor and a bichromate battery were employed, and a speed of eight miles an hour was reached.

Next came Captain Charles Renard, who made marked progress by building an envelope with a 'true streamline.' The car was suspended by means of a huge sheet placed over the back of the airship, to which were attached suspensory cords. The cubic capacity of the airship was 66,000 feet. It was kept rigid by means of an internal air ballonet, which was kept full by a fan blower coupled to a motor. It had a car 108 feet in length, which helped to steady the airship, and indeed played a somewhat similar part to the spar employed in later airships of the semi-rigid type. An electric motor, weighing 220 lbs., was installed, which developed 9 h.-p. The first trial trips were made in 1884, and were considered at the time remarkably successful so far as navigation was concerned. Indeed, it is recorded that on one occasion this dirigible flew round Paris at an average speed of 14½ miles an hour—a remarkable achievement at the time.

Clearly there was now a future for airships. Germany had recognised this for some while, and had not been idle. Baumgarten and Wolfert built an airship in 1879 with a benzine motor, but when making an ascent at Leipzig the vessel got out of control, fell to the ground, and was hopelessly wrecked.

In 1897 Wolfert made further experiments, which cost him his life. A fire broke out in the benzine container of the new ship, with the result that the inventor and his assistant were killed.

The same year saw an effort on the part of an Austrian named Schwartz, who built an airship of sheet aluminium. This, however, proved a leaky structure. It descended and came to a sudden end. Schwartz, however, was the first to build a rigid airship with a petrol motor, and there is a sense in which his efforts led to the modern Zeppelin.

With that airship—the modern Zeppelin—with its intricate construction and remarkable capacities of speed and distance, its carrying powers, its evil missions, its tactics when under fire—we shall deal later.

THE PIONEER WORK OF M. SANTOS DUMONT

The efforts of M. Santos Dumont call for special reference. He contributed greatly to the science of aerostation, and may be considered one of the foremost of the flight pioneers. He was a man of remarkable industry, perseverance, and courage.

His first noteworthy effort in construction was in 1898, when he made a cylinder of varnished silk, 82½ feet in length, with pointed ends, and measuring 11½ feet in diameter. An internal air ballonet was fitted, and an engine giving 3 h.-p. A balloon basket was hung beneath the envelope. There was a two-blade propeller, whilst shifting weights controlled the poise of the ship, steering being effected by means of a rudder composed of strong silk over a steel frame.

Comparative success greeted the venture. The airship left the Zoological Gardens in Paris and performed various evolutions, in spite of a gentle wind. Later, however, disaster threatened the ship and its distinguished pilot, owing to too rapid contraction of the gas whilst the ship was in the act of descending. But a calamity was averted by some schoolboys, who with commendable foresight caught hold of the tail rope of the airship and drew it along kite fashion with such speed that a gentle landing was effected.

At a later date, being encouraged by the offer of a prize, M. Santos Dumont built a new and larger airship with the view to flying from St. Cloud, round the Eiffel Tower, and back to the starting-point within thirty minutes. This new ship was 109 feet in length and 17 feet in diameter. It was fitted with a 4-cylinder air-cooled motor, driving an enormous propeller of 26 feet in diameter, which gave a thrust of 120 lbs. at 140 revolutions per minute. Among other novelties, water ballast was used, and piano wires replaced the old type of suspension cords.

An attempt to earn the prize was made in July, 1901. At 6.30 in the morning the airship started from St. Cloud, reached the Eiffel Tower, and made a successful turn. But the weather conditions were adverse to the venture. A wind arose, and the return journey took thirty minutes.

Not to be outdone, Santos Dumont made another attempt in August of the same year. He failed again, but soon got to work upon yet another airship. This developed an ascensional force of 1,158 lbs., and was driven by a 12 h.-p. 4-cylinder motor which gave a thrust of 145 lbs. With this ship, on October 19, 1901, Santos Dumont started for the Eiffel Tower hampered by a side wind of 20 feet a second. Nevertheless, he reached the tower in nine minutes, but owing to allowing insufficient clearance he barely missed colliding with it. However, he got the airship under control and returned to his starting-point in 29½ minutes, thus winning the Deutsch prize of 125,000 *francs* and an additional reward of 125,000 *francs*.

The greater part of the money was given by the aviator to charity, showing clearly that in his experiments M. Santos Dumont had other aims than self-gain. A wit has observed that he was a 'man of high-soaring motives,' which is, in fact, entirely true. His aim was to construct an airship that would prove of real service to mankind, and in his experiments, he sacrificed both time and money, and, of far greater importance, he made his ascents at great risk to his personal safety at a time when 'air courage' was comparatively new, and in conditions which made no immediate call to patriotism and duty. He was of the 'stuff' of which the true hero of the air is made, taking with a brave heart, serious risks, and going from flight to flight with no other thought than achieving the end he had in view.

FURTHER LINES OF PROGRESS

Progress toward the modern airship has, as we have seen, been by short and laborious flights. The disappointments and disasters have been almost numberless. Endless patience, perseverance, and dauntless courage have been demanded. Moreover, in the past the would-be master of the air has needed very considerable resources. On account of a lack of funds many promising designs have come to no definite end. In the earlier days of flying the work of construction was done chiefly by men of leisure and means. Not till a comparatively recent date has the work been put on a commercial basis and done by large manufacturing firms.

One of the chief difficulties to be overcome was to discover an object of sufficient strength to be driven through the air, and yet so light that it could displace more than its own weight of air. No very great difficulty was experienced in constructing the spherical balloon, for the sphere is, of course, the natural shape which any flexible envelope will take. No framework was needed to stiffen the flimsy covering of such a balloon. The sphere is, in itself, a natural shape, and it has no tendency to change. The distorting action upon it is that due to the weight of the car; but by using a large net bag, enclosing the whole balloon, this has been so spread that the distortion is very slight, and the natural shape not interfered with to a very appreciable extent.

The great pressure of the air has, of course, constituted many difficulties. At sea-level the air pressure is 14-7 lbs. per square inch. A vessel containing a vacuum has therefore to be strong enough to support 15 lbs. on every square inch of its surface. To make the envelope of a balloon strong enough to contain a vacuum is impossible for the purpose. Too great weight would be required.

It has been found that the best course is to fill the balloon with hydrogen, the lightest of gases. In this way the difficulty as regards pressure is overcome, for the hydrogen presses upwards as strongly as the air presses inwards. Stated in round figures, 1,000 cubic feet of hydrogen weighs about 5½ lbs., and the same quantity of air about 80 lbs. It has been found, then, that 75 lbs. represents the gross lifting weight, and that from it must be deducted the weight of the envelope to arrive at the desired lifting effect.

With the increased size of the balloon many difficulties have been removed, for the lifting weight increases faster than the superficial area of the envelope. The contents of a sphere increase as the cube of a diameter, but the area grows only as the square of the diameter. Therefore, if you double the diameter of a balloon, you increase its capacity and consequently its gross lift by eight times. Even if it should be necessary to increase the thickness of the fabric of which the balloon is made, there is still a good margin left in favour of the larger balloon.

But the aim has been to obtain something more than the ordinary spherical balloon, which simply drifts in the air-currents. Such a balloon is helpless as far as direction is concerned. It simply 'goes with the wind.' Its weight may be varied, but not its direction. The aim of the inventors of steerable balloons has been to overcome helpless drifting by means of propellers and rudders, and by various means designed to avoid loss of gas in ascending and descending.

Inventors in time past found that it was no easy matter to drive a large spherical object of a light and flimsy construction through the air. With the huge area which a spherical balloon offers to the wind, it was found impossible to make any headway at all, except in perfectly calm weather, or with the wind behind. Consequently, the steerable balloon took on an elongated shape, the nose growing more and more pointed, so that it could 'cut' the air.

But now a fresh call arose for new ways and means of construction.

The simple bag, which served in spherical form, was useless for the new design. A rigid framework of suitable lightness and strength was called for—an extremely difficult matter. Indeed, even in the case of a ship built for the sea there are troubles in this direction.

'The water supports it all along, while the load which it carries is more or less in lumps, distributed irregularly from end to end. A ship in still water, without any attacks by storms from without, is in danger of breaking its back. If it be divided up into short sections some will be found to possess great buoyancy and little load, while others will be carrying loads far in excess of their buoyancy. The ship must therefore be strongly constructed, so that the lightly loaded parts may be able effectually to assist the heavily loaded parts. As great longitudinal stiffness is required in a ship as in a bridge. In fact, the modern ship is actually modelled upon a railway bridge. The method of construction which made the great liner of today possible was invented by I. K. Brunei, who got the idea from the Menai Straits Bridge of Robert Stephenson.'

Longitudinal stiffness is, then, an absolute essential to any structure of the kind now in mind. The buoyancy must be fairly constant from end to end, the cars being suspended at intervals. That is to say, it has been found that the necessary stiffness must be attained whereby the weight of the suspended cars will be distributed in due proportion to every part of the balloon, not simply to the parts immediately above.

This has been attained by means of a cleverly constructed framework of aluminium, and on a line with this improvement have come a number of drum-shaped gas-bags, made of rubber fabric and placed in allotted spaces in the framework. A kind of keel has also been introduced beneath the frame, giving additional stiffness and keeping the airship from rolling, just as in the case of seafaring craft.

Improvement has followed improvement. In some designs two light frames have been spread out from the main structure of the airship, each carrying a propeller. Frames have also been introduced at the back of the airship, thus giving four propellers in all—two forward and two aft. With these have come fins or planes, designed with the view to keeping the nose of the airship foremost to the wind. Moreover, groups of planes have been employed, lying in horizontal position but capable of movement, and making it possible to steer upward at both ends or at one only, as required.

Whilst these structures, which led to the Zeppelin, were in course of preparation, other designs of importance were being made, which led by degrees to airships of the nature of the *Parseval*. In these designs there was no elaborate framework. The balloon portion was in one—a huge shape, stout in the middle with a pointed tail and rounded nose, and carrying triangular planes, placed horizontally. This strange shape, not unlike a fish, was maintained simply by the formation of the bag, distended by pressure of the gas. Difficulties as regards the car were overcome by long ropes, the car being suspended some distance below. The ropes were attached to the balloon at intervals, thus distributing the weight of the car throughout almost the full length of the balloon.

Later came improvements which permitted the car of the airship to slide, so to speak, upon the suspending ropes, thus giving greater freedom to the action of the propeller. To the design were also added two smaller ballonets, inside the large one, carrying air-ballast. And by means of clever manipulation these bags made it easier to keep the airship at an even keel. This aim was also aided by a small horizontal plane or elevator placed beneath the bow. Underneath the stern was hung a vertical plane, to the end of which the rudder was hinged. The motor was in the car, and drove two propellers, supported upon a framework, between the car and the balloon. These craft gradually grew to about 300 feet in length, and about 50 feet in diameter at the thickest parts.

Other designs, which led to the Astra-Torres, an airship of French origin, had a balloon of 'trefoil' shape. The car was hung low, as in other models of the kind, and was distributed by a number of wires, some of which passed into the balloon itself and were attached inside. Indeed, it was this mode of attaching the car that led to the trefoil shape. Two planes were attached to the rear, and two elevators and the rudder were placed beneath the rear end.

In another fairly successful design of a similar nature a long girder ran underneath the balloon, supported by wires from the balloon, the car being attached to the centre, thus distributing the weight throughout the whole length of the balloon.

Many of these designs had their origin in France, but the British have not been idle. Many improvements have had their birth in England, and we know that these, as in the case of other designs here mentioned, have led to definite results. Out of persevering efforts, checked again and again by misfortune and often by disaster, have come the modern airships with which we are familiar. In their wake are many victims. Yet, as we have seen, and shall see afresh in these pages, they have called forth many heroic deeds.

It is to the honour of the British nation that one of the first principles of the biplane was proposed and explained by a British subject, Mr. F. H. Wenham, as far back as 1866. He pointed out that the lifting power of a surface can be economically obtained by placing a number of smaller surfaces one above another. Indeed, flying-machines were built by Wenham on this principle, with appliances for the use of his own muscular power. He did not, however, accomplish actual flight, although valuable results were obtained as regards the driving power of superposed surfaces.

After various further experiments in the same direction, it fell to H. von Helmholtz to emphasise the improbability that man could drive a flying-machine by his own muscular power. A period of stagnation followed. But interest was revived later, and fresh efforts were made, varying in importance, down to the experiments of Sir Hiram Maxim and Professor Langley.

These two eminent men, who took up the subject of flying in the last decade of the last century, came to their task with great scientific knowledge. Hitherto flying was associated in the minds of the public with failure and folly. Indeed, Sir Hiram Maxim once remarked that at the time he took up the subject it was almost considered a disgrace to anyone to think of it. It was thought 'quite out of the practical question.' But the two great men now in mind were not to be turned aside by ridicule. 'They rescued aeronautics from a fallen position, and fired in its cause the enthusiasm of men of light and learning.'

Sir Hiram Maxim's experiments were on a large scale. He built the largest flying-machine that had then been constructed. It had 4,000 feet of supporting surface and weighed 8,000 lbs.; the screw propellers measured 17 feet 11 inches in diameter, the width of the blade at the tip being 5 feet. The boiler was of 363 h.-p. This remarkable machine had wheels and a railway line, and was restrained from premature flight by a system of wooden rails. But it proved unruly. It burst through the wooden rails, and flew in a wholly unexpected fashion for 300 feet!

Professor Langley's experiments carried flying still further. In 1896 he built a machine that flew for more than threequarters of a mile. In this machine there was only 70 square feet of supporting surface, and the weight was only 72 lbs. It had a 1 h.-p. engine, weighing 7 lbs.

But Professor Langley had still to build a machine that would carry a man. This he did in due course, but when the machine was being put to the test over water, and at the very moment of being launched, it

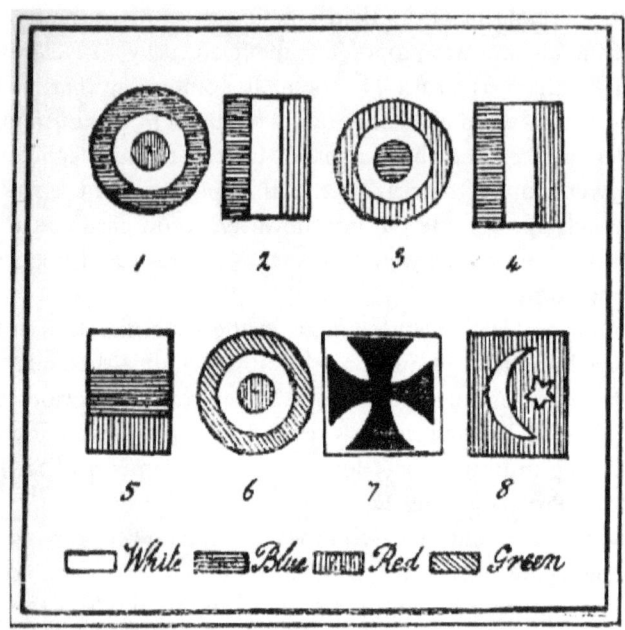

DISTINCTION MARKS USED BY THE BELLIGERENTS IN THE WAR.

1. BRITISH. 2. MARKS ON RUDDER OF BRITISH MACHINE.
3. FRENCH. 4. MARKS ON RUDDER OF FRENCH MACHINE.
5. RUSSIAN. 6. ITALIAN. 7. GERMAN AND AUSTRIAN. 8. TURKISH.

The British marks consist of circles, having a red and blue circumference, with a white or (occasionally) the natural colour of the fabric in between. The positions for these circles are:—Two on the upper surface of the top plane near the wing tips; two on the lower surface of the bottom plane, also close to the tips; one on each side of the body between the pilot's seat and the tail. Sometimes simply a red circle is used on naval machines. The rudder is painted with three vertical stripes in the following order counting from front to back; blue, white, red. The French distinction marks are similar to the British, with the exception that the centre of the circles is blue and the circumference red. The Belgian, Serbian, and Roumanian marks are similar to the French. The Russian marks are lateral stripes on the planes in the order from the leading to the trailing edge of the wing: white, blue, red. Our Italian Allies incorporate their national colours in a rosette on their machines. The device has a red centre, then a white ring with a green circle outside.

caught in the launching ways and was pulled into the water. Progress had, however, been made, and it is well worthy of note that of recent date an American aviator has unearthed Langley's machine and flown on it, thus giving posthumous honour to the inventor.

Following the professor's efforts, further progress was made by Mr. Octava Chanute, who introduced the important principle of making moveable surfaces. He also made use of superposed surfaces. But it was reserved for the two famous aviators, the brothers Wright, to bring the desired conquest of the air to a definite point.

Their first practical experiment was with gliding machines at Kitty Hawk, North Carolina, in 1900. They endeavoured with comparatively small surfaces to raise their machines like a kite by the wind. But they found that the wind was not always in their favour and often blew too strongly for their method. Consequently, they abandoned the idea, and resorted to flight by gliding. Their machines now had two superposed surfaces. They also introduced two highly important principles, namely, a horizontal rudder in front for controlling the vertical movements, and the principle of warping or flexing one wing or the other for steering purposes. Later a vertical rudder was added.

Writing of these improvements, Mr. Eric Stuart Bruce, Vice-President of the Aerial League of the British Empire, remarks that their importance cannot be overestimated:

> We have only to look at nature for their *raison d'être*, and observe the flight of seagulls over the sea. How varied are the flexings of nature's aeroplanes in their wonderful manoeuvrings to maintain and recover equilibrium!

A feature of these early experiments was the placing of the operator prone upon the gliding machine, instead of in an upright position, to secure greater safety in alighting and to diminish the resistance. This, however, was only a temporary expedient while the Wrights were feeling their way. In the motor-driven aeroplanes the navigator and his companion were comfortably seated. After the experiment of 1901, the Wrights carried on laboratory researches to determine the amount and direction of the pressure produced by wind upon planes and arched surfaces exposed at various angles of incidence. They discovered that the tables of the air pressures which had been in use were incorrect.

As the result of these experiments the Wrights produced in 1902 a new and larger machine. This had 28.44 square metres of sustaining surfaces, about twice the area of previous experiments. At first the machine was flown in the manner of a kite, with the view of learning whether it would soar in a wind. Experiments showed that the machine soared whenever the wind was of sufficient force to keep the angle of incidence between four and eight degrees. Later, in 1903, screw propellers were applied and four flights made. Definite progress favoured the venture. Two hundred and sixty metres were covered at a height of two metres!

In the following year, 1904, there was further marked progress, many successful flights, some 'circular,' being made. In the next year came an astonishing achievement: the Wrights flew no less than 24¼ miles in half an hour. This was rightly deemed at the time a great flight forward. But a period of silence and seeming inactivity followed. It was not until 1908 that further revelations were made. It was then seen that the Wrights had not been idle. Indeed, it is said (and with obvious justice) that to the labours of the Wright brothers we owe the advent of the mobile and truly efficient military air scout.'

Further Developments and Certain Enemy Machines

The earliest experiments in the construction of aeroplanes were, as we have seen, to a considerable extent made in France. The United States have also played an active part. Meanwhile England had not been idle. Mr. Henry Farman, the inventor of the Farman Biplane, was the first to apply the now famous Gnome motor, in which seven or more cylinders revolved. The influence of this motor in facilitating flight generally has been remarkable. The early forms of aeroplane engines had proved unreliable, owing to the great speed demanded. Indeed, it is said that if the aeroplanes of the great European War were flying over the enemy's line with old-fashioned engines they would drop down into hostile hands as quickly as dying flies from the ceiling on the first winter day.

Side by side with the efforts of Mr. Henry Farman in the construction of biplanes, M. Bleriot gave his attention to the construction of monoplanes. After attempts, which unfortunately brought disaster and disappointment, he produced a machine which astonished by its remarkable performances the whole aeronautical world.

Simplicity was the keynote of the Bleriot monoplane. The machine in which M. Bleriot flew over the Channel in 1909 has been described by a well-known member of the Aeronautical Society of Great Britain as:

Stretching like the wings of a bird on either side of a tubular wooden frame partly covered with canvas and tapering to the rear, with two supporting planes, rounded at the ends. At the front was placed the motor, geared direct to a 6 feet 6 inch wooden propeller, and on a level with the rear end of the planes. Immediately behind the engine was a petrol tank, and behind that the aviator's seat. Near the end of the frame and beneath it was the fixed tail, with two moveable, elevating tips. The act of moving a lever backwards and forwards actuated the tips of the fixed tail at the back of the machine, and caused it to rise and fall. Moving the same lever from side to side warped the rear surfaces of the supporting planes. The act of pushing from side to side a bar on which the aviator's feet rested put the rudder into action and steered the machine.

Still fresh in the memory is the flight in which the Bleriot monoplane carried M. Prior from London to Paris, covering 250 miles in three hours and fifty-six minutes. Later, a Bleriot monoplane carried M. Garros up to a height of 5,000 metres. At this height the engine broke down, but in virtue of wonderful gliding powers the machine was landed safely. It was this same type of machine that flew over the Alpine peaks, and later carried the first aeroplane post, flying from Hendon to Windsor in seventeen minutes.

Another monoplane which calls for special reference is the Latham Antoinette monoplane, which enjoyed the great distinction of being the first to fly effectively in a wind. Before the invention of this machine, aviators had only dared to fly in favourable conditions. It consisted of large, strongly constructed wings. The motor was about 60 h.p. At the rear of the machine were fixed horizontal and vertical fins. At the end of the tail there were hinged horizontal planes for elevating or lowering the machine. The machine, with its ability to withstand high winds, gave great impetus to the adoption of the aeroplane for military purposes. Latham, the inventor, performed some remarkable feats, and must be accounted an heroic pioneer in the more recent history of flying.

Progress continued on the lines indicated. But it is impossible, for obvious reasons, to touch upon the modern types of machines employed by Great Britain and her Allies. We may, however, deal briefly with certain outstanding types of enemy machines.

One of the most familiar German machines is the Aviatik biplane.

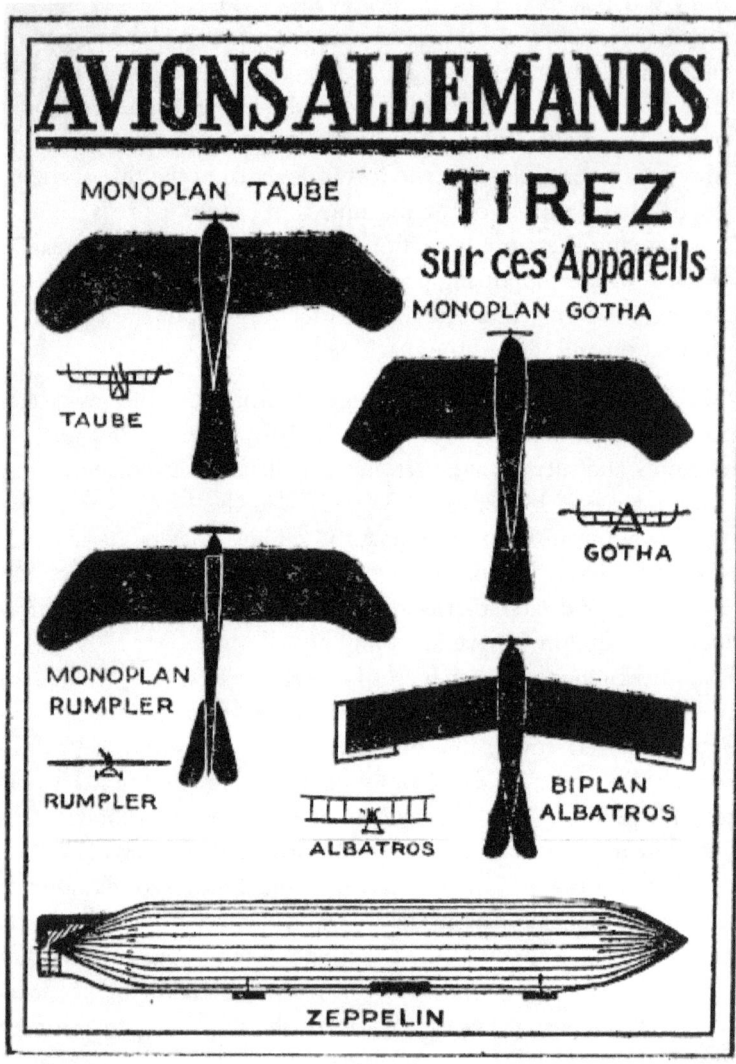

REDUCED REPRODUCTION OF A DIAGRAM ISSUED AT THE EARLY PART OF THE WAR BY THE FRENCH WAR OFFICE, BEARING THE WORDS: 'GERMAN AEROPLANES, FIRE ON THESE MACHINES.'

The vital parts of this 'fighting dragon' are fortified with metallic 'capot.' The rest of the fuselage is also armoured. In the forepart of the fuselage a space is provided allowing the observer free movement for scouting, photographing, &c. The machine can be quickly erected and dismantled. The supporting surface consists of two planes of unequal dimensions, the upper plane being the larger. Stability is assured by a fixed plane prolonged by a rudder. Two 'ailerons' at the back of the upper planes give lateral stability. Steering is effected by means of a vertical rudder placed between the two portions of the horizontal plane rudder.

Another familiar type, the Etrich monoplane, is on the lines of the German bird-shape design. The wing-shaped supporting planes have upturned wing tips at the back, which are flexed up and down for the purpose of lateral stability. The back part of the tail planes is also moveable, and can be flexed for elevating.

The Germans also have large numbers of the well-known Albatross biplanes and various monoplanes of the Taube design, and also many waterplanes of the Albatross type. An interesting feature of these machines is the fact that they are all double seated with the exception of the Argo type of monoplane.

The swiftly dashing scouting monoplane did not at first find favour with the enemy, but the war has brought many sudden and sweeping changes, and, following the much-vaunted Fokker, we learn of a German machine able to attain the astonishing speed of 120 miles an hour!

The Albatross, a much-used type of German machine, was first made at Johnnisthal, near Berlin (about 200 of these machines were made in 1913). Mercedes motors are fitted, capable of attaining a high speed.

In the Rumpler monoplane, another well-known German type, the wings are again in the shape of a dove's wings, the ends being flexible. A well-known authority writes:

The stability of the apparatus, is assured both by the shape of the wings and their flexibility. It is at once a combination of the inherent stability type and the depending on the warping of surfaces.

The Rumpler biplane, as in the case of the Aviatik, is remarkable for the space provided for the pilot and observer. In this case also the fuselage is strongly protected. The upper plane varies from that of the majority of German machines; it is not made to move in the centre. There is a short moveable central plane, attached to the fuselage by four tubes. The other planes are fixed to this central plane.

The Rumpler monoplane is shown, together with other German designs, including the Gotha monoplane, in a diagram issued in the early part of the war by the French War Office, bearing the words: *German Aeroplanes. Fire on these machines.* (See diagram earlier.)

The Zeppelin and Other Modern Airships

The keenest interest and curiosity is very naturally felt in the Zeppelin airship. Much has been written concerning its peculiar construction—much that is founded on doubtful evidence, and much that is mainly true. At this point we shall limit ourselves to a brief description of the construction of the Zeppelin, and seek to show in simple terms how the type of airship rises and falls. With the heroic acts the Zeppelins have called forth we shall deal later.

Now, imagine a long cage tapering to a rounded point at either end. At intervals are thin walls or partitions of aluminium sheet, dividing the cage lengthwise into a large number of drum-shaped compartments, while every part is stiffened and straightened by crossed bars forming diagonal bracing, tying and holding all together into a structure of remarkable strength. Such is the basis of a Zeppelin airship.

The whole of the framework is covered with waterproof fabric, the length of some of the patterns being 492 feet in length and 47½ feet in diameter.

Beneath is fixed a light framework, forming a kind of keel, and giving additional stiffness. In some designs a cabin is formed in the keel. The cars, which are not unlike the form of a boat, are hung under the keel, one near either end. Near the front, on either side, two light frames spread out, each of which carries one of the propellers, and another pair of frames are fixed in like manner toward the end. At the after end are a number of fins or planes, the purpose of these being to keep the nose of the ship foremost to the wind, as shown in a previous chapter.

Now as regards rising and falling. To many people the manoeuvring of a Zeppelin in the air is still a matter of mystery. It is certainly not easy for the lay mind to grasp and hold the fact that a monster vessel made of metal, and weighing nearly 20 tons, can float in a medium through which a feather falls. The Zeppelin, in effect, is lighter than a feather, volume for volume, and this lightness is obtained by creating an enormous space within the carcase of the ship and filling this space with hydrogen gas, which is about fifteen times lighter than air.

If we imagine that a steel boiler 50 feet long has the same width and height as a Zeppelin and weighs 20 tons, it is easy to understand that if this were filled with hydrogen gas it would not float in the air. But imagine the boiler to be drawn out until it was 500 feet long, and one gets some idea of the lightness of the Zeppelin structure. Each plate of metal in the boiler would be increased to ten times its normal length, and thus would become exceedingly thin. Of course, in the Zeppelin lighter materials are used, with the result that for a small weight we get an enormous volume.

Then, by filling this space with hydrogen the ship displaces its own volume of air, but this volume of air is so much heavier than the ship's weight that the vessel rises.

The most remarkable feature of the Zeppelin is the ingenious manner in which the volume of hydrogen is controlled, and through this control the altitude of the ship is regulated. In principle the method resembles that of the air bladder of a fish. When the eighteen gas-bags of a Zeppelin are filled with hydrogen the ship is at its maximum of buoyancy or lightness. It then has a lifting power which unless restrained by heavy weights would take the vessel high up into the air until a thin atmosphere was reached, where the ship would float motionless in a medium of less density. But if we replace the hydrogen with air when the ship is held to the ground, we increase the weight of the vessel so much that it will not rise.

Thus, in the Zeppelin, by the alternative use of light hydrogen and heavy air, we can so alter the weight that the vessel can be made to rise or sink. By a highly-developed system of tanks, pumps, and valves the relative volumes of hydrogen and air can be controlled with wonderful accuracy.

In the older system of airships, the hydrogen was allowed to escape when it was desired to make the ship heavier, but the modern Zeppelin, when it takes hydrogen from the gas-bags, is able to store the gas in metal tanks under pressure, and it also has a reserve supply to make up for unavoidable leakage.

Each gas-bag is mounted above an air-bag, and when the gas-bag is inflated to the maximum the air-bag is almost empty. The ship is then at its most buoyant stage. To reduce this buoyancy the air pumps are put in motion, and they force air under pressure into the air-bags. This pressure, acting on the gas-bags, forces out the hydrogen through pipes and non-return valves to the storage tanks. If at any time it is required to make the vessel ascend, the air-bags are deflated and the gas supply pipe with its pump is employed to force more hydrogen into the gas-bags. One thousand cubic feet of hydrogen have a lifting power of nearly 75 lbs. at sea-level, and this lifting power acts very quickly. Thus, a Zeppelin changes its altitude rapidly when the weight is altered, and at the same time there is automatic control whereby the vessel can be kept at the same level if necessary.

When a Zeppelin drops a bomb, it suddenly becomes lighter, and it rises in consequence. This circumstance is very disconcerting to gunners, for if, say, a 200 lb. bomb were dropped, the ship would leap up nearly 200 feet in the air, unless the captain desired to check the ascent. The discharge of water ballast produces the same rising effect, and with almost equal suddenness the ship can sink by using its powerful air pumps to press out the hydrogen. Moreover, when the Zeppelin is in motion it can use its elevating planes for changing altitude in the manner of an aeroplane. Thus, in addition to its power of steering from left to right in the same plane, and of climbing and descending along an inclined path by the use of the elevators, the Zeppelin can rise and fall vertically, and by its system of storage tanks these manoeuvres can go on for a long period.

There is a good deal of difference of opinion as to the altitude which the Zeppelin can attain. When fully loaded in war trim the latest ships can rise to about 5,000 feet, but by the time they reach London, for example, and have used nearly half their fuel, ammunition, &c, they are several thousand feet higher. The practical limit to airship work is said to be about 10,000 feet. Above that height the cold is so intense, the air so rarefied, and the conditions for men, engine, and ship so distressing, that there is no inducement to rise further.

It is noteworthy that the latest type of Zeppelin is fitted with a switchboard for dropping bombs, as, for example, in the airship brought down in the north of London in the early part of October, 1916.

The German *Schütte-Lanz*, a well-known type, is an attempt to secure the advantages of a rigid type, without the fragilities of the Zeppelin. The framework is made of fir wood, and contains separate gas compartments. Exceptional strength is claimed for these compartments. A centrifugal pump is employed for distributing the gas. The volume of the airship is 918,000 cubic feet—an extremely large structure, surpassing even some of the largest types of airship. It is believed

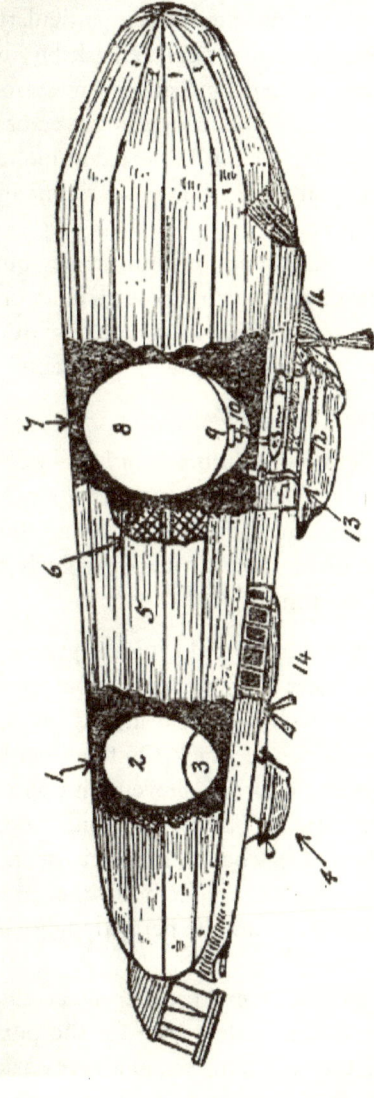

SECTIONAL VIEW OF ZEPPELIN AIRSHIP, SHOWING THE ARRANGEMENT OF THE HYDROGEN AND AIR BALLONETS WHICH CONTROL THE WEIGHT OF THE AIRSHIP, THUS ENABLING IT TO RISE AND FALL AS REQUIRED.

(1) Section of one of the eighteen ballonets. (2) Hydrogen gas-bag partly inflated. (3) Air. (4) Rear gondola. (5) Outer covering of fabric. (6) Metal work. (7) Air space between gas-bag and frame. (8) Hydrogen gas-bag fully inflated. (9) Flexible gas-pipe. (10) Inner ballonet deflated. (11) Metal gas tank into which hydrogen is pumped under pressure. (12) Forward gondola. (13) Flexible pipe rom pump to ballonet. (14) Keel cabin.

(Diagram from a photograph taken from a point at the forward part of a Zeppelin Airship.)

in authoritative quarters that one of the first airships brought down in flames on British soil was a ship of this type.

The German Gross airship has been described as more or less a reproduction of the Lebauchy type, which is, of course, of French origin. It is built partially on the rigid and partly on the non-rigid system.

The *Parseval* airship is portable, and therefore a particularly useful type. On account of its subtleness, it has been remarkably free from accidents. It is small in size, and is fitted for many purposes for which larger airships would be useless. The dimensions, however, of the *Parseval* vary considerably, the smallest being 3,200 cubic metres. (This particular ship was built in the year 1908.) The more recent and larger designs have a far greater capacity.

There are, of course, many other types on similar lines, but we are chiefly concerned in these pages with the purpose and fate of airships of the rigid type, and in our next chapter we shall see how our airmen have fitted themselves for the task of dealing with Zeppelins.

The New Arm in Warfare

It was clear some while before the outbreak of hostilities that the aeroplane was destined to play a prominent part. Mr. Sydney F. Walker, R.N., M.I.E.E., remarks, in a useful little volume on aviation, published before the war, that the first important work to which the aeroplane has been put is that of scouting.

When armies are manoeuvring in the field, it is the great object of each general to find out what his opponent is doing, exactly where his forces are, where each particular arm is weak, and where, above all things, he is open to attack. On the other hand, each general makes the greatest efforts to prevent his opponents from finding out all about himself. The art of hiding men, and even of artillery and of horses, has been brought to such success that the non-military observer might be in the midst of an army of 30,000 or 40,000 men and be perfectly ignorant of their presence.

Every inequality in the ground, every natural object, such as a tree, a mound, a house, &c, is made use of for the purpose of concealing the presence of men, horses, and accessories. It will be evident that with an aeroplane flying at anywhere up to eighty miles an hour, and that has been exceeded at the time of writing, and viewing the surface of the ground from above—provided the pilots, or passengers accompanying them, are trained to observe the ground and the bodies of men on the ground from above—practically any disposition of the enemy could be discovered.'

We are now able to judge by results and appreciate the work done. A point of primary importance in active warfare, as we have seen, is the use of the aeroplane for reconnaissance work. Other duties, and there are many, are set forth with admirable clearness by Mr. W. E. Dommett in his little work, *Aeroplanes and Airships*. The book was written at the early part of the war, and on that account is particularly instructive at this point; for it enables us to trace the progress made and the victories won by our airmen.

Reconnaissance work for the purpose of co-operation with artillery, forms the most important function next to scouting. An aerial observer is sent out to determine the position of hostile batteries whose existence may or may not be known by its fire, to determine the strength of the batteries, and how the units composing them are grouped. In addition, it is the duty of the observer to look out for troops, stores, or other matters which could and should be subjected to the fire of one's own batteries. He should supply as far as possible details as to range and elevation necessary for clearing intervening high ground. In addition, the observer can report as to the effect of his own side's artillery, and the manner in which it is failing or succeeding in its object.

The value of this form of observation is beyond calculation, in view of the fact that the artillery have not to waste time and ammunition in getting the target. Moreover, the time during which the opposing batteries or forces can do damage is correspondingly reduced. Naturally, much depends upon the accuracy of an observer's report as to its value, and in this respect, it appears that the allied forces are superior to their opponents, and it would seem that this superiority is due not so much to the superiority in the observer's machine, but to the better self-reliance, intelligence, and powers of initiative possessed by the men themselves. Observation work, it may be said, is generally accompanied by some offensive action on the part of the pilot or accompanying observer.

Observation in naval warfare is of course also of great importance. In the work of detecting submarines, for instance, aeroplanes have

171

proved of great value, for it is possible to detect submerged objects with greater ease from considerable heights than from the water surface. Writing to the *Matin*, a correspondent stated in the early part of the war that an aviator flying several hundreds of feet above the sea off Cape Helles, saw a black spot in the water beneath him. Circling round, to enable him to observe it more closely, he at last made out the form of a German submarine, under water, moving towards a British transport, which was heavily laden with troops and munitions.

Immediately the aviator flashed a wireless signal to the transport, and then, swooping down to a few feet of the surface of the water he dropped two bombs. These did no damage to the submarine, but taking warning she sank to greater depths. When the enemy thought enough time had passed, he raised his periscope above the surface, but the aeroplane was still circling close at hand and once more a couple of bombs fell close alongside the boat. Then the submarine finally disappeared. Many incidents of a similar nature have been recorded.

It is, moreover, sometimes necessary to find out the position of our own submarines in such a case as when a submarine has disappeared and not returned to its base. Before the war, when one of our A Class boats sank off the Cornish coast, whilst out from Devonport for exercise, an aeroplane was successfully employed for finding its whereabouts. The boats in company with the lost boat laid buoys to indicate the position, but these had become shifted by heavy seas, and had become useless for the purpose.

Observation work is frequently accompanied by direct offensive action; but the work is sometimes done purely with the view to the offence. For example, as early as September 23, 1914, naval airmen, namely, Squadron-Commander E. F. Briggs, Flight-Commander J. T. Babington, and Flight-Commander S. V. Lippe, carried out a raid over a mountainous route of 120 miles upon the Zeppelin sheds at Dusseldorf. And at a later date a similar raid was made on the sheds near Lake Constance.

In the early part of the war the Paris correspondent of the *Times* wrote as follows:

A feature of the operations along the front is the active use by the French of their air service, and the many indications given of the progress which has been accomplished in this branch of the service since the outbreak of the war. Realising that for fighting purposes the chief mission of the aeroplane is to act like a gun of immense range, and that bombardment requires swarms of aeroplanes and not an isolated machine, the French have equipped and organised a number of air squadrons with the object of disturbing and destroying the enemy's communications, either during or on the eve of military developments, so as to impede the arrival of men and shells from the reserve points during the progress of operations.

For this purpose, the squadrons are composed of three different types of machines, the names of which indicate the special duties of each type. These squadrons, in spite of the boisterous weather which has prevailed throughout the month, have raided no less than ten important German railway centres in the area of operations, throwing over 400 bombs in their flight, while the chaser planes engaged any protecting enemy aircraft that tried to interfere with the operations.

A glance at a map will show how effectively the air services are able to act as an extension of artillery in upsetting the enemy's transport. Thus Challerange, an important junction on the Vouziers—St. Menehould and Vouziers—Apremont Railways, whence are served the requirements of the army operating in the west of the Argonne; Arnaville and Bayonville, to the south-west of Metz; Vigneuvelles les Hattonchattel, the railway centre for the south-eastern armies operating against Verdun; Autruy, to the north of the Argonne; and Conflans-en-Jarisy, on the Verdun—Metz railway, have been regularly bombarded by aerial squadrons, which in some cases have numbered thirty-five air machines.

In this connexion it is interesting to recall an extract from an official *communiqué* that was issued early in the war: July 20—

Thirty-one aviators yesterday bombarded the railway station of Conflans, an important junction. Three shells of 155 mm. and four of 90 mm. were observed to have been neatly dropped on the station. The engine shed was struck by a shell of 155 mm. Three *Aviatiks* were put to flight by our pursuing aeroplanes, which accompanied the squadron. One *Aviatik* was compelled to land rapidly.

In the place of an enemy camp or railway junction the attack is made by the Naval Air Service on the submarine base or the dockyard. On many occasions naval airmen have bombarded German submarines in Ghent harbour. In the raid on Cuxhaven, seven seaplanes were conveyed to the vicinity of Heligoland and thence flew over Cuxhaven and dropped bombs on the docks.

A report issued at a comparatively early date of the war stated:

Quite one of the features of the campaign, on our side, has been the success attained by the Royal Flying Corps. In regard to the collection of information it is impossible either to award too much praise to our aviators for the way they have carried out their duties, or to over-estimate the value of the intelligence collected, more especially during the recent advance. In due course certain examples of what has been effected may be specified, and the far-reaching nature of the results more fully explained, but that time has not yet arrived. That the services of our Flying Corps, which has really been on trial, are fully appreciated by our Allies is shown by the following message from the Commander-in-Chief of the French Armies, received on the night of September 9 by Field-Marshal Sir John French:—

Please express most particularly to Marshal French my thanks for services rendered on every day by the English Flying Corps. The precision, exactitude, and regularity of the news brought in by its members are evidence of their perfect organisation, and also of the perfect training of pilots and observers.

FROM VICTORY TO VICTORY

At a later date (September 12, 1916) a writer in the *Daily Chronicle* remarked:

All reports, official and unofficial, concur in warm praise of the daring, resourceful, and effective work of the British airmen. Our supremacy over the Germans in the aerial arm is incontestable. Every day's fighting brings evidence of it. Not only are the exploits of our airmen the theme of admiring comment by our own soldiers, but they also extort reluctant tributes of admiration even from the enemy. Were it not for the accurate observation of these fearless, hawk-eyed scouts of the air, the marvellously effective results achieved by our gunners in the recent fighting would not have been possible, and the difficulties in the way of our heroic infantry would have been vastly increased.

174

By general consent, then, our aerial scouts far surpass those of the enemy in this work. Our aeroplanes have constantly hovered over his lines, his seldom over ours. Casualties have been inevitable in these perilous enterprises, but such is the dexterity of our fliers that the price paid has not been nearly so high as the risks run would suggest. In point of fact, our losses in the air have been less than those of the enemy, despite the greater enterprise and the bolder initiative of British airmen. 'From July 1 to September 17 in France we destroyed no fewer than 104 German aeroplanes.' These figures, compiled from the official reports, are the more impressive when it is remembered that it is the British rule not to include enemy machines damaged as lost, but only those that have, in fact, been actually destroyed.

It is not surprising, in the light of the remarkable achievements of the British Air Service in the battle-line, that its critics, so loud-voiced a few months ago, have been silenced. Fresh in everybody's recollection is the ridiculous fuss made by some sensational newspapers over the Fokker and its wonderful qualities. Where is the Fokker now? Where have those scribes vanished who were daily 'crabbing' our air service, now admittedly the best in the world? Will they, wherever they are, have the assurance to claim that it is their criticisms that have wrought what they would call the change? If so, it would be a baseless claim, absolutely without justification of any kind.

Our Air Service has evolved steadily in strength and efficiency ever since the outbreak of war. Of course, mistakes were made in the process of evolution and expansion. They could not be avoided in a new service, rapidly extending, and necessarily involving experimental changes in design and structure. But the progress has been steady and uninterrupted ever since the war began.

The truth is, the original expeditionary force was well equipped with aeroplanes and well-trained pilots. Later came the rapid expansion of the army, which imposed heavy new demands on the Royal Flying Corps. Those demands have all been met. It is to the credit of the late Lord Kitchener that from the first he recognised the great importance of the aeroplane in this war.

When in the early autumn of 1914 authorisation was sought for the manufacture of a sufficient number of machines to equip thirty new air squadrons, he at once doubled the number, ordering not 720 aeroplanes, but 1,440.

This was a notable instance of Lord Kitchener's prevision as to the scale of the war. Early in 1915 a very large new constructive pro-gramme was embarked upon, and the output since then has progres-sively increased. At first, we relied chiefly on France for the engines of our flying-machines. Now some of our best engines are made at home.

The interim report of Mr. Justice Bailhache's Committee, issued early in August, 1916, said:

> There has been an enormous expansion of the Flying Service since the war; and all the critics of the Service, without excep-tion, have borne testimony to the great progress made in its efficiency—a progress which, although most noticeable since the beginning of this year is, in the opinion of the Committee, the result of many months of strenuous work. To this efficiency the recent reports from the front bear eloquent witness.

Early in September, 1916, one who enjoyed facilities for visiting flying centres, and learning at first hand of the progress of aviation in the country, remarked that:

> There was no need to be an expert to appreciate the remark-able change that had come over certain districts, where, what a few months ago were mere country villages or stretches of pine wood, have been transformed into industrial centres, with as many signs of bustle and industry as are to be found in the great shipbuilding centres of the British Isles.
>
> A really remarkable thing is the enterprise and adaptability of firms who had never tackled the job before in organising their work so that Britain's output of machines was marvellously in-creased. Now the fruits of long and costly experimental work are being reaped, and the rate of output increases every week. This applies not to one establishment, but to the hundreds of works throughout the kingdom. So much is this the case that a country which at the beginning of war was believed to be behind in this branch of warfare is able not only to supply its own needs but also those of its Allies.

The same careful, persistent, and unobtrusive research work that has brought British aircraft to the top has also resulted in great im-provements in the construction and invention of bomb sights and dropping appliances. British engines, too, are now second to none in point of power, and great improvements are to be recorded in carburettors and special appliances for flight at high altitudes. The same progress is to be recorded in the matter of speed. The average speed of aeroplanes as used by our Air Service two years ago was from sixty-five to seventy miles per hour. Nowadays it is much higher.

As regards the future, a British officer remarked at the time now in mind:

> With all the results achieved so far, and the knowledge gained by this great war, there is no reason to doubt that the British Air Service—like the British Navy—will be the premier in the world. That is our constant aim.

An Observer in the R.N.A.S.

Further light is thrown on the work of naval pilots by an observer writing in the *Border Telegraph*.

> Most of us know, what the pilot of an aeroplane does. But have we as true a conception of the observer's duties? The man who makes his mark nowadays is the specialist. There are first-rate aeroplane observers and first-rate seaplane observers. Common-sense plays a great part in the affairs of both. Any man may recognise a haystack from a moderate altitude, but how many can tell a topsail schooner from a barquentine, a flotilla leader from a light cruiser, or a German ship of the line from one of the Entente? Therein lies the secret.

> It is abundantly clear that a very necessary feature in a pilot is a thorough working knowledge of wireless telegraphy. The days of returning to report are passing. The observer ignorant of wireless is no longer classed as an observer. He is becoming a 'back number.' It stands to reason that if a British seaplane sights a hostile squadron, and is, say, forty miles from her base, or from the nearest unit of the home fleet, then a precious forty minutes at least is going to be lost if the observer does not understand wireless telegraphy.

> Conversely a radio message, travelling at something like thrice the circumference of the earth in one second, will reach a receiving installation forty miles off while you cough, and a great deal quicker. That is one point, and the time was when it was thought any one could qualify in wireless. Quite a number of wise men have since then given up the attempt.

> The observer must recognise ships at sight, and from a reasonable

height, with the aid of prisms, be able to note their type, direction steering in, nationality, whether armed or otherwise, and their distance from the nearest mark, probably a buoy. He has, of course, to recognise and name the buoy.

Sometimes he will make a hazard at the cargo carried by detecting a clue somewhere. In a channel recently swept clear of mines, and just open to traffic, when scores of merchant-men and patrol craft are under way, the observer has got to get busy on the job. Very often if the pilot is daring and gets down to 500 feet, even the names of the ships can be discerned. Also, the observer has got to discriminate between a U Boat and an E Boat and an S Boat.'

The writer of the article in the *Border Telegraph* goes on to point out that bomb-dropping is a difficult matter:

Anyone can drop bombs, you say. "Just heave 'em overboard!" Exactly. But it's no use dropping a sixteen-pounder on a battle-cruiser. It mightn't like it. Besides, it won't wait till you drop it. You can take it that long before you get within dropping distance anything from a centimetre to a six-inch shell is up searching for you. The same when you spot a submarine. If you take too long calculating and guessing what curve the dropping bomb will take or how long it should take to reach the objective if the speed increases thirty odd feet per sec, they'll sling out the six-pounder at you, and mighty smart, too. A young man once dropped a few bombs for practice where he thought was well out in the bay. Alas! he forgot the curve a bomb makes in its flight. Don't ever forget that curve when you watch a hostile machine dropping bombs.
On this occasion the friendly bombs struck the water a couple of hundred yards from a fairly crowded esplanade, and caused something analogous to a panic. You see, those bombs, having had the pins extracted, made water spouts when they burst, not to mention noise. Rumours flew so fast that the District Brigade Major, being informed that the German fleet were shelling the port, called out the military. Why, it is not for me to say, and I'm not quite sure if the special constables were not called out, too, because I was making tracks, like Huckleberry Finn, for the back country shortly—very shortly, indeed—after the occurrence.

GUARDING OUR COASTS.
A Naval Patrol in difficulties in the North Sea.

It is, of course, highly important that the observer should be able to tell the difference between the ships of Britain and her Allies and an enemy ship. Moreover, at 1,000 feet in a fairly good light the observer has to distinguish between a floating mine and a war channel buoy. 'Then he will never cause his machine to descend to 200 feet for the purpose of informing his pilot that *it's a buoy.*' All this time communication has to be maintained with the wireless telegraphy station ashore or afloat. Instructions sent to the 'plane are taken down and given effect to, or the observer's report sent, as required.

Furthermore, the observer must be a master of aerial gunnery, and he must withal be an air mechanic in the best sense. One can readily imagine what would happen if an aeroplane had to alight fifty or sixty miles out to sea with a stubborn engine, if the pilot had no knowledge of motor mechanism.

Finally, the observer must possess and use sufficient intelligence and aptitude to write a report satisfactory to the exacting minds of the Admiralty every time he returns from his patrols. The work, in brief, is not for every man. Many high qualities are required, and above all the naval observer must have the spirit of daring enterprise. He must be a man of heroic mettle.

HEROES OF THE ROYAL NAVAL AIR SERVICE

Here we shall see afresh that the British Naval Air Service is rich in men who possess to a remarkable degree the qualities named in the foregoing chapters. Flight Sub-Lieutenant Dallas, for example (who in addition to performing consistently good work in reconnaissances and fighting patrols since December, 1915), has been brought to notice by the Vice-Admiral Dover Patrol for the specially gallant manner in which he has carried out his duties. Amongst other exploits is the following:

On May 21, 1916, he sighted at least twelve hostile machines, which had been bombing Dunkerque. He attacked one at 7,000 feet, and then attacked a second machine close to him. After reloading he climbed to 10,000 feet, and attacked a large hostile two-seater machine off Westende. The machine took fire and nose-dived seawards. Another enemy machine then appeared, which he engaged and chased to the shore, but had to abandon owing to having used all his ammunition. For these heroic exploits he has been awarded the Distinguished Service Cross.

The same honour has been conferred upon Sub-Lieutenant Oxley, who acted as observer with Flight-Lieutenant Edward H. Dunning, D.S.C., as pilot, on escort and reconnaissance patrol for a flight of bombing machines on the Bulgarian coast, on June 20, 1916. Two enemy machines were engaged at close range and forced to retire, and as our machine withdrew Flight-Lieutenant Dunning was hit in the left leg, and the machine itself was badly damaged. Sub-Lieutenant Oxley, having first improvised a tourniquet, which he gave to Flight-Lieutenant Dunning, took control of the machine, whilst the latter put on the tourniquet. The pilot was obliged to keep his thumb over a hole in the lower part of the petrol tank in order to keep enough fuel to return to the aerodrome, where he made an exceedingly good landing.

The Distinguished Service Cross has also been awarded to Flight-Sub-Lieutenant Donald Ernest Harkness, R.N.A.S., and Flight-Sub-Lieutenant Ralph Harold Collett, R.N.A.S., in recognition of their services on the morning of August 9, 1916, when they dropped bombs on the airship sheds at Evere and Berchem St. Agathe. Flight-Sub-Lieutenant Collett dropped all his bombs on the shed at Evere from a height of between 300 and 500 feet, under very heavy rifle, machine-gun, and shrapnel fire from all directions. Flight-Sub-Lieutenant Harkness could not descend so low owing to the very heavy antiaircraft fire which had by this time been opened on the machines, but he dropped some of his bombs on the shed, and then proceeded to Berchem St. Agathe, which he also bombed.

Honour has also been conferred upon Flight Commander T. Harry England, R.N.A.S., in recognition of his services on August 26, 1916, when, accompanied by a military officer as observer, he flew a seaplane forty-three miles inland from the Syrian coast, crossed a range of hills 2,000 feet high, with clouds at 1,500 feet, and after dropping bombs on the station of Horns, returned safely to his ship. The machine was exposed to rifle fire at extremely low altitudes for long periods, and Flight-Commander England showed remarkable pluck, determination, and skill in carrying out the flight under very adverse conditions.

Another officer to be decorated is Flight-Sub-Lieutenant Ronald Grahame, R.N.A.S., for exceptional gallantry in attacking and beating off four enemy seaplanes whilst on escort duty off the Belgian coast, September 22, 1916.

Mention must also be made of Flight-Sub-Lieutenant Stanley James Goble, R.N.A.S., who has been decorated in recognition of his services on September 24, 1916, when he attacked two hostile machines in the vicinity of Ghistelles at close range, and brought one of them down on fire in a spiral nose-dive.

With each passing day the list of R.N.A.S. heroes grows, calling forth just pride. Further reference to individual cases will be given later on in these pages. It may be stated here, however, that the following officers, together with many others in the Royal Naval Air Service, have been decorated by the king:—

Squadron-Commander Reginald Bone, Flight-Commander Redford Mulock, Squadron-Commander Francis Haskins, Flight-Commander Douglas Evill, Flight-Commander Vincent Nicholl, Flight-lieutenant John Petre, Flight-Lieutenant Roderic Dallas, Flight-Lieutenant Ralph Collett. The first two officers named have been invested by the king with the Insignia of Companions of the Distinguished Service Order. The last-named officers have been awarded the Distinguished Service Cross.

TOLD BY THE ADMIRALTY

Official communications are apt to make cold reading, but how much may be 'read into' them! Considered in the light of a lively imagination they convey a great deal. Between each line a story of considerable length and great interest might be written. Take, for instance, the following communication issued by the British Admiralty in the latter part of October, 1916:

> Yesterday afternoon, one of our naval aeroplanes attacked four enemy seaplanes off Ostend. Our machine was under fire from all four seaplanes, but succeeded in bringing down one, which was completely destroyed, and in driving off the others.

This was the second British aerial success against odds in the same week. A few days previously a naval single-seater machine attacked a large German double-engined tractor seaplane. The enemy pilot and observer were shot, and the seaplane dived vertically into the sea two miles off Ostend. Another British naval aeroplane destroyed a kite balloon in the same locality on this occasion.

We may crave for further details, but the time is not yet. Naval and military censors, though subjected to much adverse criticism, are wise in their generation.

Experience has shown that it is far better to give a light touch or two of romantic colouring, than to fall into the fault of conveying the kind of direct and definite information which might by some chance prove of service to the enemy. The following communications are above suspicion in the direction named, but they are not devoid of colour. They enable one to appreciate in a very real sense the heroic achievements of our naval aviators:

Between August 25 and 31, 1916, a series of attacks were carried out by naval aircraft upon the Bulgarian lines of communication beyond Kavala.

On the twenty-fifth the railway station and bridge at Buk (about twenty-two miles north-east of Kavala) were successfully bombed. On the twenty-sixth a similar attack upon the railway station at Drama (twenty-two miles north-west of Kavala) resulted in the burning of a large petrol store and considerable destruction among the rolling stock in the sidings. Bombs were also dropped on the billets of the enemy's troops at Doksat (fourteen miles north-west of Kavala).

On the twenty-seventh, Okgilar (twenty-five miles north-north-east of Kavala) railway station, where the headquarters of the 10th Division were situated, was successfully attacked. The station buildings were set on fire and considerable damage was done to the permanent way.

On the twenty-eighth Drama Station was again bombed. The station buildings were considerably damaged. On the same day Kavala forts were attacked with excellent results.

On the twenty-ninth a large body of infantry and transport concentrated at Porna (about thirty two miles west of Kavala, on the Seres-Drama line) were attacked. Considerable havoc was caused in the village and among the troops.

A large fire was started among the stores in the transport park. The moral as well as the material effect of this bombardment seems to have been considerable, as a reconnaissance made on the following day showed that all troops, camps, and transport had been removed from this district.

On the thirty-first an attack was made on Angista railway station (twenty-five miles west-north-west of Kavala). Direct hits were made and extensive damage was caused.

Further communications issued by the Admiralty in the same month showed that between August 25 and 29 a series of attacks and reconnaissances upon the enemy railway communications in Palestine were carried out by a British Seaplane Squadron. These fights were made under hazardous conditions, due to the fact that the railway runs, for the most part, behind a range of mountains difficult for seaplanes to surmount. Bombs were dropped on Afuleh Junction, where considerable damage was done to the rolling stock, permanent way, and to stores in the vicinity. A railway engine and fourteen carriages were also set on fire and destroyed.

The railway stations at Tulkeram and Ardana and an enemy camp four miles north-west of Remleh (thirteen miles from Jaffa) were successfully bombarded and severely damaged. And on August 26 a seaplane bombarded the railway station at Horns (about eighty miles north of Damascus). This flight, carried out at a distance of forty-five miles inland under extremely adverse conditions and through clouds low down on the mountains, was a singularly fine performance for a seaplane.

At a later date, from September 13 to September 22, further series of attacks were carried out by naval aeroplanes operating against the Bulgarian coast. On the thirteenth the headquarters of the Bulgarian 10th Division at Bademli Chiftlik were attacked, with considerable effect.

Subsequently these headquarters were removed elsewhere, but were discovered, and attacked three days later, with excellent results. A large explosion was caused, and a fire, which lasted for a considerable time, broke out among the buildings. On the sixteenth considerable damage was caused to transport proceeding on the road towards Drama, and on the same day the shipping in Foujes harbour was bombed. On the seventeenth and eighteenth the rolling stock, gun emplacements, and stores at Drama station were bombarded and considerable damage done to them. On the nineteenth a column of troops and transport were thoroughly plied with small bombs, which caused considerable damage and confusion.

In October, 1916, a hostile seaplane was shot down and destroyed by one of our naval aircraft. The enemy machine fell into the sea. This was evidently the raider that approached Sheerness at 1.45 p.m., flying very high. Four bombs were dropped, three of which fell into the harbour. The fourth fell in the vicinity of the railway station, damaging several railway carriages. No casualties, however, were caused. Naval aeroplanes went up and the raider made off in a north-easterly direction. But our men of the Royal Naval Air Service pursued the enemy machine, and after a short, sharp battle in the air, sent it diving into the sea.

Here we come into still closer contact with the work of the Royal Flying Corps on the various battle-fronts. On September 3, 1916, the fighting in the air on the Western Front was continuous. Again, the enemy's aircraft were forced to remain some miles in rear of their own lines, and entirely failed to interrupt the work of our machines. On two separate occasions our aeroplanes opened fire on the enemy's troops on the ground. As a result of many combats, three hostile machines were brought down and many others were driven down in a damaged condition.

On the previous day, in spite of the very unfavourable weather conditions, our aeroplanes carried out successful co-operation with our artillery. One of our patrols, consisting of four machines, encountered and drove off a hostile patrol of thirteen aeroplanes. A few days later British machines bombed an important railway junction on the enemy's lines of communications, causing great damage to the station and rolling stock. One of the enemy's aerodromes was bombed, one machine being destroyed on the ground and others damaged. Many other points of military importance were bombed. Some good work was also done from low altitudes, locating the positions reached by our troops. Three hostile machines were wrecked and four others driven down in a damaged condition.

Again, on the fifteenth of the month our pilots kept up constant and successful co-operation with our artillery and infantry, and frequent and accurate reports were furnished of the course of the battle. Hostile artillery and infantry were effectively engaged by our aeroplanes with machine-gun fire. Many bombing attacks were also carried out against hostile aerodromes and railway stations, in the course of which troop trains were hit and transport railway sidings attacked with machine-gun fire. A German kite balloon was brought down. The total number of hostile aeroplanes destroyed was fifteen. Nine others were driven down in a damaged condition.

On the twenty-second of the month there was again great aerial activity. A highly successful raid by about fifty of our machines was carried out on an important railway junction, where much damage was done, two trains containing ammunition being destroyed and many violent explosions caused. A number of other raids on enemy railway works and sidings, aerodromes, and other points of military importance were equally successful. In addition, many fights took place in the air, in the course of which three hostile machines were destroyed, and five others driven to earth in a damaged condition, besides many others which broke off in the middle of the fight and were seen to be descending steeply, but could not be watched to the ground owing to our machines being too busily engaged.

On the following day five bombing attacks were carried out by our aviators against railway stations on the enemy's communications. Much damage was done. In the course of an air fight one of our aviators collided with his opponent. The hostile machine fell vertically. Our machine fell for several thousand feet, when the pilot managed to regain control and re-cross the lines, safely flying over thirty miles with an almost uncontrollable machine.

The month closed in brilliant fashion for our Flying Corps. On the thirtieth, two of the enemy's aerodromes were successfully bombed by our aeroplanes, and at least one machine destroyed. In the fighting over the front, four enemy machines were brought down. Enemy troops and transport were repeatedly attacked from the air with machine-gun fire, and in one case several hundred infantry were dispersed. Another enemy kite balloon was brought down in flames. There were many fights in the air, in the course of which two enemy machines were destroyed and many others driven down. On this particular day we suffered no losses.

Referring to the work of the month, Sir Douglas Haig said:

Our aircraft have shown in the highest degree the spirit of the offensive. They have patrolled regularly far behind the enemy's lines, and have fought many battles in the air with hostile machines and many with enemy troops on the ground. For every enemy machine that succeeds in crossing our front, it is safe to say that 200 British machines cross the enemy's front. A captured Corps report described our aeroplanes *as surprisingly bold,* and their work has been as conspicuous for its skill and judgement as for its daring.

The opening days of the following month were unfavourable to aerial activity. On the tenth, however, our aeroplanes showed activity and destroyed, by bombing, two enemy battery positions, and damaged many others. They penetrated well behind the enemy front and bombed railway stations, trains, and billets with good effect. There was now much fighting in the air, and in one case two of our machines engaged seven hostile aeroplanes and drove down or dispersed them all. One of these hostile aeroplanes was seen to be destroyed and two others severely damaged.

The clear weather of the middle of October, 1916, gave scope for great aerial activity. On the seventeenth our machines made a large number of reconnaissances and bombed enemy railway lines, stations, billets, factories, and depots. There were numerous fights in the air, three enemy machines being destroyed, another driven to earth, and many dispersed. Two more enemy kite balloons were attacked and forced down, one being afterwards seen in flames.

Later in the same month, in spite of adverse weather conditions, our aeroplanes co-operated successfully with our artillery. This indeed has been one of the chief parts played by our heroic airmen. They have acted as 'the eyes of our artillery,' observing, directing, and reporting as only efficient aviators can.

RUSSIAN PRAISE AND RUSSIAN ACHIEVEMENTS

The Russians have been most generous in their praise of the work done by the Allied aviators in France. A correspondent of the *Bourse Gazette*, writing in the *Daily Chronicle*, has said:

One need only stay at the British front one single day to be convinced that the verdict is right. The Allied aviators dominate the air. This is a phrase no longer. It is as much a reality as the British Battle Fleet or the Allied artillery. The Allied aeroplanes are everywhere. They guide and direct the artillery fire, make bold reconnaissances, photograph the enemy positions before and after the bombardments, fill the enemy trenches with grenades, and combine with the infantry to attack the German fortifications. During the first two months of the Somme offensive the British aviators covered more than 100,000 miles in the air, and that in spite of the fact that for a whole fortnight there was no flying at all because of the heavy mist and rain. According to careful military statistics, the British airmen covered not less than 1,000,000 miles over the German lines in the first two years of war.

The correspondent of the *Bourse Gazette* goes on to remark that the history of the struggle for mastery in the air is very instructive.

At the beginning of the war the supremacy in aviation undoubtedly belonged to the British and the French. But during the first year of the war the Germans, availing themselves of their superior industrial organisation, went ahead of the Allies.

187

For a brief period, German aviation surpassed not only the British and French aviation separately, but both combined. That period coincides with the appearance of the Fokkers and the activity of Immelmann and other prominent German pilots.

But the Germans, as we have seen, could not maintain their superiority. Towards the end of the second year, the supremacy passed to the Allies once more. By the quantity and quality of their machines, as well as by the quantity and quality of their pilots, the British and French now so much surpass the Germans that at present one can speak of the absolute superiority of the Allied aviators. The writer in point continues:

The Allied aviation, is divided into three separate branches or three kinds of fighting—the attacking battle-squadron, something like aerial cavalry; the scouts, rather like aerial infantry; and a division of aerial photographers. The pilots of the aerial battle-squadron are the real fighters of the air. Most of them are young. And the lives of all of them are filled with unprecedented adventures.

Of all branches of aviation, however, the most important in the estimate of the writer of the article is that of photographing from an aeroplane:

Before the bombardment of any enemy position, the headquarters make a detailed map, drawn up from photographs taken from the aeroplanes. Then, while the bombardment is in progress, the aviators continue to take photographs of the position at fixed intervals. The bombardment continues until the photographs taken by the aviators show them all the *points d'appui* of the positions have been demolished. I saw these photographs and the maps of the German positions prepared from them. The making of these photographic maps is one of the greatest technical miracles of the present war. But its realisation demands indomitable courage and *sangfroid*.

Photographing the enemy positions is at once the most ingenious and the most dangerous of aerial operations. The aviator-photographer having risen to a great height above the enemy position, settles his aeroplane almost vertically above the position he is going to photograph. Descending a certain distance, he arranges his camera, takes his photograph of the German defences, and at once climbs up at top speed in order to regain his own lines. One can imagine with what a fire the Germans meet their uninvited visitor. All the while his dizzy manoeuvres over the German positions are going on, he has to face the fire of anti-aircraft guns, machineguns, and rifles.

As I stood on a hill, I noticed a tiny spot in the sky far above the German lines, around which small white clouds exploded. I asked my officer-companion if this was a fight between aeroplanes in the air. "No," he said, "it's our man photographing the German positions, and the Germans are firing at him from their trenches." . . .

All day long the British aviators rushed through the air. At certain moments, when they closed together, I could count up to thirty aeroplanes. From below they appeared like a flight of some mighty birds. Several of them evidently formed an aerial patrol. They circled round the kite balloons. The others flew away, singly or in groups, to the line of the German trenches. During the whole day only one single German aeroplane flew over the British lines and tried to attack a kite balloon. But it was driven off by the aerial patrol.

As regards the praiseworthy work done by Russian aviators, it is noteworthy that on September 14, 1916, a squadron of four Russian giant aeroplanes of the Slyr-Murometz type bombarded the German seaplane station on Lake Angern, in the Gulf of Riga. Seventeen seaplanes of various sizes and models were discerned. The Russians dropped seventy-three bombs, of a total weight of sixty-two *poods* (about one ton). The sheds were soon concealed in smoke and flames. Eight enemy seaplanes attacked the Russian machines, but were speedily put to flight by machine-gun fire.

As the result of the bombing and the air fight not fewer than eight enemy machines were destroyed or put out of action. The Russians returned safely, notwithstanding a hail of incendiary shells from anti-aircraft guns. On a previous occasion one Slyr-Murometz and one Ilya-Murometz, with a crew of five, routed seven attacking German seaplanes.

On the twenty-ninth of the same month Russian aviators carried out a raid on the rear of the enemy's cantonments in the Bourgunt Krevo district (about forty-five miles south-east of Vilna). The bombs dropped caused explosions and fires in the enemy's depots at various points. Bombs were also dropped on convoys, a narrow-gauge railway, and on wagons. In the course of the raid there was an air fight in which four German machines were brought down.

Russian airmen who call for special mention are Sub-Lieutenant Orloff, Lieutenant Gorkovenko, Captain Kayakoff, Captain Schifkoff, and Midshipman Safonoff . Captain Schifkoff in particular has many aerial victories to his credit.

ITALY'S PART

Italy has fought many air battles. Her sons are men of the right mettle. Her beautiful cities have suffered from raids, but the enemy has been made to pay the price. Italian airmen have not only put up a strong defence, but have made their power felt far beyond Italian territory.

On September 13, 1916, enemy aircraft bombarded Venice, Pordenone (thirty-five miles north-east of Venice), Latisana, Marano, Cervignano, and Aquileia on the marshland between Venice and the Isonzo. The Italians replied with a raid on Trieste and Parenzo, in which French aviators took part. With the departure of heavy Capronis for Trieste, squadrons of seaplanes set out from sea-bases for Parenzo. Five French machines joined forces with eleven Italian seaplanes. Shortly after 5.30 p.m. the first of them were over Parenzo, dropping explosive and incendiary bombs on the enemy's defence batteries and seaplanes station.

Only one enemy 'plane succeeded in getting off the water, and was immediately forced to come down by the attacks of the French aeroplanes and to take refuge among a squadron of Austrian torpedo-catchers, which continued to hug the coast. In spite of the lively fire of Austrian Army gunners, all the allied aeroplanes returned to their bases. For a long time on their return journey could be seen the useful effects of the bombing carried out by the Italian and French pilots in broad daylight, the hangars and batteries being shrouded in the smoke from the fires.

Scrupulous care was taken not to do damage to the unredeemed city. The Caproni squadron arrived over Trieste about 4 p.m., and, supported by other squadrons of light machines, began from some 9,000 feet the bombardment of the arsenal, the technical dockyard offices, the timber yards, and the depots housing the rolling-stock and kerosene supply, this latter at St. Sabba. Photographs and the dense columns of smoke showed with what results!

On the thirteenth of the same month an Italian aeroplane squadron fought a hotly contested battle, in the course of which two enemy 'planes were brought down. On the seventeenth of the same month, Italian aviators scored further victories.

On the same day an Italian squadron dropped bombs on the works and sheds of the narrow-gauge railway in Comignano (Komen on the Carso, ten miles south-east of Gorizia). Effective results were observed. It was also on this day that another squadron of Caproni battle-planes, escorted by Nieuport chasers, dropped bombs on the stations at Dottogliano (about eight miles north of Trieste), and Scopo (about two miles farther north), on the Carso, hitting the railway establishments, the adjoining stores, and the water tanks and trains standing in the stations. All the Italian aeroplanes returned safely, although chased by the enemy and fired on by anti-aircraft batteries.

Later it was made known that Italian squadrons of seaplanes in the course of a general reconnaissance, carried out by them along the west coast of Istria on October 16, succeeded in spite of unfavourable weather in successfully bombarding detached naval units near Rovigo, as well as military works at Rovigo and at Punta Salvore. At one point they became engaged in a fight with enemy aeroplanes, and damaged two of them, one of which was seen to fall into the sea. In spite of enemy artillery fire all the seaplanes returned safely to their bases.

On the first day of the next month, Italian aviators engaged in numerous further air fights, in the course of which several enemy machines were driven down. On the same day fourteen Italian battle-planes, escorted by Nieuport chasers, bombarded with marked success the railway stations of Nabresina (coast railway, Gulf of Trieste), Dottogliano, and Scopo (on the Gorizia-Trieste Railway), on the Carso. The aviators were fired on by anti-aircraft guns and attacked by enemy aeroplanes, but all returned safely to the Italian lines.

Again, on November 8, 1916, squadrons of Italian aircraft carried out an offensive reconnaissance on the enemy coast. Bombs were dropped with good results on the aviation station at Parenzo-Istria, and on craft used for military purposes in the harbour of Cittanuova. In spite of the violent fire of the anti-aircraft defences and of a counter-attack by enemy seaplanes, all the machines returned safely.

Many battles in the air were fought during the days that followed, various enemy machines being driven down by the skilful Italian aviators. Amongst those who have earned special notice are Lieutenant D'Annunzio, the son of the poet; Second-Lieutenant Garros; Capitaine de Fregate Arturo Ciano; and Baron Mario de Bratti, of the old nobility, who lost his life while serving his country. His funeral was attended by all connected with the Italian Aviation Corps and the technical and constructional side of the science, from General-in-Command to mechanics and artificers, so widely was his loss felt.

ENEMY ACTIVITY

In November, 1916, a series of brilliant conquests by British and French aviators had reduced the Germans to a secondary, if not actually a futile, part in the air. But after a period of bad weather and a lull in the fighting, German aviators again ventured over the Allies' lines. Their enterprise, however, was short-lived. Proof of the Allies' superiority was again seen on November 10 in an important aerial victory over the German lines. Thirty British machines defeated a greater number of the enemy—his strength is believed to have been between thirty and forty—while on a bombing expedition between Bapaume and Arras. The fact worth remembering is that the British airmen were not turned off, but that they punished their assailants decisively and then fulfilled their obligations as ordered, delivering seventy-two high explosive bombs on Vaulx-Vraucourt with satisfactory effect.

Mr. Percival Phillips, special correspondent of the *Daily Express*, writes:

It is a pity, that such a thrilling episode of aerial warfare cannot be told in detail—but there are very few details to be had. The only eye-witnesses at close range were the intrepid airmen involved, who were so fully occupied with their own individual opponents that it was impossible to follow the fortunes of the entire enemy fleet until its ignominious disappearance. I am told, in the dry, matter-of-fact language of our airmen, that the British bombing 'planes, flying at pre-arranged altitudes in a westerly wind, surrounded by their escort, sighted the German battle machines climbing through the rising mist to try to intercept them. The British fleet dropped to accept battle, and they closed a mile above the German trenches.

Then followed a breathless, furious duel, fought at a dizzy speed as the opposing 'planes swirled and eddied through the clouds, intent on each other's destruction. Machine-gun bullets ripped their hulls. They circled and dived with amazing confidence and accuracy. British and Germans alike drove their craft with superb skill, for the science of fighting in the air has become as intricate and difficult as handling a group of Dreadnoughts. No longer do the aeroplanes barge blindly at each other, firing point-blank, like old ships of the line. The expert crews twist and dodge in a manner undreamed of even a few short months ago, working their guns with nice discrimination, perhaps putting in one skilful shot where the pioneer guns of the air would have wasted half a drum. The battle was won as much by good airmanship as by the work of individual gunners.

The German pilots were outmanoeuvred. When at last their machines had enough of the fight—three of them had reeled earthwards, smoking wrecks—they dropped beyond range to examine their wounds, and the victorious British fleet passed on its way, in full view of the great army of spectators gazing upwards from the fields, road, and trenches below.

Besides the three German 'planes destroyed, others were sent down more or less damaged, but the full extent of the enemy casualties could not be ascertained. A broken aeroplane does not drop like a stone. It takes three or four minutes to reach the earth, and there is not time during an engagement for the men who are fighting to follow the progress of every crippled machine in its aimless descent.

The British casualties for the day's work were two bombing machines and two escorting machines missing, one observer killed and two pilots wounded. Of the latter, one managed to alight inside the British lines; the other came down in 'No Man's Land.'

The special correspondent of the *Times* describing the same battle writes:

It is a long time since the German initiated anything new in the air. Now, in his recrudescence of activity he is doing his best to learn from us. He copies exactly our methods, formations, and air tactics. In the recent moonlight nights especially, his airmen have been penetrating behind our lines, trying to bomb railheads and transport, and so forth; and individual Germans are even getting so bold as to do what we have done for the last four months, namely, fly low enough to use their machine-guns on troops in trenches or on columns on the road.

So far, they are making little by it; and they are having a most exciting time. One of the chief evidences of the new activity has been the great aerial battle, wherein some seventy aeroplanes were engaged, which the official *communiqué* has already mentioned. It took place between nine and ten o'clock on the morning of November 9, well over the German lines in the direction of Vaulx-Vraucourt, whither certain of our aeroplanes were bound on a bombing expedition. With them were fighting machines and scouts, making in all a fleet of thirty sail. Near the villa of Mory, just before reaching Vaulx-Vraucourt, they sighted an enemy squadron somewhat outnumbering themselves, the actual strength being something from thirty-six to forty aeroplanes.

They attacked at once. Some of our machines were flying at a higher level than the enemy, and they plunged headlong to join in the general engagement, which was fought at an average height of not much above 5,000 feet. Of the *mêlée* which followed, it is impossible to get any coherent account, for no man in it had time or thought for anything except the enemy machines with which he was successively engaged; but for twenty minutes there raged among the clouds such a battle as the world has never seen before: an inextricable tangle of single combats, of darting, swirling machines, the air filled with the roar of seventy propellers and the chatter of guns.

Four of our machines were lost, that is to say, that they were compelled to descend in German territory, a strong westerly wind drifting the battle as it raged more and more over enemy's soil. In the ships which came home, one brought a dead observer, and two others, with wounded pilots, had difficulty in beating up against the wind and landing in our lines. Of the enemy we know that six machines were sent to earth, of which three are known to have crashed. What happened to the other three, beyond that they were falling out of control, is not known. In yet another the pilot was seen to be shot dead. What further casualties the enemy suffered he only is aware; but the best evidence that the victory was ours lies in the fact that the whole enemy formation was broken and scattered.

The Germans fled for safety in all directions, leaving us in possession of the sky. Then we went upon our business; we punctually dropped our bombs on the stores and ammunition depots of Vaulx-Vraucourt, and then came home proudly flying in regular formation, no German daring to interfere.

Again, and again the Germans have made desperate efforts to

snatch the control of the air from the firm grasp of the Allies, but without the desired result. The Allies' aviators are not to be beaten. Their enterprise, their courage, above all their heroic bearing, are proof against all attacks.

LEONAUR

ALSO FROM LEONAUR

AVAILABLE IN SOFTCOVER OR HARDCOVER WITH DUST JACKET

WINGED WARFARE *by William A. Bishop*—The Experiences of a Canadian 'Ace' of the R.F.C. During the First World War.

THE STORY OF THE LAFAYETTE ESCADRILLE *by George Thenault*—A famous fighter squadron in the First World War by its commander..

R.F.C.H.Q. *by Maurice Baring*—The command & organisation of the British Air Force during the First World War in Europe.

SIXTY SQUADRON R.A.F. *by A. J. L. Scott*—On the Western Front During the First World War.

THE STRUGGLE IN THE AIR *by Charles C. Turner*—The Air War Over Europe During the First World War.

WITH THE FLYING SQUADRON *by H. Rosher*—Letters of a Pilot of the Royal Naval Air Service During the First World War.

OVER THE WEST FRONT *by "Spin" & "Contact"* —Two Accounts of British Pilots During the First World War in Europe, Short Flights With the Cloud Cavalry by "Spin" and Cavalry of the Clouds by "Contact".

SKYFIGHTERS OF FRANCE *by Henry Farré*—An account of the French War in the Air during the First World War.

THE HIGH ACES *by Laurence la Tourette Driggs*—French, American, British, Italian & Belgian pilots of the First World War 1914-18.

PLANE TALES OF THE SKIES *by Wilfred Theodore Blake*—The experiences of pilots over the Western Front during the Great War.

IN THE CLOUDS ABOVE BAGHDAD *by J. E. Tennant*—Recollections of the R. F. C. in Mesopotamia during the First World War against the Turks.

THE SPIDER WEB *by P. I. X. (Theodore Douglas Hallam)*—Royal Navy Air Service Flying Boat Operations During the First World War by a Flight Commander

EAGLES OVER THE TRENCHES *by James R. McConnell & William B. Perry*—Two First Hand Accounts of the American Escadrille at War in the Air During World War 1-Flying For France: With the American Escadrille at Verdun and Our Pilots in the Air

KNIGHTS OF THE AIR *by Bennett A. Molter*—An American Pilot's View of the Aerial War of the French Squadrons During the First World War.

LEONAUR

ALSO FROM LEONAUR
AVAILABLE IN SOFTCOVER OR HARDCOVER WITH DUST JACKET

THE FALL OF THE MOGHUL EMPIRE OF HINDUSTAN *by H. G. Keene*—By the beginning of the nineteenth century, as British and Indian armies under Lake and Wellesley dominated the scene, a little over half a century of conflict brought the Moghul Empire to its knees.

LADY SALE'S AFGHANISTAN *by Florentia Sale*—An Indomitable Victorian Lady's Account of the Retreat from Kabul During the First Afghan War.

THE CAMPAIGN OF MAGENTA AND SOLFERINO 1859 *by Harold Carmichael Wylly*—The Decisive Conflict for the Unification of Italy.

FRENCH'S CAVALRY CAMPAIGN *by J. G. Maydon*—A Special Correspondent's View of British Army Mounted Troops During the Boer War.

CAVALRY AT WATERLOO *by Sir Evelyn Wood*—British Mounted Troops During the Campaign of 1815.

THE SUBALTERN *by George Robert Gleig*—The Experiences of an Officer of the 85th Light Infantry During the Peninsular War.

NAPOLEON AT BAY, 1814 *by F. Loraine Petre*—The Campaigns to the Fall of the First Empire.

NAPOLEON AND THE CAMPAIGN OF 1806 *by Colonel Vachée*—The Napoleonic Method of Organisation and Command to the Battles of Jena & Auerstädt.

THE COMPLETE ADVENTURES IN THE CONNAUGHT RANGERS *by William Grattan*—The 88th Regiment during the Napoleonic Wars by a Serving Officer.

BUGLER AND OFFICER OF THE RIFLES *by William Green & Harry Smith*—With the 95th (Rifles) during the Peninsular & Waterloo Campaigns of the Napoleonic Wars.

NAPOLEONIC WAR STORIES *by Sir Arthur Quiller-Couch*—Tales of soldiers, spies, battles & sieges from the Peninsular & Waterloo campaings.

CAPTAIN OF THE 95TH (RIFLES) *by Jonathan Leach*—An officer of Wellington's sharpshooters during the Peninsular, South of France and Waterloo campaigns of the Napoleonic wars.

RIFLEMAN COSTELLO *by Edward Costello*—The adventures of a soldier of the 95th (Rifles) in the Peninsular & Waterloo Campaigns of the Napoleonic wars.

LEONAUR

ALSO FROM LEONAUR
AVAILABLE IN SOFTCOVER OR HARDCOVER WITH DUST JACKET

A DIARY FROM DIXIE *by Mary Boykin Chesnut*—A Lady's Account of the Confederacy During the American Civil War

FOLLOWING THE DRUM *by Teresa Griffin Vielé*—A U. S. Infantry Officer's Wife on the Texas frontier in the Early 1850's

FOLLOWING THE GUIDON *by Elizabeth B. Custer*—The Experiences of General Custer's Wife with the U. S. 7th Cavalry.

LADIES OF LUCKNOW *by G. Harris & Adelaide Case*—The Experiences of Two British Women During the Indian Mutiny 1857. A Lady's Diary of the Siege of Lucknow by G. Harris, Day by Day at Lucknow by Adelaide Case

MARIE-LOUISE AND THE INVASION OF 1814 *by Imbert de Saint-Amand*—The Empress and the Fall of the First Empire

SAPPER DOROTHY *by Dorothy Lawrence*—The only English Woman Soldier in the Royal Engineers 51st Division, 79th Tunnelling Co. during the First World War

ARMY LETTERS FROM AN OFFICER'S WIFE 1871-1888 *by Frances M. A. Roe*—Experiences On the Western Frontier With the United States Army

NAPOLEON'S LETTERS TO JOSEPHINE *by Henry Foljambe Hall*—Correspondence of War, Politics, Family and Love 1796-1814

MEMOIRS OF SARAH DUCHESS OF MARLBOROUGH, AND OF THE COURT OF QUEEN ANNE VOLUME 1 by A. T. Thomson

MEMOIRS OF SARAH DUCHESS OF MARLBOROUGH, AND OF THE COURT OF QUEEN ANNE VOLUME 2 by A. T. Thomson

MARY PORTER GAMEWELL AND THE SIEGE OF PEKING *by A. H. Tuttle*—An American Lady's Experiences of the Boxer Uprising, China 1900

VANISHING ARIZONA *by Martha Summerhayes*—A young wife of an officer of the U.S. 8th Infantry in Apacheria during the 1870's

THE RIFLEMAN'S WIFE *by Mrs. Fitz Maurice*—*The Experiences of an Officer's Wife and Chronicles of the Old 95th During the Napoleonic Wars*

THE OATMAN GIRLS *by Royal B. Stratton*—The Capture & Captivity of Two Young American Women in the 1850's by the Apache Indians